This book is entirely a work of fiction.
Any correlation with real people or events is
coincidental

Andrei Livadny

The SHADOW of EARTH

Thank you FOR your support and inspiration! They mean so much to me,

AndRei LivAdny.

The History of the Galaxy
Book#2

Magic Dome Books

The Shadow of Earth
The History of the Galaxy, Book # 2
Copyright © Andrei Livadny 2018
Cover Art © Vladimir Manyukhin 2018
English Translation Copyright ©
Sofia Gutkin 2018
Published by Magic Dome Books, 2018
All Rights Reserved
ISBN: 978-80-88231-70-7

TABLE OF CONTENTS:

Prologue

THE SHORT MAN STOOD in front of a panoramic window, listening to the report as he looked at the skyscrapers forming the famous Square of Five Corners, which was unfailingly repeated on the many levels of the urbanized anthill.

Earth was an eternal city. This was the name of a planet where the shell of the technosphere had completely enclosed it, uniting all the continents.

Ever since the problem of the industrial fog

had been overcome using absorbents, transparent walls had again come into fashion. The megasuburbs soaring into the clouds looked like enormous terrariums, where millions of people hurried about their day.

Looking at them, John Winston Hammer experienced intense and contradictory emotions.

"Everything could have turned out differently," he couldn't help thinking in moments like these.

Three hundred and fifty years ago, when the Great Exodus ended, humanity's fate seemed sealed. Thousands of colonial transports had vanished into the unknown. Hyperspace swallowed them up without a trace, and the rush to expand fizzled out, with even the most ardent optimists turning into sceptics, and the theory of the hypersphere thrown into doubt. Dozens of unfinished starships were left standing on the Moon's shipyards.

Back in that distant time, the Genesis Corporation was still trying to master the dust storms on Mars while Earth's cities were completely enveloped in the toxic atmosphere. Humanity's last generation was living out its final days in the in-modes.

The inexorable end was drawing close.

John Hammer had studied that period of time in detail, which had shown the great importance of specific people in history. Ulrich Fitzgerald, the founder of Genesis, a 120-year-old man who had never turned his dream of completely terraforming Mars into reality, prevented the utter collapse of civilization.

There were only a billion people left on Earth when ships from Genesis' Martian fleet appeared in orbit around the planet and dropped containers with a unique strain of genetically-constructed bacteria into the poisoned oceans.

For a year, the microorganisms frenetically multiplied, consuming waste and creating oxygen. Then the absorbents, developed to fight the dust storms on Mars, were released into Earth's atmosphere, murky from the industrial fog.

Ulrich Fitzgerald lived for another thirty years. He left Mars alone but saved Earth. He resurrected the World Government and conducted radical reforms. He blocked the cyberspace Layer and forced people to leave the in-modes. Fitzgerald ruled the world with an iron fist, clamping down on any signs of dissent and laying the foundations for civilization's golden age.

It was also the time when the technosphere closed completely over the planet. The oceans, sealed in steel and reinforced concrete, now served as sources of oxygen and organic material for the primitive organisms that felt perfectly well in the dark and cold waters. Their genetic code was created in Genesis's off-world laboratories, based on the ancient forms of life discovered deep in the frozen seas of Europa, one of Jupiter's moons.

New cities rose above the oceans, while the old, historical megacities underwent reconstruction.

Earth's atmosphere gradually became clean and all the dangerous manufacturing was taken off-planet, to technology parks on the Moon and Mars.

The technological Renaissance and the following Golden Age of civilization didn't last long, however. The harsh reality quickly reasserted itself. The planet's population began to grow again, while deliveries of resources decreased significantly. The inhabitants of the Moon, Mars, the Asteroid Belt, and then the mining colonies on Jupiter's moons declared their independence. By controlling the sources of raw materials, they thought that they could dictate their conditions to the ancestral homeland, and they were right. Their dominance over the metropolis lasted for almost three hundred years.

Earth's technosphere became a massive multifaceted cybernetic system during this period, which independently formed a controlled ecosystem. The unified machine network replaced the destroyed nature, created and maintained acceptable living conditions on Earth but consumed an extraordinary amount of resources. The smallest malfunction, setback or delay in the delivery of resources had serious consequences for the lives of billions of people, who depended on the technosphere.

John Winston Hammer won the elections in 2561 and got the right to form the next World Government.

He had inherited a truly dire situation. In that time, the natives from off-world settlements would kick open any door - the little kings of small moons, the owners of mining asteroids, the industrial magnates from Mars and large space freighters felt that they were in control on Earth, and they exploited the resource shortage and the population's growing needs mercilessly.

None of them were concerned about the latest change in government, which turned out to be a mistake.

LONG BEFORE he became the Head of Government, John Hammer began his career as a trade representative of Earth. He often visited Mars and the distant space settlements, making connections and drawing his own conclusions.

One day, while sitting in a bar on the Phobos Orbital Station, he met a pilot who had just arrived from the asteroid belt. Alexander Nagumo was killing time as he waited for his load to be accepted, a thousand-ton block of ice. Hammer's flight was delayed and they started talking, just idle chatter, until a message arrived on the pilot's cyberstack.

"Frayg be damned!" the man swore, looking at the numbers. "The gall of these people!"

"What, they're not giving you a decent price?" Hammer asked.

"No," Nagumo muttered darkly. "Have a look, a hundred credits per ton. And that's considering the constant shortage of water on Mars. I'll barely have enough to pay for the fuel that I've spent!" he added grimly.

"The Martian Mining Company has a monopoly," Hammer noted for the sake of fairness. "It's hard to argue with them."

Nagumo waved him off in irritation.

"It's certainly possible!" he answered hotly and then added unexpectedly: "You know, I would cast the whole Solar System down at the feet of the person who gave me a couple of military ships!"

Hammer noted more than just rage in the young pilot's eyes. That phrase was no accident, it looked like he knew what he was talking about.

"And what would you ask for as payment?"

"The title of admiral," grumbled the pilot, making it out like the conversation had been a joke. "Well, I better go. Be well."

FOR THE FIRST few years after being elected, John Hammer didn't conduct any reforms, and the resource magnates of the Far Outlands dictated their terms as usual, feeling like masters of the situation. That is, until March 2564, when a fleet of five military ships appeared in orbit around Mars. The half-erased logos of Genesis, Rimp Cybertronics, Megapool and Cryonics could be discerned on their darkened hulls — the names of corporations that ruled the world before the Great Exodus.

After shooting down the few defense satellites, the fleet rapidly attacked and destroyed a cruiser of the Martian Mining Company. While fragments of the most ferocious ship in the Solar System burned up in the atmosphere, the frigates crushed the anti-space defense of Phobos Station and landed an assault force on the orbital base.

The industrial empire of the Martian Mining Company fell in one day. The Moon settlements hurriedly capitulated next, as Earth's satellite was approached by another fleet, made up of the ancient military ships.

After the first victories, John Winston Hammer announced the creation of the Terran Alliance. From this moment on, all space settlements had to accept the rule of the metropolis and follow one set of laws. The Asteroid Belt became a problem, however, where every mine was well defended.

The ensuing war rapidly devoured the precious resources, with not many of them left on the Moon and Mars. But Hammer couldn't stop without finishing what he had started. He gave the order and the space shipyards began working again, now building the military cruisers of the Terran Alliance.

HE WON THE INTRASYSTEMIC war but this didn't solve the problems of a lack of resources and overpopulation. Mars was in ruins, the Moon had been hollowed out like a worm-ridden apple, and most of the deposits in the Asteroid Belt had been exhausted during the six centuries of the space era.

"A civilization trapped inside its own star system is doomed to disappear..." John Hammer had heard this phrase when he was a teenager and had remembered it his whole life.

Looking at the human anthill encased in steel and glass, John Hammer didn't think of himself as a god, quite the opposite. He was a realist and understood that the power of the crowd should not be scorned.

He had come from the urbanized depths

himself, and ever since then had felt the pulse of the life bustling around him, wanting it to succeed as much as himself.

To love and despise, to understand and beware — what could be more painful and yet sweeter than the narrow path of power? He was responsible for the *humanity* swarming around him, which had come so close to self-destruction and was now looking with unhealthy curiosity at the abyss that it faced.

He turned away from the window and pushed aside the memories, glancing at the gray-haired Admiral Alexander Nagumo. The old man was listening attentively to the speaker, while Tiberius Nadyrov and Max Gornev, the young shoots that had come up after the last victories, looked bored.

A quarter of a century ago, in the midst of the fighting for the Asteroid Belt, John Hammer had asked for the hypersphere theory to be tested again. A separate research division of the World Space Forces had to be created but specific results had only been obtained a few years ago.

The holographic monitors were showing equations, graphs and schematic diagrams of the propulsion units.

No wonder that the faces of Nadyrov and Gornev showed boredom.

"Make it shorter, more accessible and to the

point," Hammer ordered, making the speaker fall silent mid-sentence.

"But..."

"Put this away!" Hammer indicated the equations irritably. "Enlarge the star map!" He demanded. "And now, tell us the gist of it! The engineers and scientists can pore over the rest."

"May I, Mister President?" Edward Nechaev, Head of Earth's Intelligence Agency, stood up from his armchair. Seeing the nod, he changed the display image and pointed to a 3D map of space, where the stars were linked by thin lines. "The hypersphere theory has been confirmed," he began. "Hyperspace, as we understand it, is the carrier of all gravitational connections in the Universe, but from a strictly practical viewpoint, we are only interested in star-sized objects. By possessing enormous mass, they are the ones that form stable power threads in the hypersphere, which can be found by our instruments."

"What does that give us?" Hammer asked.

"After activating the hyperdrive, a ship finds itself in alternative space. There are no stars but their gravitational connections still exist." A network of thin lines appeared on an additional screen. "This is our Sun." A bright spot appeared in the center of the image. "As you can see, sixty-four power lines lead away from it through hyperspace. All the stars that we can jump to are located between five and fifteen light years away."

"Have they been explored?" Nagumo asked.

"Certainly. Most of the systems have planets but they are unfit for life."

"Wait," Hammer interrupted. "If there are only 64 power lines running from the Solar System to the nearest stars, then where did the thousands of colonial transports go?"

"They became victims of the 'blind punch'," Nechaev explained. "Once we make a jump to any of the neighboring stars, we'll see new routes and a new region of hyperspace. If a ship doesn't surface in time at a node, indicating a solar system, the ship can float along this net until it runs out of energy. Hypersphere navigation had not been studied at all in the time of the Great Exodus, and as a result, most ships became victims of circumstance."

"So, they could have ended up hundreds of light years away from Earth?" Tiberius Nadyrov asked.

"Precisely."

"What if the energy runs out while travelling between two nodes?" Gornev inquired.

"Then the ship leaves the hypersphere somewhere between two stars. It's thus easy to see the importance of the power lines in hyperspace. They are the only reliable form of guidance."

"Fine." Hammer was impressed but now he

had numerous questions. "Why didn't any of the colonial transports return after so many years?"

"As I said before, a new section of the hyperspace network opens up in a new star system. The number of new routes can vary, depending on the star density, but they all look identical on the screen of the mass-detector — the only device that can note and display the power lines in the hypersphere. I'm sure that attempts were made to return to the Solar System, and more than one, but they were unsuccessful. We've needed a quarter of a century to add practical findings to the theory of Johann Ivanov-Schmidt. We lost two hundred and seventeen reconnaissance ships. I'm assuming that the colonists didn't have the capacity to conduct such experiments.

"I understand." Hammer sat down in his chair. "Now, explain to me why a jump is limited to fifteen light years? What do we do if we need to go further?"

"The ship's energy equipment is the deciding factor. If we had an unlimited source of power, we could float along the network from one star system to the next, without 'surfacing' in-between. Theoretically, we can reach any of the stars in our Galaxy this way..."

"But?" Hammer interrupted him.

"The accumulators lose charge quickly.

We're currently working on a two-reactor model. One power source supplies the hyperdrive, while the second is meant for the other systems on the ship. One jump consumes almost all the energy..."

"Well then, make a ship with ten reactors," Tiberius Nadyrov butted in with his suggestion.

Nagumo smiled crookedly.

"Better keep quiet and listen," he advised the young admiral.

"Why?" the man bristled.

"Because. Nechaev, tell him what will happen to a ship that has ten reactors."

"It'll become very large and incredibly vulnerable. It'll be about ten kilometers in length. All the usable space inside will be occupied by the energy accumulators and the control systems for the power units. Experience has shown that a two-reactor system is optimal. I'll say right now that the colonial transports of the Great Exodus only solved one task, and that is completing the jump. The had incredibly strong power units mounted on, which ensured the function of the cryogenic chambers. During our explorations, we found one such transport, which didn't leave the hypersphere at the first node. All the energy had been diverted to the hyperdrive. The result was the death of the crew and passengers. We have a different goal. Our construction anticipates a successful jump and stable function of the onboard systems after resurfacing in normal space.

"So," John Hammer looked closely at the star map, "how can we go about settling the other planets?"

"It has to be done in two stages, Mister President. First, we'll have to reach one of the sixty-four explored systems. Then the ship will need a day to recharge the hyperdrive accumulators, after which..." Nechaev looked uncomfortable, "we will have to select one of the navigational lines and perform a 'blind punch'."

"So, we don't know which star system the ship will end up in? Whether there are hospitable planets, and if they haven't been occupied during the Great Exodus?"

"That's right," replied Nechaev.

"How long do you need to explore the routes in detail?"

"At least ten years. And so far, there are no guarantees. We haven't yet learned how to 'label' navigational lines in the hypersphere."

"What about the systems accessible in one jump?" Nagumo asked. "Have you sorted them out, at least?"

"Yes," Nechaev nodded. "But the planets circling around the nearest stars are mostly unsuitable for colonization. We found only two planets with an oxygen-containing atmosphere. One is Yunona, where we found the wreckage of the colonial transport Yuna, which crashed during landing, and Dabog, a well-developed colony from the time of the Great Exodus."

John Hammer stared intently at the 3D star map and thought of the current problems.

Despite the success of the Alliance, the sixty billion people trapped within the Solar System could not be provided with enough resources, jobs and reasonable living conditions. The situation would begin to rapidly deteriorate in another few years. Eighty percent of the population was currently surviving on government subsidies — they were the 'extra people', who hadn't been taught to work and to strive to reach their goals.

"What did you find out about the colonies?" he asked drily.

"Dabog is an agrarian planet," Nechaev replied. "We positioned our spy satellites on distant orbits and are scanning their communication frequencies; we have also managed to infiltrate their information network."

"Are they exploring space?"

"Yes. Moreover, they are in contact with several more advanced colonies from the time of the Great Exodus. About once a week, passenger and freight ships from other worlds appear in Dabog's airspace. We have concluded that trade is only episodic at present. We have discovered from intercepted conversations that at least four planetary civilizations have managed to go into space and are actively exploring the hypersphere," Nechaev continued. "We're currently conducting reconnaissance, identifying their navigational methods and trying to determine the location of these worlds. For now, we only know their names: Elio, Kjuig, Rory and something called the Moon Stellar, presumably an airless satellite of one of the listed planets. Thanks to the combined efforts of several civilizations, a space shipyard has been built there."

"A shipyard?" Nagumo perked up. "Does that mean they're designing and building their own ships?! But the preliminary report stated that 'all settlements on other planets will inevitably go through centuries of regression', so how the frayg do they suddenly have high technologies?!"

"You are right, Admiral, most of the planetary civilizations founded during the Great Exodus either perished or are quite primitive at present." Nechaev responded. "But there are exceptions. We have discovered that Dabog — let's focus on this world as the one most studied — was settled by people from the Fugitive Colonial Transport, which carried the majority of staff from Rimp Cybertronics Corporation, including Catherine Rimp herself and her inner circle, which, by the way, included Hans Gervet, the most famous engineer of his time. It makes sense to assume that many technologies, now considered lost, have been preserved on this planet."

John Hammer paced the office.

"How does the population feel about Earth?" he asked, stopping in front of the window again. "Did our agents investigate this?"

"Yes, we managed to initiate a discussion on this topic using the computer networks."

"And?"

"If there is contact with their ancestral homeland, they are willing to accept a small number of immigrants from Earth. But only through a competitive selection process."

"They want to get our best people?" Nagumo smiled crookedly. "And leave us the scum?"

"I can understand the inhabitants of the colonies. Their history consists of centuries of fighting for survival," Nechaev uttered incautiously. "I doubt that they would agree to accept just anyone, and turn their world into a dirty flophouse for layabouts."

"So that's how you see Earth?!" Hammer glowered. "A dirty flophouse?" Touching a sensor, he brought up an image of the planet. It showed pulsing splotches of varying brightness, indicating the current population density. A number appeared at the bottom of the holographic screen, showing slightly over 60 billion. "These are all people, you know!" Hammer burst out, losing his cool for just a second. "Whose only fault was being born! The resources of the Solar System have been completely exhausted. So let's think about Humanity, but decide, first of all, where it is! Is it here or is it over there?!"

Nechaev wisely kept silent, while Max Gornev spoke, looking at the image of Dabog. "One terraformed planet would solve most of our problems. Dabog is within the reach of our fleet. I don't think we have anything to argue about."

"There is an important nuance that you need to understand," Nechaev had to join the conversation again. "None of the worlds that we've explored match Earth Standard. All the colonists on Yunona died from an epidemic caused by an unknown exovirus."

"But they survived on Dabog!" Tiberius Nadyrov noted.

"Yes, however, the planet is only partially terraformed. Due to the colonization, it now has a hybrid biosphere. I'll say this plainly: the least that a person from Earth can expect is a severe allergic reaction. I have to remind you that for the citizens of our modern cities, the Earth Standard is a controlled living environment."

John Hammer frowned.

"Can we at least protect our assault units?" he asked.

"Yes, of course. We have developed an

external metabolic implant," Nechaev brought up an image of a small device. "It is strapped to the leg and connected to the femoral artery. It cleans the blood, conducts a heuristic biochemical analysis and synthesizes antibodies as required. This technology has been tested but it's only a temporary form of protection. We need serious studies..."

"That's enough," Hammer interrupted. "We possess military terraforming technology, which we inherited from Genesis." He switched to the star map again. "Gentlemen, I would like to hear your opinions."

"Dabog is the key to everything," Alexander Nagumo stated firmly. He enlarged Earth's neighboring star systems, which were within a radius of one 'jump'. The chain of dead planets formed a sphere. "We have no idea who we might meet as we travel along the energy lines of the hypersphere," the admiral continued. "How developed are the civilizations that we don't yet know about? That's why we need an industrial base in another star system. Dabog is perfect for this purpose. Take the bunker zones, where the colonists lived for several centuries. If our intelligence is to be believed, the plants for manufacturing planetary technologies are located there. We would be able to modernize them to serve the needs of our fleet. I agree with Gornev.

There should be no doubts." He snapped. "We're talking about the survival of billions."

"We can negotiate with the government on Dabog," Dmitry Stolyarov disagreed, the President's Advisor on Colonial Policy.

"Negotiate about what?" Nagumo said sharply. "About the fact that their world will undergo combat terraforming?"

"No, of course not! Their biosphere, the result of four hundred years of effort, will be destroyed in this case. Nobody would agree to that!"

"And we can't accept anything less!" Nagumo snapped back. "We're in the midst of a resource crisis! The raw materials in the Solar System have been depleted. Hunger in Earth's megacities is no longer a sign of things to come but a pressing issue! Look at the star map again. Dabog is the only planet where we can begin combat terraforming in the shortest possible time. A year later, this colony will accept inhabitants from Earth. And we will continue our expansion from there."

"You mean, we will wipe out the population on Dabog?" Stolyarov asked bluntly.

"We still need to work out the mission details. But the planet will be captured and terraformed to match Earth Standard," Nagumo retorted. "If we hesitate any longer, we'll have another intrasystemic war on our hands."

The advisor kept silent but now Tiberius Nadyrov threw back his head. "Not everyone will agree with this decision. When we were putting down the revolt on Mars, we had cases of open insubordination. Officers in the fleet refused to carry out orders that would lead to mass civilian casualties."

"We'll keep that in mind," Nagumo replied. "We'll ensure the necessary rotations so that the ship crews in the assault groups carry out orders and not question them!"

JOHN WINSTON HAMMER considered himself a deep and progressive thinker. He wasn't wrong in general but from the peak of absolute power, many problems appear simpler and smaller than they actually are. Just like human figures meld into a faceless, gray mass, so do separate fateful decisions lose their intense acuity when they have to be made daily.

The intrasystemic war had finished. The military machine of the Terran Alliance stood idle, which could lead to grave consequences in the near future. Young and energetic corporations that blossomed in the war grew in strength and strove for power, breathing down his neck and watching the stars hungrily.

John Hammer believed that the lives of

billions of people, trapped in Earth's supermegacities, were more important that the fate of a handful of colonists, scattered throughout the Galaxy by the cruel whim of the hypersphere.

He knew that he would be cursed by some, and hardly win the love of those for whom he was opening the door into infinite space.

Now, after hearing Nagumo's words, the star map appeared differently before his gaze: in the pattern of the tiny silver specks, John Hammer saw the phantom of future events — new waves of expansion, a great movement of nations, which he was going to initiate by his personal decision...

Part One

Act
of Intimidation

Chapter One

THE OLD ROAD, laid down in the early days of colonization, led into a tunnel that ran through a low mountain range, and exiting, circled down to the base of a shallow crater.

The signs of the past were everywhere. The cliffs still bore signs of melting. Two ancient robotized complexes rose above the squat, single-level buildings.

This morning, a comfortable multiseat flycar

stopped in the parking area, and a group of children got out, accompanied by a young teacher. The sky was cloudless and the autumn air was crisp and clear. A faint breeze stirred the leaves of the carelessla, the first hybrid plant created by the colonists as a mix between the Terran ivy and a local shrub.

Every detail in the surroundings captured the imagination, and the children fell quiet as they looked around them. The ancient reinforced concrete was cracked in places. A massive fragment of the ceramic plating, pitted by its contact with space, rose like a wall in front of them. Embossed letters could be still be seen on the armored plate: Fugitive Colonial Transport.

A sign hanging slightly higher stated:

Entrance to the Colonization History Museum of Dabog.

The high wall was pitted with holes. The frame of a planetary machine, crushed by an enormous force, rusted under an open sky. The guard turret was half buried under the dully glinting used shell casings, with the endoskeleton of an android lying nearby.

An alley of carelessla led to a ramp that sloped downwards, ending at the tightly shut armored gates.

"Daria Dmitrievna, what happened to it?" asked one of the students, a boy of about ten, as he stopped and stared at the android. "Why did it break down?"

"This robot, like many others, protected the humans," the teacher raised her arm to attract attention and continued. "Our ancestors came from deep space, but their ship crashed during landing. The planet was completely different back then, hostile and unfriendly. Now, we're going to descend into the colonial bunker and I will show you how Dabog looked four hundred years ago..."

With these words, the massive gates trembled and began to move apart with a vibrating hum. A small room was revealed, pierced with sterilizing radiation. The children were informed about this by the personal nanocomputers on their wrists.

Daria Kretchetova, a recent graduate from the State University of Dabog, tucked a lock of hair behind her ear, smiled reassuringly at the children and stepped forward as an example.

The children followed their teacher timidly, crowding around her as the gates shuddered and began to close again, cutting off the sunlight.

It looked fascinating and terrifying at the same time. One of the girls squealed...

"Right now, we are in the so-called airlock, a chamber located between the outside world and the interior of the bunker," Daria explained.

The children crowded together, curious,

puzzled and a little frightened. Everything that they were seeing was so different to their familiar Dabog! Could it be that this warm and friendly planet had once been so hostile to humans that they had to hide underground in these gloomy bunkers?!

A long and dimly lit corridor with a low ceiling led from the airlock. Its walls seemed to emanate cold and damp.

One of children couldn't help but shiver.

"Yes, this is exactly how the history of Dabog began," said Daria. "The colonial transport crashed and many cryogenic halls and storage rooms were inaccessible due to the deformation of the ship. The specialists, who were supposed to be woken up right after landing, remained in cryogenic sleep, and the first people landing on the planet were the ones whose cryogenic chambers had failed during the accident."

With these words, she touched a sensor and doors opened into a huge hall, where modern devices recreated the atmosphere of those days, based on preserved archival records...

...It grew dark.

The first stars appeared in the sky. A full moon hung low above the horizon. Its cold light was reflected in the sparkle of small lakes scattered here and there, while the rest of the continent was hidden under a tangle of grass-like plants, vaguely reminiscent of horsetails and ferns, and reaching 5-6 meters in height.

Humming, chirping, the rustle of wings and other sounds, unfamiliar to humans, came from the mysterious, shadowy, damp thicket. A warm wind brought sharp smells and someone's heavy tread was accompanied by sucking noises, as if a large animal waded through the swamp mud, beneath the spreading boughs.

Occasional weather-beaten cliffs rose above the waving ocean of plants. The greenery changed radically near them, with the appearance of tree-like vines, which clung to the rocks and climbed upwards, creating arches and hanging bridges, and connecting the edges of the cliffs.

The moisture evaporating from the water-logged soil formed a haze that drifted between the spreading leaves, condensing into streaks of night time fog.

The moon kept rising. Staccato sounds now came from the direction of the cliffs, as if hundreds of hammers were working in the depths of the forest.

From time to time, the flexible plant trunks began to shudder, their tops swaying from side to side, revealing the short but ferocious fight between some large creatures, then everything became still again. Only the persistent hum, too loud to be the usual insect drone, continued without pause.

A new star appeared in the sky that night. It quickly grew in size until it became a bright pea, then it suddenly changed direction, crossing the face of the moon as it dropped a handful of fireballs, and disappeared over the horizon.

THE LIGHT IN THE HALL went out for a second. There was movement as parts of the diorama shifted and changed, and new 3D images appeared. The children could now see the site of the Fugitive's crash.

A reddish sun peeked through the breaks in the purple clouds. The heat streamed upwards like a curtain. The blackened side of the colonial transport dropped sharply downwards.

The crater floor, formed by a solidified glass-like mass, was intersected by numerous cracks and breaks. Some were so wide that the planetary vehicles leaving the access ramps had to move along the edges of the chasms, looking for places to install temporary bridges and keep going further.

People were climbing out individually and in small groups. Having just woken up from cryogenic sleep, they were disorientated and bewildered. Nobody was in charge of the situation.

A flock of large flying lizards swarmed over the horizon.

"I know, those are raptors!" one of the girls exclaimed.

"That's right," replied her teacher. "But it was the planet's microscopic inhabitants that were a much greater threat to humans. The bacteria and viruses caused new diseases in the very first days. Our ancestors simply could not survive on the surface, so they had to hurriedly build sealed shelters."

The teacher skipped over a lot of details. In reality, the first few years of colonization on Dabog were full of tragedies, since most of the colonists had come from the Layer, and had spent all their lives in the in-modes, among the illusions of cyberspace. They were utterly unprepared to face the reality of an alien world and to fight for their survival.

The children would learn about this later, in history lessons and exobiology classes, but now, another change in the decorations allowed them to skip over decades.

"After the first epidemics, the humans split up. Some developed immunity to the diseases and were able to live on the surface, and others were forced to spend precious resources on the creation of a controlled environment. Thus, several colonization centers were formed, located quite far from each other. At the beginning, they developed separately, while the numerous fantastic specialists on board the Fugitive, who could have affected the situation, remained in their cryogenic chambers."

"Why weren't they woken up?"

"It wasn't possible. But when their stores became depleted, our ancestors had to look for new ways to survive. They had to conduct experiments and transform the planet. Now you will see how it happened. Please, don't get scared, just stand beside me and watch. We're not in any danger. Everything that you'll see are just copies, models and holograms controlled by the computer..."

✳ ✳ ✳

Long-range orbit around Dabog
October 9, 2607
One hour before the invasion

THREE CRUISERS FORMED the head of the fleet's battle formation. They looked simply like bright lines at a distance, with a stream of harmless silver specks drifting behind them.

The ships had just changed formation and were on an approach course with the planet. The phantom generators that switched on a few minutes later hid them from any observers.

Now the invaders looked as black as the night, with only the occasional flash from the correction engines briefly illuminating the sinister outline of the many combat structures.

The fleet's flagship Endgrouse exhaled a dissipating atmospheric cloud — it was the opening of the electromagnetic catapults' diaphragms for the launch of the space fighters. The armor plates of the ships moving alongside it also began to shift: Titan opened its vacuum docks in preparation for the launch of its assault modules, while rocket battery ports were revealed on the front of the Shadow of Earth.

It was a force that could crush a star system as easily as a tank tread crushes a children's toy lying in its path.

Admiral Alexander Nagumo paced along the flagship's bridge, occasionally glancing at the screens and sensors of the tracking systems.

The star, shaded by the light filters, blazed on the left side. The planet slowly grew in size directly in front of them, splattered with gray streaks of cloud. The scanners recorded about ten civil satellites and one freight ship in low parking orbit.

It was nothing complicated. This world looked like an overripe apple ready to drop at their feet, but a different fate awaited Dabog. Its cities would be ground into dust and its biosphere would undergo combat terraforming. Only the bunker zones held any practical interest for the fleet, where the factories producing agricultural technology were located and where (it was highly likely) the lost technologies of the Rimp Cybertronics Corporation were hidden.

The strike on Dabog was to be quick and heartless. John Hammer planned to use this planet as an example to the other colonies, founded during the Great Exodus, of what would happen if they refused to accept the rule of the mother planet.

The admiral had never been a humanist. He didn't feel guilty. He was fully aware of what he was going to do. Nagumo believed that the future generations would figure out what's what and it would be up to them to decide whether to put up a monument to the admiral or to turn his name into a curse...

He touched a sensor and contacted Nadyrov.

"Go ahead, Tiberius," the phrase that began a new era sounded calm and ordinary.

The launch tubes of the Shadow of Earth cruiser were illuminated by dim splashes of static. The rounded contours of the space-to-surface missiles could be just barely seen in the depths of the massive tubes. Pilots called them 'megacity killers'.

* * *

Dabog
Colonization History Museum

A VIRTUAL RAIN was pelting down.

Low, heavy clouds sailed over the hushed children. Findings themselves in the depths of the primordial jungle, among the tall grasses, they timidly observed the huge insects that lived hundreds of years ago in the tropical forests of Dabog.

Their teacher smiled reassuringly and drew the children after her, and soon the path running through the holographic jungle brought them to the marshy flood plain of a wide river.

Through the yellow haze of vapor, they could see a stony ridge with dark openings of several caves, encased in steel and concrete. It appeared that humans had made their dwellings there, for why else would there be two soil transformers on the shore?

A swarm of 'perforators', creatures that belonged to the insect kingdom, circled over the rocky outcrops, occasionally trying to break into them and producing a loud, staccato sound — the insects were trying to reach the tunnel worms, which lived in the cracks.

The soil transformers were sinking in the mud. Their wide caterpillar tracks got sucked into the mire, and one of the robotized complexes titled over to one side, became stuck in a deep hollow and fell silent.

People in protective suits came out of the cave, accompanied by androids. Two rumbling all-terrain vehicles followed them. They attached cables to the soil transformer and attempted to pull it out onto a sloping hillock, but the sound of the motors attracted an unexpected and dangerous guest. A huge lizard suddenly appeared above the cliffs.

Its appearance was terrifying. The giant reptile watched the humans without fear, clearly seeing them as prey.

"Mommy..." one of the girls unwittingly took a few steps backwards.

"Don't worry, this is only a show, an imitation," Daria tried to calm them down. "We're surrounded by holograms. Who can tell me the name of this lizard?"

"Dicort," one of the boys said hollowly.

"That's right. It is one of the largest and most dangerous representatives of our planet's indigenous fauna," the teacher agreed.

Meanwhile, the events on the riverbank were unfolding rapidly and dramatically. The dicort paused, leaning on its powerful back legs and tail, covered in horny scales. It looked vaguely like a tyrannosaurus, but despite its impressive weight and size, it could climb cliffs, using the suctioned tendrils growing from its abdomen.

The lizard climbed up the rocky outcrop and looked down, belching out a wheezy and stinking breath, and nervously scratching its claws as it readied itself for a jump.

The people noticed the danger but it was too late, as the body weighing dozens of tons landed on the marshy shore, throwing up fountains of mud.

The sinking soil transformer was swamped by a wave of silt and mud, one of the all-terrain vehicles flipped over, while the dicort, stung by the unexpectedly snapped cables, went mad and attacked the closest planetary vehicle, crushing its frame...

The androids opened fire while the humans hurriedly withdrew to the cave, but the shots from the ARG-8 did not cause much damage to the incredible beast, instead enraging it further. The lizard grabbed one of the robots with its tentacles, flung two more away with a swipe of its tail, and bit the last one in half, spitting it out with a growl when it realized that the android was inedible.

Soon, it was all over. The hungry lizard didn't find any food but had inflicted significant damage: one soil transformer had sunk and the second one was belching smoke. The all-terrain vehicles were seriously damaged and would take weeks to repair. The colonists had managed to make it to their shelter but the androids covering their exit had been destroyed, their broken bodies swallowed up by the marsh.

"There you have it." the teacher's voice interrupted the silence. "How could our ancestors fight the hostile environment, when even the most powerful planetary vehicles were helpless before the inhabitants of the jungle?"

None of the children answered. They were staring around them, clearly frightened of *this* version of Dabog.

"Now we'll move on to the next hall. There you'll see how the planet's flora and fauna changed, as well as people's technology, after several decades of colonization..."

✳ ✳ ✳

The internal launching area of the Shadow of Earth cruiser
Ten minutes before the start of the invasion

THE SIREN HOWLED continuously.

The regular flashes of the warning lights outlined the launch beds with the affixed assault modules. Hundreds of fighters in armored camouflage suits went up the ramps and disappeared into the reddish glow of the landing force compartments.

"Quickly! Get a move on!" the officers' shouts flooded the communicators.

People's faces showed conflicting emotions. Some were angry, some were focused, others looked depressed and some were shaking. Beads of sweat, unnatural flushes or, on the contrary, a deathly paleness, revealed the emotional tension of these minutes.

"Quickly! Hurry up! Hurry up!"

The hangar gates hissed open along the perimeter of the internal launching area. The howling of the siren was drowned out by a low-pitched roar. A planetary combat vehicle with the number 1 on the contoured tower of the plasma generator appeared from the most distant compartment.

In the age of high-tech, engineers had turned away from the caterpillar track. The PCV moved on eight cast ribbed wheels, but thanks to the inbuilt anti-grav, possessed unique passability and maneuverability, since the weight of the combat vehicle changed depending on its surroundings. The variable gravitation module could make it very lightweight, reducing its pressure on the ground, or could make it sink into the earth. Intrasystemic wars had convincingly shown that it was the most reliable and deadly planetary technology. It was believed that only another PCV could stand against a PCV.

The loading finished a few minutes later, and the launch beds with the affixed assault modules began to slowly turn around.

One of the walls of the internal launching area split into four wedge-shaped segments. It was the opening of the cruiser's vacuum dock.

Dabog. Colonization History Museum
The same time

A DIFFERENT ERA AWAITED the class in the next room.

The river still flowed in the center of the panorama, but now its shores were edged by thickets of carelessla, which leaned towards the water. The jungle on the left side of the river had retreated, and on the right side, greenhouse domes sparkled among the gray cliffs.

The children's eyes glowed in admiration.

Having felt timid before the wild and hostile nature of ancient Dabog, they welcomed the unimpressive but familiar trees with excited approval. The teacher looked pleased too, for the children had correctly absorbed the first lesson. Now they will undoubtedly learn to value everything created by their ancestors, to love and care for modern nature.

"And now, let's see how human technology changed over the decades of colonization," she uttered, inconspicuously touching a sensor on the hologram control panel.

A familiar rhythmical sound came from the depths of the jungle, and soon the wall of plants parted to reveal something huge, powerful, and looking completely different to the modern agricultural servomachines!

"I know! I know! It's a monument! We saw one in the park but it was a small one!"

The teacher smiled.

"No, you're mistaken, Sasha. It's not a monument but a real machine, preserved from that distant time. We'll be able to look at it a bit later, in a different room of the museum."

The cybermechanism kept moving, swaying slightly from side to side. Apart from the sound of the working servomotors, the ancient machine had nothing in common with the elegant modern agricultural robots. Powerful, tall and heavily armored, it would have looked ridiculous on the modern Bao tree plantations, but the children suddenly felt an earlier unknown pride. They had gotten over their fear and had lifted slightly the veil of history, seen the bravery of their ancestors... and now they were genuinely happy to see the giant that could conquer the marshy jungle!

"We are all very lucky. The first generation of colonists consisted of many clever, talented and brave people, like Max Bourne, Catherine Rimp, her daughter Chloe, who created the first hybrid plants, and of course, Hans Gervet, a real genius of engineering. He created a prototype of the universal servomachine, basing it on the giant loader, which was designed to remove the armored plates from the colonial transport and build shelters out of them. The universal servomachine was not only able to replace the soil transformers but also resist the large lizards."

The children listened to her, watching in wonder as the powerful cybermechanism, whose cabin rose above the plant life, walked through the jungle as if it was nothing more than forest shrubbery. The two legs left deep pits in the boggy soil. It simply stepped over the small rocky ridges that frequently appeared in its path.

"Miss, it's not going to trip and fall, is it?" the children fretted.

"No, no, don't worry," Daria reassured them. "The construction has been carefully designed and tested over centuries. The science that allowed us to create a completely new type of machine is called bionics," she continued. "Hans Gervet and the exobiologists helping him researched the anatomy of the lizards, which weigh dozens of tons and yet walk easily through swamps and even climb cliffs that none of the all-terrain vehicles can cross."

Confirming her words, the ancient walking mechanism stopped by the edge of the river and then easily waded across.

"Who controls it? Is it a computer?" the children bombarded her with questions.

"No, a person controls it. Moreover, each ancient robot has a name. In the old days, when the planet was first colonized, each family on Dabog owned a cybermechanism like this. They were manufactured in underground factories, in deep bunkers."

"What's this one called?"

"Aquila. It is the family robot of the Rokotov family, one of the few remaining servomachines."

The holographic decorations changed again in the meantime. Now, three cybermechanisms similar to Aquila were clearing the ground on the left riverbank: one pulled out the plants, the second sprayed around a whitish substance, while the third dried the swamp — it turned out that the giants could use different agricultural implements as attachments.

Things moved quickly. The swamp became

shallower, leaving behind silt drying in the sun, while the special reagents and bacteria spread by the robots prepared the obtained layer of soil for the Bao saplings, the main agricultural crop on Dabog.

Daria could have told the children a lot more but this lesson was meant to be an introduction and overview. Later on, when they would study separate subjects, they would discover that the Bao tree was the result of genetic engineering, a hybrid of a local plant and the breadfruit tree from distant Earth, and that modern nature on their planet was a synthesis of the two biospheres...

"Miss, does this mean that all the lizards died out?" the children watched as the reagents made the impassable jungle wither and disintegrate.

"No, they didn't all die out," the teacher reassured them. "To destroy the native wildlife would be cruel and wrong. That's why our ancestors left an enormous island untouched, far to the south, in the middle of the ocean. It's so huge that many people call it a continent. This is where all the native inhabitants of the planet live, while scientists care for them, study the evolution of Dabog and conduct different experiments."

Meanwhile, the attention of the students was drawn to another walking servomechanism, which appeared on the right riverbank. This robot was equipped with tunneling lasers. It projected a holographic layout onto the cliffs and began to cut the stone, making a tunnel through the mountain range.

"Oh, look, look!" the children became alarmed again, noticing how several huge lizards suddenly appeared from the jungle. There were three of them this time!

Nevertheless, only one servomachine stopped working as the pilot turned it around to face the threat.

The cybermechanism, which had just been spraying fertilizer, transformed as it moved. Additional plates of armor covered the sloping front of the control cabin. It dropped the agricultural attachments and weapon pylons extended on both sides, with electromagnetic weapons suspended from them.

Things were heading towards a fierce battle. The dicorts were rapidly approaching but the servomachine pilot kept his cool. Having assessed the situation, he made three single sniper shots, which penetrated the lizards' natural armor but would have hardly stopped them...

This only angered the dicorts further but after several seconds their movements suddenly became sluggish and hesitant. The special drug contained in the bullets had paralyzed the lizards.

Soon came the hum of motors and a

transport module appeared in the sky.

"It's going to take the lizards to the island?!" one of the children guessed.

"That's right," nodded their teacher. "But not all such meetings ended so quickly and without loss of life. Quite often, especially during the seasonal migrations, the lizards attacked in large groups and the humans were forced to have whole battles with them. That's why all the ancient servomachines were so well armored and armed. It was thanks to this dual purpose technology and the bravery of our ancestors, that you and I can live under the open skies. Now, let's move on to the next hall, where we will see the real Aquila, which..."

In the next moment, the walls of the ancient bunker suddenly shook. The holograms twisted and then went out.

Sparks flew from some of the wires, the red emergency light came on and went out, and everything was plunged into darkness.

Chapter Two

Dabog
October 10, 2607

IGOR ROKOTOV TURNED thirty-seven this year.

Leaving his flycar in the museum's parking lot, he made his familiar way to the service lift.

There were frequent excursions at the start of the school year. Children not only liked to look at Aquila but also see it in action.

For Rokotov, studying the history of his home planet and filling in the existing 'blanks' had become not only a beloved job but also his life purpose.

It sometimes happens that an unexpected meeting, a devoured book or sudden circumstances completely change a person's life. This happened to Igor in his youth, when he first entered the control cabin of his family's Aquila.

The ancient agrobot was stored in one of the more distant hangars, together with the other relics. It stood silent and imposing, surrounded by service towers, having lost its former purpose and meaning, for modern Dabog was a peaceful planet where humanity was no longer in deadly danger and where the Bao tree plantations were serviced by a new generation of machines, very different from the relics of the past.

Igor remembered that day very clearly. It had been autumn back then as well, and heavy rain thrummed on the wet hump of the old hangar. Igor had been walking home and dashed into the hangar to wait out the downpour. The hangar roof had worn out in places and the water dripped from overhead, droplets spraying against the cover of the ancient robot and leaving an orange stain on its leg.

Igor didn't feel like running home in the cold rain, so he decided to look around. He'd been in here before, of course, but hadn't paid much attention to the outdated technology, seeing it as nothing more than a phantom of the past.

He came closer and the outline of the cybermechanism appeared in the gloom. He could see the numerous scarring and pitting on the giant's ceramic armor, and then... reacting to the human's approach, the system suddenly switched on: there was a squeak of the cyberstack signal and Igor's personal nanocomputer began to receive a fragmented report about the state of the system nodes.

"This can't be happening!" he thought. How was it possible that after so many years of disuse, the servomachine still had some power left?

Intrigued and puzzled, Igor clambered up the struts of a service tower and reached the emergency hatch located in Aquila's base.

Something screeched and the remains of the seal showered down like trash. One of the segments of the technical corset that held the ancient robot in place turned around, forming a small platform and as if inviting Igor to step onto it and climb inside the cyber behemoth.

Igor couldn't resist. He was overcome with a burning sense of curiosity.

The light was dim inside Aquila's cabin. The dark screens reflected the light from the indicators of reserve power. The base with the piloting chair on it looked worn, the paint peeling in places and the metal darkening with age.

A tiny scanning screen glowed on the wide

armrest, covered with sensors, and Igor's cyberstack began to receive further messages:

Connection with the colonial shelter is lost. Server not found to synchronize date and time.

Attention, to activate the Inheritance Protocol, a DNA sample is required.

Igor felt an inner tremor but overcame his trepidation and intuitively touched the scanner with his finger. He felt Aquila's system take a drop of his blood and then...

One of the screens began to glow and a message appeared on it.

Rokotov family genetic line has been confirmed.

Inheritance Protocol has been activated.

Welcome, pilot.

Reactor power at 3%.

Scanning the surrounding environment — exosystem not identified. Database update is required.

Subsystem status — urgent repair is required.

* * *

THAT EVENING COMPLETELY changed Igor's life. The unexpected event made an incredible impression on the young man.

When Rokotov came home, he immediately began questioning his parents but they couldn't give him any clear answers. According to his father, Aquila had been put into storage back in his great-great-grandfather's time and had been standing in the hangar ever since.

Igor then decided to look for information online and discovered to his surprise that almost nothing was known about the early period of the planet's colonization. It was possible that the technological relic, which had belonged to his family for many generations and had been unfairly forgotten, was the last example of cybernetic mechanisms from a bygone era.

How could this have happened?!

The answer didn't come straightaway. This evening became a catalyst for the start of a long and difficult yet fascinating search.

Apart from the history of his home planet, Igor Rokotov became very interested in technology, engineering and servomechanics.

Trying to repair Aquila and its transport module, which rose like a mound of dead armor behind the hangar, Igor read all the ancient technical manuals, but the majority had been written back on Earth and dealt with the construction of the colonial transport.

Now, in his search for the necessary information and spare parts, he regularly went on risky forays. All up, Rokotov managed to find and explore nine ancient, semi-submerged colonial shelters.

A great discovery for Igor were the books by Hans Gervet, which he found in one of the bunkers, and the diaries of Max Bourne, who became the pilot of the very first servomachine on Dabog.

Nowadays, Igor's personal collection contained over a hundred microchips with documentary recordings from those years.

The history of the desperate struggle with the planet's native biosphere, the mind-boggling experiments in biology, the conflicts between the different settlements — Rokotov gradually got a better glimpse into those distant and dramatic times.

Nobody had hidden the history of Dabog on purpose, but the link between generations was disrupted about two hundred years ago, when a series of controlled mutations allowed humans to leave the colonial shelters and live on the surface.

Far from everyone had agreed to the 'biological adaptation' and society had split in two, with conflicts erupting and some of the bunkers even being destroyed. Then came a period of rapid change, the growth of cities and the exploration of endless territories, and the events of the past grew dim and lost their intensity, becoming forgotten.

Igor just smiled at his own thoughts. It was stupid to think that modern civilization had appeared in a day. The search for the grains of truth, lost among the centuries, was what he had dedicated his life to.

* * *

ENTERING THE LIFT, Rokotov touched a sensor. The cabin moved gently down towards the underground hangar, where Igor kept the restored Aquila for demonstrations.

...The sudden strike, like the jolt of an earthquake, took him by surprise. The emergency brakes activated with a screech, the cabin stopped sharply and Igor was knocked off his feet, falling and hitting his shoulder.

In the next moment, a series of crushing vibrations shook the ancient bunker. The lights went out and pieces of broken constructions rained down, with several cables snapping. The lift cabin dropped several meters with a grating sound and then became stuck. Its internal lining burst, exposing the fine mesh of the protective net, and Rokotov was thrown painfully against it at the next jolt.

Everything went quiet for a minute, only a torn cable sparking in the dark, and the drumming of small cement pieces, falling onto the cabin roof.

Grimacing with pain, Igor got up from the tilted floor. He could taste the salty tang of blood on his smashed lips. Darkness encased him. Turning on the cyberstack light, he looked at the tiny display. The wireless network was down. There was no connection. What happened?! An earthquake? But this area was always considered earthquake-resistant!

Several large shards fell from above. One of them burst through the roof of the lift and became wedged there. Now Igor couldn't use the emergency hatch!

What was he going to do?!

He turned on the cyberstack's torch. The dull light played over the plastic splinters that the cabin's interior lining had turned into, the sharp edges of the torn metal mesh, the bent loadbearing beam and the cables snaking alongside it.

"If I try to squeeze through sideways, I'll probably fit," Igor thought. He was actually very frightened. Even during his expeditions to the ancient colonial shelters, he had never found himself in such dire circumstances. Right now, tons of cement shards were pushing down on the cabin from above. The bitter dust irritated his throat and made him feel like he was choking. He couldn't tell where the accident had occurred.

The thunder of falling rocks came again and this spurred Igor into action. He pulled back the edge of the torn mesh. The lift's frame had become twisted. There was a gap between it and the wall, which could fit a person.

"Hey!" he hoped for a reply but heard only a distant echo. He was quite high up but he had to take the risk. There was no other way out. Good thing that the bunker's elevators hadn't been converted to modern ones. The light from the torch illuminated a bundle of cables, hanging from the bottom of the cabin. None of them was throwing out sparks, which meant that the automatic fault protection had kicked in.

Igor reached out, grabbed the cables and found himself hanging in total darkness. His legs automatically wrapped around the thick bundle of cables. He had descended to greater depths in the past, but now, without a belay or safety equipment, it wasn't as easy.

Fear flooded him when the lift's frame dropped again and he barely held on, swaying at an unknown height. His breathing caught and a cold sweat beaded his forehead. Small stones showered down. Judging by the sound of their falling, the shaft descended another thirty meters at least!

His arms soon began to tremble from fatigue. The ominous screeching frayed his nerves. The descent seemed endless... until a weak flash of light came from below!

The light of a pocket torch swept over the walls, illuminating the bottom of the shaft, strewn with fragments, and the electromagnetic damper built into its base.

"Daria?"

"Igor Vladimirovich? Is that you? You're alive!"

The light shone in his face and blinded him.

"I'm fine. How... are the children?"

"They're OK. They're frightened but not a scratch on them. What happened?"

"Daria, can you put down the torch so that it's illuminating the bottom of the shaft, and step back? It's dangerous here."

"All right... But please come as fast as you can, the children are afraid of the dark."

✳ ✳ ✳

A MINUTE LATER, Igor Rokotov jumped onto the shaft floor, picked up the torch and tried to brush off his torn and dirty clothing. Then he shrugged, annoyed at his own habits.

The server room was located behind the technical hatch, and beyond it lay the main museum floor.

It was pitch black everywhere. The emergency generators hadn't turned on like they were supposed to. The children huddled together, whispering about something among themselves. The light from the tiny cyberstack screens made their frightened faces look unhealthily pale.

"Everyone in one piece?"

"Yes! It's just dark. And scary... Will someone come and get us out?"

"Of course. Here you go, Daria," he gave the torch back to the teacher. "We need to take the students to the technical boxes, they're better protected."

"Igor Vladimirovich, what happened?

He could barely make out her features in the gloom. She was as scared as the children and trying hard not to cry. Rokotov's appearance had weakened her resolve, for here was a person who was undoubtedly braver and more decisive, who knew exactly what needed to be done...

She had no idea that Igor felt equally confused and overwhelmed.

"I think there was an earthquake," he said.

"But this has never happened before!" Daria whispered. "There's no connection to even the rescue services... What are we going to do? The exit's been buried under, right?"

"Don't forget that Aquila is here. Get the children and follow me. The most important thing is to calm the children down and try not to panic yourself, all right? We'll have to be strong for a little while, but we'll definitely get out of here."

She didn't reply, only nodded and stared at him anxiously for several more seconds.

In orbit around Dabog

"PHANTOM-1 REPORTING, enemy transport has been destroyed!"

The pilot of the lead fighter plane watched the remains of the freight ship as it burned up in the atmosphere and then assessed the overall situation. The assault modules were on an approach course with the planet. The communication satellites had been shot down and orbits were clear, but something was going wrong down below.

Two mushroom-shaped clouds, piercingly bright at their base and streaked with flames, tightly woven with plumes of black smoke, had already reached the edge of the stratosphere.

'What the frayg?' thought the pilot, 'did they actually shoot a nuclear warhead?'

Admiral Alexander Nagumo was wondering the same thing as he stood on the bridge of the flagship cruiser.

"Recordings from the reconnaissance probes!" he ordered, refusing to listen to anyone's bumbling explanations.

A holographic screen appeared before him. The operating windows showed images of two large cities. They still looked whole on the recording from five minutes ago.

The 'megacity killers' appeared in the morning sky as two rapidly glowing arcs and immediately splintered into a multitude of fiery parts. The rocket warheads had split and now thousands of flaming missiles were falling onto the cities of Dabog.

A crawling sensation swept over Nagumo's scalp. He had last seen this on Mars. The outlines of the buildings suddenly shook and became hazy: they fractured, the facades exploded in a sparkling shower of glass, and clouds of cement dust boiled up from the street — level after level, suburb after suburb, the residential areas turning into rubble.

The projectiles were the result of military high-tech and consisted of layers of a special alloy. When they struck an object, the outer shell turned into plasma, burning a crater in the city's cover, while the missile kept moving deeper and deeper, creating further explosions, punching through residential levels and felling the load-bearing constructions through multiple strike waves...

A thick smoke rose from the burning plastic. The concrete turned into dust, which was immediately burned up. Innumerable columns of smoke rose into the azure sky, flakes of ash and soot were flung up to the stratosphere, plunging this part of the continent into darkness.

Suddenly, in the wake of the destruction, a series of particularly bright flashes appeared in the dust clouds that obscured the ruins — a powerful impediment of some sort stood in the way of the weakening missiles.

A dazzling blaze swept along the ground and the sensors on the reconnaissance probes recorded strong energy signatures. Ancient underground constructions, equipped with nuclear reactors, lay at the base of the cities!

Nagumo watched in helpless fury as the plan of invasion collapsed.

Underneath the ceramic cover (made from the dismantled armor plates of the colonial transport) lay well-protected and securely shielded energy stations. Unsurprisingly, orbital scanning hadn't picked them up but no amount of explanation would help now. The 'megacity killers' burned through this obstacle. The probe sensors were blinded by the nuclear explosions.

They could forget about military terraforming the continent now. The act of intimidation, designed to break the will of people on other planets, had turned into a nuclear disaster. 'At least Dabog's capital wasn't attacked and is quite far away from the epicenter of the two explosions,' the admiral thought in annoyance. 'Who would have thought that these idiots would build modern cities on top of ancient colonial shelters?!'

Nagumo didn't even briefly think about the people who had perished in that terrifying moment. He was more concerned about the underground factories, so necessary for the fleet.

The bunker of the Colonization History Museum of Dabog
An hour after the catastrophe

"MR. IGOR, WHAT ARE you doing?" a child's breaking voice sounded behind him.

Rokotov stopped the hand winch and turned around.

He hadn't managed to start the emergency generators. The avalanches had blocked many of the rooms. The only source of power right now was Aquila's engine, which was being used to charge the batteries that Igor had found in one of the technical boxes.

The boy that had sneaked into the hangar was called Sasha.

"There's been some sort of accident up above, you see," Igor squatted down and patiently repeated himself. "I need to get to the surface and call for help. That's why I'm setting up the lasers. They'll help clear the tunnel."

"Can he do it?" the boy glanced at the silhouette of the ancient cybermechanism.

"Aquila is very strong. He'll manage."

"Really? Can you ask them to rescue us quickly, then? It's cold and we're hungry already."

"Don't worry. Go back to the other students, I've still got a lot of work to do."

"OK." The boy looked at Aquila again, then smiled shyly and bounced away to the entrance of the lit room, where the voices of other children could be heard.

Rokotov felt a lump in his throat. He no longer believed that everything would end so simply. The communications were still down. Nobody had tried to come to their rescue although enough time had passed. The emergency services knew the timetable of the excursions and should have reacted immediately.

None of mechanisms worked. Igor's hands were covered in scratches and shook from fatigue. He picked up the hand winch again, lifting a massive piece to the required height.

Finally, the locking plates clicked into place. Now he just had to connect the control unit and everything would be ready.

The hollow echo of approaching steps sounded again.

"Igor Vladimirovich, how is it going?" Daria asked worriedly.

"I'm finishing up. I've installed the tunneling lasers. I was preparing them for a performance at the next anniversary celebrations of the Fugitive's landing. It's ironic that I removed Aquila's technical manipulators a few days ago..." he wiped his hands and climbed up, where he began connecting the cables.

"Will you really be able to climb out?"

"There is a tunnel leading from the hangars, designed to fit servomachines. It has partially collapsed but I'll clear the way," Rokotov replied confidently. "The charged batteries will last you three or four hours," he connected the last socket and came back down. "Take the children deeper into the hall. I'll activate Aquila now."

"All right," Daria caught his gaze and held it for a second.

Igor wanted to reassure and cheer her up

but the words wouldn't come out.

"Go," he forced himself to say. "I'll send help soon. I'll have to seal the doors to this part of the shelter since the tunnel will fill up with smoke when I start cutting the rocks."

Daria hugged him suddenly and whispered, "Be careful... and come back soon."

Their lives took place on different planes. They barely knew each other, with only a brief nod whenever they met. In these short moments, they had become so close to each other and so needed...

"Leave the communicator on. I'll get in touch as soon as I find anything out."

✳ ✳ ✳

THE DRONE OF ELECTROMOTORS and the rustle of servodrivers broke the silence of the technical box. With a pneumatic hiss, Aquila's body became free of the station's equipment supports. Its legs straightened, testing the recently replaced parts.

Rokotov turned the servomachine towards the tightly closed control gates, beyond which lay the emergency tunnel, stretching through the mountain range.

He immediately noticed the cracks in the sturdy reinforced concrete vault. Water was already seeping through them in several places. Fragments of the shattered lighting panels crunched under Aquila's feet.

Igor piloted the ancient cybermechanism confidently. It must be said that Hans Gervet created a genius construction, which (with a certain level of skill) could even be operated by a teenager. Nevertheless, Aquila's system had plenty of secrets which had yet to be discovered. For example, it's neuronal component. The chips, obviously borrowed from the Hugo BD-12 series of androids, formed the neural system of the servomachine and were responsible for many of the important functions, such as maintaining balance. But did Aquila possess artificial intelligence?

The question so far remained unanswered. Many of the neural chips were damaged. Rokotov had recently replaced them but this didn't have an immediate effect. It took time for the artificial neural network to piece together the fragments of the past and show itself...

...The distance gauge beeped shrilly. The avalanche was blocking Igor's way. The columns of light indicating the surrounding temperature and radiation levels suddenly leapt up into the yellow zone.

Igor was dumbfounded for the first few moments. The avalanche was to be expected but what about the increased temperature and radiation? Where did that come from?

The indicators didn't stop there — trembling, they slowly approached the red zone. The cabin sealed automatically as Aquila's system continued to process the obtained data.

Predicted surface temperature: 53 degrees Celsius.

Lethal radiation level!

Igor couldn't believe that this was truly happening. He manually reset the sensors but repeat scanning produced the same result.

Normal human fear now looked like a pale shadow compared to the sense of impending doom that flooded his brain. His heart beat like mad. His breathing sped up. His palms were sweaty.

No, this must be a mistake, a fault in the sensors.

Dust particles spun in the light of the projectors. The communication frequencies crackled. The uncertainty drove him mad and he reached for the control joysticks again. His trembling fingers touched the laser tunneling controls.

Two ruby red lines pierced the cement, cutting into it like a hot knife through butter.

There was thunder and fragments showered down. The way was soon clear but Igor hesitated. Through the opening in the rocks, he saw low-lying, crimson-colored roiling clouds.

The sensors went crazy.

Rokotov forced Aquila to take several steps. The tunnel opening flashed on the overview screens. The torn down gates lay on the black, and in some places, smoking hillside. A little further down the slope, he saw the burnt trunks of trees, flung to one side, and thickets of carelessla that had lost their leaves and looked like frayed rolls of burnt wire.

Large flakes of ash spun through the air like snow.

AQUILA FROZE on the blackened slope. The flattened cabin of the servomachine slowly turned around as it scanned the surroundings. The hot gloomy air shimmered and wavered, the large amount of ash obscured visibility and Rokotov had to release probes to obtain an image of the nearby city.

What he saw shocked him.

There was almost nothing left of the megacity, only mounds of wreckage, and the stunted, jagged ruins of the lower levels of buildings, which stretched along the edge of a huge, fire-breathing pit.

For a second, Igor thought that he had died and ended up in a mythical hell.

The low, crimson clouds pressed down like a stone slab over his head. Hundreds of smoke pillars reached up to meet them. There was no contact with the satellites and the automatic frequency search could not find a signal.

Igor's mind glitched. He was overcome with shock and terror. The absolute destruction spoke of hundreds of thousands of deaths. Nobody had survived — the radiation level left no space for hope.

Rokotov's gaze went blank while Aquila's scanners impassively picked up more and more details: a thermal map overlay the surroundings, letting him see the numerous glowing craters, which had already been covered by ash.

The earthquake theory clearly wasn't right, but what had really happened?!

A strange flash appeared and then faded on the horizon. The wind grew stronger. A storm of ash danced around Aquila in a devilish frenzy.

'As long as Daria and the children stay inside the bunker and don't do anything silly.' Igor's thoughts were disjointed and jumped around. He couldn't imagine what kind of disaster had befallen Dabog, that had turned the familiar area into a radioactive desert.

The craters didn't fit into the picture of an earthquake at all. His confusion and bewilderment grew, while the situation worsened with every passing second. A new series of jolts swept over the land, a distant blaze shone through the murk for a moment, but its origin remained mysterious and unknown...

'It's 300 kilometers from here to the capital as the crow flies. There are vehicle tunnels passing through the mountain range. If they haven't collapsed, I'll be able to contact someone on the other side and call for help,' these thoughts helped Rokotov to shake off the daze.

The self-stabilization gyroscopes howled dully and the three-toed legs of the ancient servomachine pressed deeply into the glowing soil and scratched against the rock. Aquila turned around and headed towards the road that had melted into the soil.

* * *

THE CLOSEST TUNNEL had indeed survived.

Rokotov passed through it without meeting anything alive. A wave of heat swept over him in the narrow space: the burned out flycars still smoked, piled up on top of each other. In some places, pools of oils burned, dispelling the darkness.

Several times, Igor had to force his way through piles of cars, crushing the smoking metal with Aquila's feet.

A plain opened up on the other side of the low mountain range. Igor thought that the cliffs had protected the agricultural farms from the catastrophe, but he had been wrong. The radiation level dropped only slightly and remained dangerous to life.

The low ash clouds blocked out the sunlight, creating a dusky environment. A blind cow staggered along the edge of a smoking field. One of its sides was completely burnt and bloodied ribs stuck out through the charcoaled hide. The animal was screaming with pain. Igor was so stunned by this scene that he forgot about the controls and Aquila stopped, a dying howl coming from its servomotors.

The blind cow stopped, turned to face the sound, and Igor was faced with a surreal image, for the animal's other side was completely whole.

A lump was stuck in Igor's throat. The animal's cry was a plea for mercy but his fingers shook and he couldn't grab the joystick. Rokotov's mind began to crack in these moments. Everything became enveloped in fog. He had been desperately hoping that things would be different on this side of the mountains, but he was wrong. The farm buildings stood without their roofs. The shattered windows were framed by pools of fiberglass. One side of the building was coated in soot with a pale human outline standing out sharply against the background: someone had stood there in the moment of the blast.

Tears came unbidden into his eyes. His misty gaze could find only more evidence of death around him. The trees planted along the road had been toppled over and uprooted, while the ones that still stood upright reached their charred branches to the ash-covered sky like broken arms.

Only Aquila's scanners continued to gather information, scant lines of data appearing on the screen.

There had been several nuclear explosions. The direction of the blast waves and the radiation indicated that the second large city on the continent had also been destroyed. Furthermore, the servomachine's sensors picked up a group of awakened volcanoes near the shore. They were the source of the flashes that intermittently lit up the horizon.

Only the probe sent in the direction of Dabog's capital showed a gradual decrease in the radiation levels.

Igor's lips shook. No matter what would happen, his previous life was gone forever.

The screaming cow, whose one side had turned into a bloody pulp and the other side glistened pristinely, was like the two halves of his broken life...

He finally pressed the switch and ended the animal's suffering.

The frequency scanner continued to crackle with interference. Ash floated through the air.

Several minutes passed before Aquila began moving again, turning towards the capital city and cutting straight through the field.

Igor didn't have much time left. The energy in the museum's bunker would only last another 3-4 hours. Thinking about the children trapped there helped to clear Igor's head and get himself under control.

I must bring help...

THE AIR ASSAULT MODULES of the Terran Alliance entered Dabog's atmosphere, descending in the direction of the planet's capital, the only large city that had been spared an attack from space.

The now reddish sun still shone over this part of the continent, but the ash front was rapidly approaching.

"This is AAM-1," Major Sherman watched the groups of volcanoes that had awakened near the shore. "We have passed the low orbit zone. We've had no resistance and no communication intercepts. The city," he switched to the data from the probes, "looks abandoned."

This inhabitant of Earth hadn't been impressed by the sudden eruptions. He'd seen worse. The huge conical pipes of the waste incinerators in Europe Megacity, for example, had a diameter of several kilometers and reached up to the stratosphere. Several times per day, a flame would burst from them that lit up the sky from one horizon to the other...

The modules began a rapid descent. The cybernetic systems were scanning constantly but not finding any targets. This was concerning. According to the plan, Dabog's capital was to be captured in half an hour, and its population, frightened by the orbital bombardments inflicted on the other cities, would turn into willing hostages, ready to provide access to the bunkers and to release data from the biological studies conducted over centuries of colonization.

It looked like there was nobody to ask... 'Where did the population all go?' the Major wondered as he studied the signature maps.

Raising clouds of dust, the air assault modules landed one after another at the edge of the city. Multi-ton ramps dropped down with a clang and planetary combat vehicles rolled down them. From a distance, their cast wheels looked like giant rotary cutters.

A minute later, the armored vehicles

reached the ring road surrounding the megapolis and surged towards their predetermined positions.

Sherman watched the situation from the tactical compartment and continued to puzzle over the disappearance of the city inhabitants. There should have been panic and chaos in the city streets, but instead they were empty!

Meanwhile, PCV-1 had reached the upper level of the nearest petal-like junction and stopped, swaying softly on its suspension. The assault team in their armored suits began climbing out. The vehicle's cybernetic system had found a target — a communications complex at the top of one of the high-rise buildings. The plasma generator turret turned sharply and a small clump of energy, similar to ball lighting, formed within the force field and was rapidly shot upwards.

There was a flash a few seconds later and shards of melted metallic constructions showered down.

"Communications node has been destroyed. No natives seen, maybe they've all died from fear," Captain Joshua, in command of the planetary vehicle division, made a nervous and clumsy joke.

There was a sharp smell of ozone in the air after the attack. Soon it would become familiar to many worlds, the smell of high-tech death.

Sherman didn't reply to the captain. He wasn't liking this silence.

***

FOR THE PAST HOUR, Igor had taken Aquila down the highway, moving at over a hundred kilometers per hour and overtaking the ash cloud front. The radiation level was steadily decreasing, which gave him hope. The foggy outline of the megapolis could already be seen in the distance. It seemed that he would soon meet people or at least catch the signal of the emergency services.

Suddenly a hot, gusty wind began to blow. Thick, billowing clouds covered the whole sky. Filled with ash, they separated into strips, passing so low that it seemed like they could touch the servomachine's cabin.

Visibility dropped again and the air around Aquila seemed to collapse. Then, on top of everything else, came a downpour of rain.

The drops of deadly water, mixed with ash, struck the servomachine's armor. The Bao tree plantations that stretched along the highway began to wither before Igor's eyes. He watched the crowns of the young and not yet sturdy saplings dropping helplessly, dying from the effects of the radioactive rain.

The frequency scanner unexpectedly picked up a communications signal.

"Finally!" Rokotov touched the communication sensor but the information channel turned out to be encrypted!

"How is this possible?! Shouldn't the emergency services broadcast on an open channel?" his thoughts faltered. An additional screen suddenly lit up on one of Aquila's consoles. Igor had never seen this subsystem in action previously, which was related to the servomachine's neural net.

Protected communication channel found.
Cryptographic subsystem activated. Analysis is being conducted.

Igor knew that Dabog's colonization history contained many dark and poorly recorded moments. Due to the crash of the colonial transport, groups of people came out of cryogenic sleep at intervals of many months and sometimes years. They took the available technology and formed the initial colonies. These enclaves often fought with each other. Nevertheless, Rokotov would not have guessed that the servomachines took part in these clashes of many centuries ago!

Despite all that, it took Aquila only a few minutes to break into the protected communication channel.

The sound of a foreign voice shocked him. Igor didn't even understand the language in the first few moments. He needed some time to understand that it was Intergalactic English, spoken by everyone of Dabog, but significantly altered, full of unusual turns of phrase and unfamiliar words.

He felt chills run down his spine as he listened to this foreign voice, gradually becoming used to the accent and beginning to make out separate words. When he understood what was being said, he bit his lip until it bled and continued to listen.

"DAMMIT, MAJOR, they've hidden away like rats!"

"Rotmistrov, frayg take you, report properly! What is the problem? Where is the population?"

There was a sharp crackle of interference and then speech again:

"...we can't reach them. There's a deeply echeloned system of bunkers here! It's like another city but underground!"

"Did they realize what was happening?"

"Yes. And they've sealed off all the entrances!"

"Are there many?"

"Sorry?" Many who?"

"Entrances, you dolt!"

"There's one in the basement of each building! That's why they managed to descend so quickly into their shelters!"

"So find some ventilation shafts or other

pipelines!"

"Everything's sealed off. There are probably closed-circuit life support systems in the bunkers. Past tech, I bet. We should have struck this city from space!"

The interference crackled again.

The meaning of what he had heard slowly seeped into Igor's brain. The words, like rocks thrown into water, sunk through the layers of terrible images seen over the past few hours, and dropped to the bottom of his exhausted soul — heavy lumps of fact that left no room for doubt...

"...Rotmistrov, get them out of there! This is in your own best interests! If you need to, blow up the seal or open up one of the shafts and pump gas in there!"

"So that they die off underground? It's an option, of course, but what will Nagumo say? The admiral needs..."

"Shut up and carry out my orders!" Sherman roared. "The admiral needs the controlled environment of the bunkers and the automatic manufacturing plants! Nagumo will have our hides if we don't report the planet's capture in due time! We'll be buried alive in the mines of Ganymede, in the name of Uncle Hammer! Do you get it now, imbecile?!"

"I get it, don't you worry, Major. But think about this, if we don't leave any captives alive, who is going to give us the access codes? Who will give us the results of the biological studies?"

"I said to frayg with it all! The information that we need must be in their computers! That's it! Go! I must report to the Shadow of Earth in an hour! Open up the bunkers! I don't care how many people die in there, get it?! It's my ass that I'm worried about!"

IGOR LISTENED to the argument between the two officers and an icy feeling grew in his chest.

A strike from space... My ass that I'm worried about... Gas...

They couldn't be human! Igor couldn't believe it. He didn't want to.

"I must have gone crazy," Rokotov whispered painfully, crushing his pulsing temples between his hands. "I've gone crazy!"

He had forgotten that his communicator was still connected to the encrypted communication channel.

"Hey, who's that mumbling? What do you mean 'gone crazy'? Who has gotten onto the command frequency?"

IGOR COULD TASTE the salty tang of blood on his bitten lip... He had never thought that a person could change so much in only a few hours.

With one strike, everything had been ripped

from his life... His mind refused to believe it but it seemed that his soul already did... He remembered the pale silhouette of a person on the wall, the blinded cow blundering along the road, and understood that the words he had heard were not an empty threat... The newcomers from the distant, long-forgotten ancestral planet had already decided that they had the right to come and murder...

Chapter Three

THE RAIN POURED down without stopping.

The planetary combat vehicle bearing the number 7 crossed the city by moving down the central avenue, and without meeting any opposition, burst from the narrow jumble of buildings onto the expansive road interchange.

This was not at all how Lieutenant Patrick Goodman had imagined landing on colony planets. There had been an aggressive information campaign prior to the invasion, where Dabog was presented as a world ready for immediate colonization. The new Promised Land remained inaccessible only due to the selfish stubbornness of a small group of colonists, according to the mass media.

The combat vehicle's sensors now showed the complete opposite. Despite the transformations performed by the colonists, a person from Earth had to beware of a multitude of deathly dangers...

"Seven, are you there? Report!"

"I have reached the southern road interchange," replied the lieutenant. "The assault team is still combing through the buildings but I think that it's a waste of time."

"Hold your position, and do less thinking," there was no triumph in Captain Joshua's voice, only irritation and worry.

Goodman looked at the screens again. He didn't know what real life was like and had never seen death. All his so-called values had been formed in virtual reality and could not have prepared the young lieutenant for a meeting with another world. He knew that many people had died on Dabog on this day but didn't feel any compassion.

The unexpected trill of the long-distance sensors startled him.

Goodman froze in the first second. It turned out that the mind can clearly differentiate between realities. This wasn't the virtual training area. In virtual space, he hadn't felt even a tiny fraction of all the sensations that washed over him.

"This is Seven reporting! We have guests! Unknown signature, fifteen kilometers away and approaching rapidly! Heading four-sixteen-south!" he announced in a rush.

His message flowed through the network of the invasion division like a nervous impulse. Major Sherman immediately turned his attention to the situation, since he was responsible for the ground operation. Looking at the signature analysis data, he switched on the comms, "Keep it cool, Lieutenant. It's probably a lost robot from one of the agrofarms. At least it's some sort of entertainment during our rainy walk, right?"

Goodman didn't appreciate the man's attempt at humor. "I consulted the intelligence database. This signature is unknown!"

"Don't panic! Just trust me on this. And don't forget that the PCV has no worthwhile opponents!"

The telemetry switched on. Now the planetary combat vehicle could be seen from different angles on the tactical module screens, with filming done by the accompanying probes.

The huge ribbed wheels skidded over the wet road and the multi-ton vehicle leapt forward with the speed of a racing flycar, leaving behind a plume of smoke.

Major Sherman liked the lieutenant's keenness, in which he could sense the trembling of a predator that had first smelled blood. No matter who was hiding in the depths of radiation-poisoned tree plantations, they were about to come face-to-face with some serious problems!

* * *

THE BAO TREE PLANTATIONS, Dabog's main agricultural crop, surrounded the city like a solid green wall. Now they were withering away. Rokotov directed Aquila over the remains of the crushed plant life.

He could not understand how one could enter someone else's house and kill without pause, and justify it somehow... Everything that he loved, everything that he believed in was dying before his eyes. Invisible death hung over everything: it fell from the sky in droplets of rain, it squelched under the feet of the servomachine in the oversaturated soil.

He felt deafened. A ringing emptiness filled his soul.

Having directed Aquila to the southern edge of the city, the location of the cargo bay of an ancient colonial shelter, Igor knew what he had to do in the nearest ten to fifteen minutes. But how was he supposed to live after this?

It turned out that these fragile seconds of hopelessness were a crucible. Igor's soul, like a rusty piece of metal, was thrown into the fire and burned away, leaving behind the cinders of the past. To keep living, he had to force down the hopelessness, grinding his teeth and accepting the irreparable damage that had been inflicted, but what would remain? What would his new inner core be made of? Hate? Madness? Desperate recklessness?

It was impossible to predict. It would be decided in seconds, for the true clash of civilizations happens face-to-face and eye-to-eye.

Right now, Igor filled the gnawing emptiness inside with thoughts of Daria and the children. I must reach the cargo bay... I'll find an all-terrain vehicle there with an untouched emergency store and send it to the museum bunker...

Igor was just a normal person. He followed the path of desperate hope, seriously believing that one could hide behind airlocks and sealed gates from a conflict between two worldviews, which is what war really is.

Igor released a probe, which disappeared among the withered trees, and a few seconds later, the terrain map lit up with a scattering of red markers.

Were they Terrans?

The system was still processing the gathered data when the wall of trees unexpectedly split into two under the force of an enormous, blunt-nosed vehicle. Hidden by its masking field, it rapidly attacked the ancient agrobot from the side.

Igor didn't have time to react. A bolt of plasma scorched the left side of the cabin, Aquila's sensors were burned away and the surrounding screens went dark. There was a fading howl of the servomotors while missiles struck the robot's armor. One of them pierced the cabin, ripped through the base of the piloting chair and blew up the edge of the chair's back.

The overwhelming strike made Rokotov's consciousness fade for a moment...

THE SEVENTH PLATOON of the colonial space troopers (this was now the name of the planetary forces) reached the southern road interchange.

The troopers were angry and tired after combing through the city blocks abandoned by the inhabitants. Their camouflage armor was covered in raindrops and blended into the gray color of the street. The closed visors occasionally flashed with electrostatic charges, which dispersed the radioactive drizzle.

The planetary combat vehicle suddenly came alive, its motors roaring hollowly as it launched forward. The phantom generators kicked in and the PCV disappeared from scanners, with only the fallen trees marking its passage.

"Where did Goodman rush off to?" the platoon's computer technician asked in puzzlement.

"No idea. I think they found some kind of signature," replied the sergeant and added, "We've been ordered to take our positions and await further orders."

The pale glow of a plasma shot and the rapid drumbeat of targeting electromagnetic weapons suddenly came from the direction of the disappeared PCV.

LIEUTENANT GOODMAN'S pale lips trembled from the stress. He was stunned by the size of the behemoth that he had managed to fell with his unexpected attack. He had never seen anything like it in his life! The cabin of the colonial machine, dribbling smoke, rose above the wilted tops of the trees, which were at least fifteen meters tall!

"I shot it!" Patrick exhaled.

The lieutenant was severely mistaken in his belief that it was all over. It was not enough to just *shoot down* a machine created by Hans Gervet. One had to do it again and again, and then cautiously approach the pile of twisted metal, in case it came alive again.

Even now, this colonial monster triggered an

unconscious sense of alarm.

"Finish him off!" came the abrupt order from Major Sherman.

"Sorry?"

"Finish off the pilot! He's still alive, can't you see?!"

Goodman looked at the summary display and swore under his breath. True enough, the scanners showed the warm outline of a person, standing out from the overall signature.

The fear was suddenly back as a sweaty trembling.

Goodman's subconscious didn't feel gleefully victorious, as if an inner voice kept whispering, *'Something is wrong, lieutenant'.*

The reactor of the enormous colonial mechanism was still working. The plasma-heated armor was peppered with holes but it was exuding a gray foam, which rapidly hardened. The behemoth's system was clearly restoring the control cabin's seal!

"Hurry up and die already!" he thought as he aimed at the pilot's warm outline.

✳ ✳ ✳

WAR IS A HELL where the phantom of near death rips away everything contrived and reveals each person's true nature.

Life grasps people and throws them into the whirlpool of war like blind kittens. Someone will swim to safety, someone else with drown, and someone, in a desperate attempt to save oneself, will climb over the heads of friends or enemies, whoever is there.

In any case, nobody knows how to swim at the start but they learn, rapidly and painfully.

Something savage burst forth from Patrick Goodman. He tried to quash the fear inside but it only grew, demanding an immediate blood offering.

Die! It was the only word he heard in the whine of the servomotors controlling the aim.

ROKOTOV REGAINED consciousness among a crimson fog of pain. His throat hurt from the acrid smoke. Something hot and sticky was sliding down his temple and cheek. The control panels doubled in front of his eyes. The ringing from the contusion drowned out all other sounds.

Cabin seal had been restored.

Reserve sensors are active.

Confirming the system message, the holographic screens switched on again.

Igor struggled to focus on the machine attacking him. Its frontal armor contained two electromagnetic guns. Their barrels suddenly twitched, jerking right and left, as if they were alive, aiming... at him!

His back was drenched in cold sweat.

It was a terrifying moment of shock, a desperate desire to live, a nagging icy feeling in his chest. Rokotov suddenly understood very clearly that if he hesitated for a few more seconds, he would be killed...

The reserve indicators glowed brightly on the control panels. The system had already bypassed the damaged links and had restored all its functions.

Igor's hands grasped the control joysticks. The right thumb flicked off the safety switch on the tunneling laser control. The servomotors howled as they straightened and rotated Aquila's frame.

LIEUTENANT GOODMAN could not believe his eyes.

The enormous servomechanism, which a moment ago had been still and slumping towards the soaking earth, had come alive and was straightening up. Lumps of sealing foam were still being forced through the jagged tears in the frame.

The PCV scanners let out a warning shriek, noting the unexpected energy spike: pumping mechanisms began to work in the depths of the colonial mechanism, while the rotary barrels of the two heavy lasers on the robot's shoulders suddenly started spinning.

"Goodman, fire!" Major Sherman screamed over the comms. The division commander watched what was happening from the tactical section of the assault ship, a safe distance away from the unfolding events.

The PCV's guns sprayed long lines of bullets but the giant servomachine shifted out of the line of fire so that only a few missiles scraped along its armor and bounced off, shredding the nearby trees.

In the next moment, Aquila's cabin unexpectedly spun around: the colonists' robot was moving along the path towards the city, but its heavy lasers stayed locked on the planetary vehicle of the Alliance.

The PCV plasma generator didn't have time to reload — a new burst of energy was still gathering in the force field...

"Goodman, move!" Major Sherman saw the whole picture and understood what was about to happen but his order came too late.

The emitting tubes of the immensely powerful rotary lasers released a storm of coherent radiation.

The air in the narrow glade boiled up. The planetary combat vehicle's armor was split open all along its length and burned right through.

"Frayg! I missed! Aaaaah!!!" Goodman's deathly scream was drowned out by the thunder.

The mud was boiling. The trees were aflame. Geysers of overheated steam shot up into the sky, everything was enveloped in a thick fog and images from the probes' cameras disappeared. Only one reconnaissance unit, moving along the edge of the plantation, continued to transmit images, automatically zooming in as much as possible.

Major Sherman could clearly see the pulpy leaves of the unfamiliar trees curling from the heat, and a burning, spinning ribbed wheel with the remains of a melted axle fly out of the fire. Another series of powerful explosions shook the ground and the blackened, twisted PCV flashed past the video camera: a fragment of the armored vehicle flew several hundred meters through the air and crashed into the base of the road interchange.

* * *

THE COLONIAL INFANTRY FORCES had barely taken their positions when a burst of automatic gunfire thundered behind the wall of rain, there was a blinding flash and the blast wave rolled over the ground.

When they saw a charred fragment of the PCV get dragged along the reinforced concrete, nobody panicked. Their amazement was too great. There were only unintelligible exclamations —

even the veterans of local conflicts had never truly come face-to-face with death. Wars in the 27th century were only demonstrations of technological might and very rarely, non-contact strikes. An orbiting cruiser could control a whole planet by aiming its guns at the cities below and forcing the inhabitants of the intrasystemic colonies to do the bidding of the World Government.

Right now, the fighters were stunned as the myth of the indestructibility of the PCV was destroyed before their eyes. Fear came a few seconds later, when the howling servomotors announced the arrival of a huge, threatening outline of a colonial mechanism that towered above the wall of trees.

Shrouded in steam, it looked like a horrible hallucination.

"Command-1, this is Infantry-7!" the sergeant pressed himself into the small cement fence that he was hiding behind and hurriedly made the report. "We've lost the PCV!"

"Do you see the opponent, Seven?"

"Y-yes," the sergeant stammered. The technological monster that had just destroyed the PCV continued to tower above the treetops. Its construction seemed inexplicable, matching none of the known combat technologies.

"Listen carefully," Major Sherman also didn't sound very calm. "It's just an agricultural robot of the colonists! Do you hear me?! Forget about what happened! Goodman was dumb enough to get in the line of fire! Hold your position until the other PCVs arrive! They're coming!"

The next phrase was lost in the interference.

The sergeant peeked cautiously over the top of the fence. The creepy servomechanism wasn't moving. Did Goodman damage it after all?

∗ ∗ ∗

A PERSON DOESN'T BREAK down in an hour, even if they are under pressure from deadly and insurmountable odds. They will keep their character and habits, everything that makes them who they are, for a little while longer.

So it was for Igor.

When he fired the shots, he saw only the enemy vehicle and acted decisively and instinctively, but when he heard the desperate, dying scream in the communicator, the thought of other people (even if they were the enemy) stabbed him like a knife.

The emotional impulse that pushed Rokotov out of the pilot chair could not be comprehended. Common sense dissipated. Igor's moral shock was stronger.

Dabog's society wasn't perfect but they

treasured life. Igor didn't understand that the invaders from the overpopulated homeland were raised with a different value system. They were cannon fodder, an easily replaceable 'human resource', much cheaper than the complex planetary technology.

He had yet to learn this truth but now he climbed outside and ran to the burning wreckage of the planetary vehicle, feeling the nightmare become reality.

"I'm coming... coming!" his bloodless lips kept whispering.

Rokotov thought that the people buried under the twisted metal could still be alive and hear him.

A radioactive rain poured from the sky. Hot mud steamed underfoot.

The storm of laser shots had cut the planetary vehicle into several parts and the internal explosions had finished off what he had started by scattering the remains all around.

Igor slowed down and then stopped, looking around him.

He glanced over the twisted interior of a compartment: he could see a hand under the wreckage, still clutching the controls.

Igor grasped it and pulled. The mound of smoking metal shifted and he saw the deathly pale and grimacing face of a stranger. Suddenly, the upper half of the body, bloodied and smoldering along the bottom edge, slipped easily into the mud.

Igor threw up. Suppressing the spasms with difficulty, he stared into the Terran's dead eyes for several seconds and then staggered back, swaying as if intoxicated. Igor leaned heavily on Aquila's leg and then was sick again.

The rain washed the mixture of blood and water off Rokotov's fingers.

In this instant began his descent into apathy and hate. This terrifying, desperate second marked the beginning of the Galactic War, the moment when the defense of Dabog began, which all the history books would write about in the future.

Right now, one man stood under a lethiferous rain, staring blindly ahead and trying to suppress his uncontrollable trembling.

Aquila rose above him. The overheated lasers were enveloped in steam. The warning signal from the scanners was transmitted to Rokotov's cyberstack but he didn't react. The bottom of the servomechanism opened automatically and an elevating segment slid down, as if the ancient agrobot was calling him back into the cabin...

Chapter Four

High planetary orbit
On board the flagship cruiser Endgrouse

"WE'VE LOST one PCV!" the report from the tactical center came as Nagumo was studying the plans of the bunkers, obtained from deep scanning.

"What?!" he turned abruptly.

"The planetary combat vehicle attached to the seventh platoon has been destroyed!"

"All information to my terminal!"

The admiral struggled to keep himself under control. He could see the shock and bewilderment in the eyes of the officers standing on the bridge.

The invasion plan was falling apart as it was. Many factors hadn't been considered. The rocket strike had been too powerful, the nuclear catastrophe had been unforeseen, while the colonized continent was under a veil of deadly precipitation due to the strength and direction of the winds.

And what happened now?!

The image of the gigantic servomechanism, armed with two industrial lasers, impressed but didn't frighten the admiral. He understood that he had been sent this angle of filming on purpose. The armored vehicles looked like toys, captured from a significant height.

"Give me a decent image!" he demanded irritably.

The panorama on the screen grew larger. Now the colonial mechanism was walking, leaving deep indents in the sodden earth and its curved body breaking the tree branches around it, while the planetary vehicle made its way through the forest, crushing the tree trunks that fell into the mud with an agonizing shudder of their leaves...

Nagumo watched the recording up to the moment when the blast wave destroyed the reconnaissance probes. He sat for several seconds, staring at the darkened screen. "How many are there?" he finally asked.

"One."

"Give me the chief fleet engineer!" Nagumo glanced over the tactical data. The Shadow of Earth's orbit was taking it over Dabog's capital in this very moment. "Give me Nadyrov on a secure channel."

Nagumo had appropriately assessed the degree of risk. There was no time to deal with the intelligence services, who had missed the fact that the colonists possessed such powerful technology. The situation had to be rectified at once!

Two communication channels switched on simultaneously and the admiral combined them with an annoyed flick of his hand. Let Tiberius look at the behemoth and listen to the opinion of the technical specialist.

The head fleet engineer had already seen the recording and now, while it was being transmitted to the bridge of The Shadow of Earth, decided to immediately begin his explanations.

"This mechanism was created by a truly genius constructor and it has no counterparts among modern technology. The machine contains a reactor that supplies the lasers, whose power is comparable to the largest guns on a frigate. The external view and the signatures recorded by the probes don't give us enough information about its construction so it's vital that we capture the robot for further studies, even if it's damaged!"

"What do you say, Tiberius?"

"There are cargo portals nearby, leading to the ancient shelters. If the robot gets in there and plants itself among the reinforced concrete, it's unlikely that we will be able to defeat it using our assault forces. I think it must be destroyed. At once."

Nadyrov's logic was easy to understand. While Earth's fleet had complete dominance in space, it had a limited number of assault subdivisions since most of the intrasystemic wars had taken place in the asteroid belt and involved small forces. For this reason, the design of the ships did not allow a large number of assault forces. If there would be prolonged fighting on the planet, the whole operation would fail.

"Admiral, sir, the sample's destruction is unacceptable! Can't you see that if we possess a prototype of such a machine, we could..."

"Tiberius, act!" Nagumo interrupted the engineer. "Destroy it! We'll figure it all out later. I need a report that the planet has been captured in less than an hour!"

"But the seventh assault platoon is there currently!" the chief fleet engineer threw down his last ace.

"You can chip in and build them a memorial," the admiral brushed him off.

* * *

THE FIRST WALL OF EXPLOSIONS came half a kilometer south of the road interchange and threw up an orange-black shower of earth into the sky.

The Aquila swayed and that snapped Rokotov out of his daze. The screens showed him the fiery hand of the orbital strike ploughing through the plain, rapidly nearing the edge of the plantations. He suddenly understood that he no longer feared death, for his mind and soul had broken down completely.

The nervous trembling was gone as if everything human had been left behind, beyond the experienced shock.

He touched the controls automatically and shuddered when he felt their soft, porous coating.

"I'm still alive..."

Aquila's right leg lifted from the mud with a sucking noise. Igor's heart bet slowly and evenly. He moved the machine out of the way of the approaching explosions.

A new wall of flame ran through the city suburbs. Several buildings on the Avenue of Fugitives suddenly shuddered and began to collapse, tossing up clouds of white cement dust.

Someone yelled angrily and wordlessly on the radio.

The clouds boiled, the glowing lines of

rockets struck the ground like a rain of fire.

"First, you bastards! Where are you shooting? We're here!"

The fragments pelted Aquila's armor.

"Withdraw!" someone's breaking voice sounded over the comms.

The orbital strike was gaining power with every passing second: it seemed as if the earth itself had reared up and was hovering in the air, contrary to the laws of physics.

Aquila's frame shuddered from the crushing vibrations but the servomachine maintained its balance: a multitude of automatic subsystems were helping Igor by making split-second decisions.

Navigating between the explosions, Rokotov was initially aiming for the cargo portal of the colonial shelter but the fire kept getting denser in that direction. Stepping over an intersection that had been shattered by a direct strike, with only its reinforced cement foundations remaining, he was forced to turn onto the central avenue.

The search and identification system was self-learning as it went. If its database had previously contained information on aggressive lifeforms on Dabog, now the list was being supplemented by a variety of cybernetic monsters: several times already, Aquila's scanners had confidently identified the signatures of planetary combat vehicles among the fire and smoke.

All around Igor, buildings were collapsing from the damage done to their walls. The sensors found another PCV among the fiery splashes: it was lurking in the ruins at the intersection, and loading up its plasma generator.

Igor found the target and gripped the tunneling laser controls.

Streaks of coherent radiation pierced the gloom. There was a shower of cement fragments and a powerful explosion.

The frequency scanner cut off the interference and emitted someone's voice, "He's coming! He's still coming! We've lost the second PCV!"

The past was burning up in the boiling hellfire of the city streets. The Igor Rokotov that had parked his flycar in front of the museum this morning was gone. The fragments of phrases he heard over the comms no longer upset him.

"Bring out the AAM! Launch the missiles at him!"

On the other side of the city, two signatures of the air assault modules began to rapidly gain power. The assault ships were a serious threat to the Aquila, but Igor had passed beyond doubts, fear and pity, he was burning up in the knowledge that he was not going to survive this battle.

His grief, bounding on madness, pushed

him to take a desperate step. Crashing through the wall of one of the buildings, he led the servomachine onto a highway segment that had somehow been spared.

The air assault modules could only be seen on the scanners as pale energy matrixes. They were landing at intervals of 500 meters. Right now, the middle pair was lifting into the air while they turned to make a pass over the target.

Rokotov launched a volley from the industrial lasers and then immediately reversed.

The elevated segment of road was reduced to pieces by the return fire while a bright glow suddenly blossomed where the scanners had noted the AAM position, illuminating the low clouds. One of the modules was clearly damaged.

Igor realized a very important fact in this moment: the invading forces were relatively small and he could fight as an equal with any of the Terran vehicles.

Navigating towards the glow, Igor headed into the ruins and then turned Aquila towards the northern edge of the city.

✳ ✳ ✳

A VOLLEY FROM the PCV's guns reached Aquila at the next intersection. The cabin had already been pierced in several places and the screens flickered as a bitter smoke seeped from underneath the damaged consoles.

Four planetary combat vehicles were shooting from inside a building, having positioned themselves on the ground floor, behind the shattered front window of a supermarket.

The frame's rotary motors worked jerkily with a screech of damaged metal. The storm of laser charges cut through the building's supporting beams, collapsing it on top of the enemy.

The combat vehicles' plasma generators exploded in blinding flashes among the pale clouds of dust, burning huge holes in the cement.

If Rokotov had obeyed rules, tactics or tricks during his terrifying march through the streets of the destroyed city, he would have died. But it was only the maddening grief that drove him. Having resigned himself to death, Igor directed Aquila toward the fire, driven by a single urge — to destroy the enemy's assault ships at any price.

They should not have come to Dabog. They had no right to be here...

Igor didn't know that the enemy was beginning to feel a mystical terror at the sound of Aquila's heavy and fatalistic sixty-ton tread.

The next explosion was only a few meters away. A spinning section of the cement curb flew past the cabin. A scraping sound came from Aquila's right leg.

"...entering Sector Four! That's a click away from the AAM's position!"

"...the planet's fuel is burning! We can't put it out..."

"... can't stop it! It struck the right leg... He has ceramic armor! It's obviously the plating taken off a colonial transport! Another successful hit! It keeps moving! I have no idea what's powering it!"

NAGUMO WAS LISTENING to the comms and glanced glumly at the tactical monitor.

"Withdraw!" he ordered hollowly, having made the difficult decision. "Start the AAM when ready! These losses are unacceptable! We'll finish it off from orbit and then launch the assault modules again."

In truth, this was a crushing defeat. Two assault ships were burning in a pool of planetary fuel at the edge of the city. Six PCVs had been lost. The admiral couldn't comprehend how one colonial mechanism could do such a thing!

APPROACHING THE LANDING site of the air assault modules, Igor noticed how people in vaguely familiar uniforms appeared and immediately hid among the ruins.

He was having trouble thinking. The severe concussion that he had sustained and the two shrapnel wounds were making themselves known.

His vision had become blurred. Aquila was leaning heavily to one side. The damaged servomotors in the right leg howled and scraped.

Something crackled alarmingly in the left laser, and its rotor was jammed. Showers of sparks cascaded off the top of the Aquila.

Crimson spots of pain floated before Igor's eyes. He was controlling Aquila with difficulty but there was almost no resistance in his path. The enemy was withdrawing and the orbital strikes had ceased.

Rokotov's drawn face and pale, tightly pressed together lips showed not only a desperate effort but also hopelessness. He truly felt that he had lost his right to live in the wreckage of the first destroyed planetary vehicle, among the ripped apart human bodies.

Signatures appeared again in the smoke. Two PCVs were approaching fast, attacking from opposite sides. They began firing from far away and the projectiles skimmed along the ruins, creating bursts of flame, before reaching Aquila and biting into its armor, causing the giant to stagger.

The right leg became completely jammed. The ancient servomechanism, created at the dawn of Dabog's colonization, genuinely surpassed Earth's technology, especially in its defenses and ability to keep functioning. This is what had allowed Rokotov to survive this long, but now the limit had been reached.

Aquila's frame was riddled with holes. The massive parts, made from the colonial transport's ceramic plates, were covered in pits and scorch marks. Most systems were still functioning, hidden deep under the armor, but one of the lasers had stopped working and the second was reloading slowly and jerkily since its reactor had been overloaded.

Ignoring the PCV, Rokotov turned the frame around. The cabin shifted with a metal screech so that it was slightly covered by the corner of a building. The target monitor showed pale crosses over the assault ships - two of them were in the firing line.

The right laser released a long volley of light with a scattering of sparks. They pierced the moist air with a hiss and struck the assault ship, burning through the defenses with a shower of molten metal.

Another powerful explosion shook the Avenue of Fugitives in the northern corner of the city.

The weapons of one of the starting AAM's growled in answer. Inversion plumes of rocket fire exploded from behind the building ruins. The air itself was boiling. One of the rockets found its target yet the damaged Aquila remained standing.

It leaned the front part of the cabin against the ruins and froze, enveloped in a cloud of poisonous green steam. Warning lights flickered on the control panels. The system had automatically shut down the overheated reactor. Hydraulic fluid squirted from the damaged power transmission of Aquila's limbs.

This is the end.

Rokotov was barely aware of reality. He had received a large dose of radiation and was bleeding from several shrapnel wounds. There was a roaring in his head and shifting his gaze to the surviving sensors was unbearably, painfully difficult.

The flames rose higher and higher in the north of the city. Igor couldn't understand why this was happening. He had shot down three modules, but the fire from the released planetary fuel could not have enveloped such a large area.

A few seconds later, Rokotov realized what was happening. The remaining ships were leaving, one after another.

They were running, abandoning the remaining assault teams and taking with them only the intact combat vehicles. It seemed that technology was much more valuable to them than human lives.

The roar of the engines drowned out everything else. The ground shook. Like burning torches, the ships soared up into the ash-gray skies and slowly faded beyond the roiling clouds.

A few troops were still running towards the destroyed avenue, hoping to reach the last landing ship, when they were suddenly blocked by people wearing ancient protective suits.

They quickly surrounded the ship that had been damaged by the laser volley.

A tear rolled down Igor's cheek. He felt overwhelming fatigue.

A Hugo-BD12 model android swiftly climbed up Aquila's damaged leg. It tried to contact Rokotov but didn't receive a response and began manually opening the emergency hatch.

Hundreds of pillars of smoke rose into the sky. The low clouds touched the jagged ruins, scattering ash over the buildings.

Igor could no longer see it. He was unconscious.

Part Two

Bitter Wormwood

Chapter Five

A RED MOON CIRCLED around a black planet.

The planet used to be green and the moon yellow.

The laser communication signal had the voice of Daria Krechetova, "Igor, the signatures have split up. Three AAMs accompanied by a squadron of Phantoms. They've launched from the Shadow of Earth cruiser and are on course towards Dabog."

"Got it," Rokotov assessed the situation at a glance. "I'll have time to intercept them. Over and out."

The cargo ship designed to transport Aquila had been rebuilt and armed. Freshly tuned, equipped with trophy camouflage systems and a hyperdrive, it now played the role of a heavy assault carrier.

Readjusting his course, Igor looked back at his home world. Beneath the thick, ash-filled atmosphere raged the bitter cold of a nuclear winter. One would think that after several unsuccessful attempts to storm the planet, Earth's invasion forces would have left the star system, but the squadrons of the Terran Alliance continued their siege.

Life on Dabog survived only in the deepest bunkers, where the reactors of the Fugitive Colonial Transport still worked. Teenagers had replaced their perished parents. The technologies that had belonged to the Rimp Cybertronics Corporation now served for war. The AIs, consisting of self-developing androids from the Hugo series, studied the corporation's archives and adapted the ancient technology for war, extracting the necessary raw materials from the planet's depths.

Rokotov looked at the screens again.

Dabog's moon grew steadily larger. It had never had an atmosphere but now a dense dust haze enveloped the planetoid. To prevent the Alliance fleet from taking the satellite and building bases and spaceships on it, they had to drop nuclear charges on its surface. Producing the charges had used up the whole store of radioactive material for the reactors, and the temperature inside the bunkers had to be reduced by five degrees below normal, but the invaders had lost a convenient site, instead getting a dust moon. The nuclear explosions threw up billions of tons of reddish dust into space, surrounding Dabog's moon with a suspension of tiny abrasive particles, which eroded spaceship armor and made engines fail.

FROM THE NOTES of John Hammer:
"Our travels beyond the Solar System and the war with the colonists showed how strong, and simultaneously, how weak our technology is. We cannot gloss over the fact that we are being held hostage by the extraordinary power of our own spaceships.

The events on Dabog, which has become a dead lump of radioactive ice, have served as an impressive lesson.

Erasing worlds - was this the purpose of conquering colonies? What is the point of our domination in space if we are unable to capture the thing that is most valuable - the living space on terraformed planets? The Second Wave of Expansion was initiated not to destroy but to conquer. This is the reason for the war with the colonies, an evolutionary war to control the much-needed living space and resources.

The complete opposite happened on Dabog... Nevertheless, the frenzied resistance of the colony inhabitants unexpectedly showed us a powerful weapon, so necessary to keep moving forward. The defeat of our assault units on the surface of Dabog turned into a technological victory. We learned a valuable lesson and now know that there is a ground analogy to our space cruisers. The walking agricultural machines of Dabog, appropriately modified and perfected by the servoengineers of the Terran Alliance, shall be the blade forged on other worlds, hard as steel, able to surgically excise the tumors of the resistance. Then dozens of new planets will be open to the citizens of the Terran Alliance.

No matter how cruel some episodes of this confrontation may be, it is inevitable. We cannot wait or else we will perish. The wheels of war are turning and nobody can stop this incredible movement of people, greater than any previously known to human civilization..."

John Winston Hammer, published diaries.

THE ASSAULT CARRIER'S supports touched down at the base of the crater, raising a cloud of regolith.

The surroundings were enveloped in a reddish gloom.

Radioactive dust circled lazily, creating a thick veil that hid him from the enemy's scanners.

Why was Rokotov taking the risk by landing in the dusty atmosphere?

The answer was simple. The number of Dabog defenders shrank with each passing day. There wasn't enough technology. Only the sudden strikes prevented the Alliance forces from landing on the planet, seizing a foothold, and storming the bunker areas.

Igor unclipped the safety belts, stood up and headed out of the control room.

A red sign lit up behind him on one of the consoles under the heading 'Cargo bay unsealed'.

Passing the airlock, Rokotov found himself in the ship's cargo hold.

Aquila stood surrounded by a carcass of stationary servicing frames, but the servomachine's system switched on as soon as it sensed the approaching pilot. Its hatch opened and a transport platform extended, the compressed air whooshing out in the silence of vacuum. The technical corset elements shifted aside and the ramp that kept the compartment closed began to open slowly.

Aquila shifted a minute later, straightened its legs and stepped into the crimson murk.

There was no time to waste.

Rokotov's daring idea could stop the attack but for he had to reach the preplanned position in time.

The servomachine picked up speed as it took long strides, and soon the terrain map showed the crater's slope with steps cut into it.

Thanks to Aquila's unique construction and the stepping propulsion method, it didn't have any trouble ascending the giant stone staircase to a small platform located slightly above the billowing dust atmosphere.

The search radar immediately displayed a scatter of red markers, indicating the enemy ships.

They were approaching Dabog without fearing a strike from space and ignoring the dust moon.

Igor assessed the situation. He had chosen his position in advance. Right now, Aquila was above the dust but after sending out a salvo, it could rapidly hide within it.

A web of the target grid lay over the screens. Numbers scrolled across its corners. The air assault modules and their accompanying fighters were underlined in red - after undergoing many improvements, Aquila's cyber system could monitor up to twenty targets simultaneously.

The servomachine's legs bent slightly to provide additional stability. The 200-megawatt laser charging devices displayed a full battery and readiness to fire.

Aquila's frame was covered in a camouflage coating and blended in with the terrain. The enemy was unlikely to have time to detect the laser salvo and calculate its coordinates for a return strike.

The goal was to shoot down the assault ships and stop them from entering the atmosphere.

Did Igor know, when he was rearming Aquila and installing additional systems, that he was, in fact, creating a new war machine that was destined to work for centuries?

No. Rokotov never considered such a thing. There was a war. He was defending his world. The rest didn't matter.

THE ALLIANCE COMBAT TEAM did not expect a strike from space. It was thought that the squadron led by the Shadow of Earth cruiser completely controlled the planetary space and that the dust moon couldn't be used for military purposes.

The Terrans were wrong. Dabog's satellite had a close enough orbit that an attack from its surface reached its target.

The power of Aquila's lasers had been increased specifically for this operation. The firing rate had reduced significantly but their destructive capacity had been maintained, and the first salvo burned through the armor of the leading air assault module.

There was a dull flash but then the explosive decompression of the compartments immediately finished off what had been started, with fragments flung into space and surrounded by gas plumes.

One of the escorting Phantoms was hit by the decompression fragments, disengaged from the action and turned in the direction of the squadron. The others rapidly regrouped and took a course towards the dust moon while scanning the surface.

Rokotov had anticipated this. It would take the fighters seven minutes to reach the moon while the laser beam struck with the speed of light in vacuum. He fired four more salvos: one Phantom disappeared in a burst of flame, the assault modules sustained serious damage and the landing was disrupted. Igor immediately took Aquila down into the radioactive gloom that filled the crater.

Only the huge four-digit prints of the

servomachine, sunk deep into the regolith, showed where it had gone.

"DUST MOON, this is Dabog calling."

"Dabog-3 here. Sending you the updated data. The Shadow of Earth cruiser has started moving towards the planet! Something major is going to happen!"

"I see it," Rokotov was carefully studying the received signature maps. "Hold on. I'll change my tactics. The Shadow of Earth will probably try to launch its assault modules from low orbit."

"We're preparing a missile attack. If the cruiser enters our battery range, we'll greet it."

"Don't risk it before then. You can't unmask our positions unless you're sure that you'll destroy it with a few hits!"

"New information: two rocket carriers are setting a course for Dabog! Another four Phantom squadrons have been sent towards the moon!"

"They're beginning their assault!"

"Dabog-3, attack the cruiser only from the fallback positions!" Rokotov ordered.

"Igor, what are you planning to do?!" Daria Krechetova couldn't keep up the dry tone and her voice trembled. "The moon's orbit is full of fighters!"

"I'll manage. Contact in five minutes at the next navigation point."

He switched off. Aquila was walking across the crater base on autopilot and Igor could concentrate on the obtained data.

He had learned a lot in the six months of war. For example, how to read energy distribution maps. The signatures could tell him which subsystems on the enemy ship were active and what technology was in the outer compartments.

Rokotov frowned.

Previously unknown energy matrices had appeared on the launch deck of the Shadow of Earth. Instead of the familiar assault modules, there were ships larger than Aquila's space carrier, but Igor's attention was drawn to the signatures appearing in front of them.

Unidentified combat unit.
Unidentified combat unit.
Unidentified combat unit.
Unidentified combat unit.
Unidentified combat unit.

'What is this technology?' A vague suspicion, bordering on apprehension, made Igor run a heuristic analysis of the uncovered signatures.

Aquila's system managed quite quickly.

The Terran Alliance had created its own version of the servomachine!

They were preparing to land a mechanized assault force, which would overrun the bunker defenses! The ships hiding in the cruiser's internal launch sites were assault carriers!

Rokotov went deathly pale and steered Aquila towards the intermediate position, from where he could transmit the information to Dabog.

* * *

A FIERCE AND UNEQUAL battle raged in space.

The Shadow of Earth cruiser was nearing the planet despite the desperate resistance of its inhabitants.

Two rocket carriers had just fired concentrated salvos at Dabog. The fiery splashes that lit up the wounded continent could be seen from space.

Aquila climbed up the stone steps to the next shooting platform, which had been prepared earlier. Igor transmitted the data and, ignoring the approaching fighters, released a firestorm towards the Shadow of Earth, aiming at its vacuum docks. If he could damage their motors, the cruiser wouldn't be able to launch the assault carriers and land the servomachine squadron!

The energy batteries emptied quickly and the recharge indicators glowed yellow. The cruiser's armor appeared to have withstood the hits, at least, Rokotov didn't notice any decompression explosions. He needed to repeat the attack, but the Phantoms had discovered his position!

Streaks of explosions tore open the cliffs. Reversing the engines, Igor took the machine down the steep slope, hiding in the clouds of radioactive dust.

The fighter pilots lost their target but the soil vibrations, silent in space, continued to transmit the enemy's furious onslaught on the crater peak, where the hated servomachine had stood a minute earlier.

He wouldn't be able to work from there anymore, but he'd see who gets who in space!

A few minutes later, Igor reached the assault carrier. He left Aquila in the cargo hold and ran into the cockpit.

The best engineers on Dabog had worked for several months on refitting and rearming the spaceship and it was the only trump card of the planet's defenders.

The Phantoms were changing formation, creating a mobile shield over the crater. One of the rocket carriers in Tiberius Nadyrov's fleet began to turn around, setting a course for the dust moon.

They wanted to finish off Rokotov and his Aquila once and for all, whatever it took.

One person can't stand against a whole fleet, of course. Igor knew this, but the ground batteries on Dabog would provide him with fire support in low orbit, and a technological battle was a rapid and fickle concept. A second could make all the difference and one correctly calculated hit could inflict serious damage to even a frigate or a cruiser.

The war had changed many things. The assault carrier that had once served the Rokotov family as an ordinary transport had been altered to break through the blockade. It now had not only a weapons system but also a hyperdrive, which had been removed from a small reconnaissance vessel on the colonial transport.

Dabog couldn't hold on forever. They needed the help of the other Great Exodus colonies but a connection with them had been lost.

A hundred thoughts flashed through Igor's mind while he was preparing to launch but the automatic subsystems were also getting ready for the fight. The scanners recorded a barrage of fighters. The combat cybernetic modules performed their tasks as they were programmed to do.

Igor set a course and touched the necessary sensor but launch was delayed for a few seconds.

The anti-air defense system kicked into action before the engines turned on. Rapid-fire air defense gun ports opened in the ship's armor and fired onto previously determined targets from the veil of radioactive dust.

The crater, swathed in a haze, became a

boiling pot.

✳ ✳ ✳

IGOR CHARGED DESPERATELY towards the planet despite knowing that he would be too late.

The Shadow of Earth, firing rapidly, came into low orbit. Admiral Tiberius Nadyrov appeared reluctant to risk the new type of equipment and was planning to land the ships with the servomachines directly over the targets, covering their descent with the cruiser's main caliber weapons.

Light flooded the cockpit. Missiles sped past, blinding the sensors for a moment.

Rokotov didn't even immediately realize that it was the missiles from his own people until the scanners picked up the direct data channels. The missiles were being controlled from Dabog's surface using the experimental technologies of Rimp Cybertronics.

"Not all is lost then," The desperate hope persisted despite everything.

Frequent strokes of cold fire filled the air - it was the cruiser's laser complexes, creating a protective barrier. Nevertheless, several missiles got through and struck the Shadow of Earth, blossoming into fiery flowers.

The cruiser shuddered but survived. It appeared that air had been pumped out of all the outer compartments.

The vacuum docks began to open.

A little longer and the squadron of cybernetic mechanisms discovered by Igor would be on its way to the surface of Dabog, leaving its defenders with no chance of survival.

Rokotov was not fast enough to intercept them. Under intense fire from the cruiser and with two Phantom echelons following him, the task seemed impossible, but Igor nevertheless turned the navigation rudder, switched the on-board system to automatic defense mode and, shuddering inside, tore the safety off on a separate control section.

Shells were drumming over his ship's armor.

Hyperdrive section is active.

High-frequency loop power is on.

Attention, jump calculation is not possible. Number of variables exceeds the allowed value. Recommendation: exit the battle and try again.

Igor's hand closed over the lever. Despite the inner turmoil, he pulled the lever.

High-frequency loop generator has been activated.

The image on the outside screens became distorted. A funnel woven from absolute darkness, threaded with energy discharges that looked like slivers of lighting, appeared over Dabog and began consuming everything: Rokotov's ship, the fighters following him, the enemy cruiser and the two frigates accompanying it...

A moment later, the darkness of the hypersphere enveloped the screens.

The indicator lights glowed faintly on the control panels. A thin green thread, leading into the unknown, appeared in the depths of the mass detector.

Rokotov's ship, drawing the flagship of the Terran fleet after it, dived into a blind punch.

Chapter Six

Planet Cassia
Eight light years from Dabog planetary
system

OLGA FELT FORLORN that evening. It was hard to say goodbye to the university and her friends.

Leaving the flycar by the side of the road, she climbed out without closing the door, tore off a stalk of grass and bit on it, staring for a long time at the horizon and the mist-enveloped distance.

The open space on either side of the road made her head spin and her breath come fast.

Everywhere she looked, the grasslands stretched out like an endless velvet carpet, flowing towards the horizon and merging with the green slopes of the hills, with the Verezhenka River sparkling between them. Unwittingly, her deepest childhood memories rose within her -- there, under the shadow of that oak, was the first time that she had timidly kissed a boy from the city, who had come to visit his parents over summer, and here -- Olga's gaze drifted down the tender birch leaves, which enveloped the snow-white trunks like a green cloud -- was where her mother had first showed her what mushrooms were. There was no shortage of memories associated with her childhood haunts. It made her head spin.

Sitting down by the edge of the road, Olga stared into the distance and couldn't look away. It was weird... as if she was seeing it for the last time.

Olga shuddered, driving the terrible thought away.

What was she worried about? So what if she was turning twenty? She had her whole life in front of her!

'I wonder if Sergey has finished his exams and is home yet?' she thought, feeling a sudden bitterness fill her mouth from the blade of grass. 'What's wrong with me today? It's like everything is leading to one thing - I'm feeling sad and pensive and the blade of grass that I tore off turned out to be bitter.' Olga wanted to return to the car and cut the worrying thoughts and vague images off with a slam of the door, but the air smelled so intoxicating... she wanted to sit there and drink it in like a magical potion...

It slowly grew dark.

'Sergey has probably arrived and might have even dropped in,' Olga thought again. 'My parents are probably worried and waiting for me,' she reminded herself.

The remaining three kilometers to the villa flashed by and she barely noticed them. Braking beside the gates, she turned off the motor and looked at the cozy glowing windows of the large two-story house. A door opened in the side of a barn with plastic roof tiles, and a German shepherd named Alpha bounded towards the car, whining excitedly, having no doubt smelled Olga.

Olga took the keys from the ignition and noticed a shadow flit across the closest window, undoubtedly her mother hurrying to welcome her home. The young woman picked up her handbag and as soon as she opened the flycar door, Alpha's cold nose poked into her palm.

"Wait a second, honey." The German shepherd stepped back obediently and sat down, watching closely as Olga locked the car out of habit from living in the city. "How are things, Alpha?" Olga squatted down beside the dog and ruffled its black and glossy fur.

The dog only glanced at her and yawned in reply, showing its white canines and pink palate.

The door of the house opened and the

wooden porch squeaked. Mom...

"Olga, darling! You're home at last! I was beginning to wonder if you had gotten lost on the way!" Olga's mother chided her daughter gently as she hugged her.

Olga pressed close to her, her heart brimming with joy and tenderness. That's it, school was over, she never had to go anywhere! "Where's Dad?" she asked.

"He went into town a few hours ago."

"Why?" Olga asked in surprise, taking her things out of the trunk.

"They called him. Some kind of emergency meeting of all the officers. I'm wondering myself what could have happened."

Olga noted the concern in her mother's voice and decided not to ask further, although she felt a little hurt. 'Well, if they called him, there must be a reason,' she thought, trying to ignore the unpleasant news. Olga didn't want to ruin this night with petty misunderstandings. She knew that her father loved her and was undoubtedly also upset that he had to leave without seeing his daughter on this important evening.

"Come on, Mom, let's go inside," she took her by the hand and her soul sang out again. "By the way, did Sergey Voronin drop in?" Olga asked matter-of-factly as she walked up the front steps.

"Why, certainly... He came by a couple of

hours ago. He was asking if you were home. He's become so tall and grown up, I can barely recognize the neighbor's rascal."

The young woman sneaked a smile and stepped onto the front porch. A sense of strange foreboding came over her again, for the coming night seemed dark and hostile.

* * *

IN THE PRESIDENTIAL PALACE, located on the outskirts of Cassia's capital city of Alexandriysk, the evening was stressful and busy.

Officers scurried up and down the marble front steps and the parking lot was full. More and more people in uniform arrived by the minute and they all looked worried.

Nicholas Polvin arrived at around nine o'clock in the evening. Entering the hall, he paused in the doorway, looking for a familiar face and at the same time, automatically slapping the white gloves in his right hand against the open palm of his left. He was baffled like all the others, as well as extremely upset by the unexpected need for him to come to the capital, as it was his daughter's birthday tomorrow.

Polvin's gaze roamed over the hall, noting the glint of bladed weapons not normally worn, and paused at the foot of the stairs. Not finding anything remarkable in the crowd, Nicholas turned back to the door but then one of the officers spotted him and shouted loudly, "Nicholas! How many years has it been?"

Polvin turned towards the hearty voice, and his features softened when he recognized the officer hurrying towards him.

"Vadim Lozin!" He exclaimed joyfully, stepping towards him. "What are you doing here?" Nicholas asked in genuine surprise as he hugged the captain. "I heard that you were in the south somewhere, fighting the jungle!"

"Yes, they dragged me right out of the jungle. You don't happen to know what's going on, what's the emergency?" Lozin asked.

"No," Polvin confessed. "I'm confused myself. Never mind that, how are you? How's your family? How's Andrew?" He showered his childhood friend with questions, leading him away from the crowd.

"Oh, me," The captain flashed his pearly whites. "I signed up to dig up trees, as you have rightly heard. Katie's berating me, saying that I'm too old and that I'm shirking my family duties but I just listen to her, nod and do my thing. I'm stuck, I just can't live without this... this bloody jungle."

"Seriously, you just can't live without it?"

"Yes, believe it or not. To be honest, I'm

afraid to quit my job. My Katie's a smart lady and she's right, I'm not as young as I was." As Lozin spoke, his lips lifted at the corners in a familiar manner and Polvin listened to him and felt the breath of time, like a breeze from his past, from the time of his youth, cadet school and his first love.

"I'm afraid of getting too comfortable and ending up with a pot belly," The captain continued. "Home is better, of course. My grandson Andrew is growing up, the little rascal is five already." Lozin grinned and his gaze lit up. "How are you, Nick?" He suddenly remembered himself. "Your Olga is probably all grown up by now. Where is she?"

"I've just missed her," Nicholas sighed. "She was supposed to come home today and she's turning twenty tomorrow, but I was called here, as you can see."

"Twenty?" Vadim repeated respectfully. "That is unpleasant, of course. You're not going to initiate her then? Or will you move the date?"

"We can't move the date, it's a bad sign, as you know," Polvin replied regretfully. "The tradition has lost all its meaning and has turned into a ritual, but it's still a pity. I had to ask Lisetsky. Maybe you remember Kirill?"

Lozin frowned. "No, I don't remember him," he admitted.

"It doesn't matter, well, he's my neighbor and the same age as me. He's got two daughters, twins... He'll lead Olga to our ASUM tonight."

"Yes, it is a shame," Lozin sighed sympathetically. "For me, it left an indelible impression. Like an imprint on my mind for the rest of my life. Whether it's a tradition or a ritual, it's still the right thing to do. One of the ancients was right to say: one can be ignorant of many sciences and still be educated, but one cannot be educated without knowing history."

Nicholas was about to reply when the comms signal interrupted their conversation.

"Polvin," he answered drily.

"You are expected in the North Wing, room 127," said a voice without any introduction.

"Sorry, Vadim, I have to go," Nicholas said. "I'll find you once this mess is over. Don't leave without seeing me again, alright?"

Lozin nodded and Nicholas shook his hand.

"Room 127?" Nicholas frowned as he tried to remember the number on his way to the stairs. "The Emergency Control Center?"

* * *

THE NIGHT WAS warm and soft.

Olga finished her dinner while sitting next to her mother at the table. They were being served by the old android called Stepan. As a child, Olga had called him Stip. She had only started talking and couldn't yet pronounce words properly, but the android had gotten used to the name Stip.

There were steps outside. Olga turned around, secretly hoping to see Sergey Voronin, but the late visitor turned out to be their neighbor Kirill Lisetsky, a retired colonel with a bald head and thick sideburns.

"Hello, Mary," He bent down and kissed the hand of the lady of the house. "Welcome back, Olga," he turned to the young woman with an unusual solemnity. Olga noticed her mother's cheeks turn pink out of the corner of her eye.

"Is it already time, Kirill?" she asked, unable to hide her nerves.

Olga couldn't understand what was going on. "What happened?" she pushed the plate away and Stip immediately came forward and began gathering the dirty dishes.

"My darling daughter," Her mother's voice shook and she smiled through sudden tears, which upset and puzzled Olga. "Your father was very disappointed that he wasn't going to be the one to take you to the ASUM, but the circumstances... Anyway, he asked Kirill... You must go with him and learn about your roots. Tonight is the eve of your coming of age. This is an age-old tradition that we have steadfastly followed for over three centuries."

What are you talking about, Mom?! Olga wanted to say but she kept silent, taken aback by the solemnity of her elders.

"Let us go," Lisetsky looked at his watch. "It's nearing midnight and we must hurry."

Olga stood up without any idea of what was happening and looked at her mother, who nodded encouragingly, "Go."

"What is ASUM?" asked the young woman. The word sounded odd and she had never heard it before.

"It's an abbreviation," Lisetsky replied. "Come, I will tell you everything as we walk."

Olga could do nothing but follow. "I'll be back soon," she promised her mother for some reason.

* * *

THE OLD ROAD led into the forest.

Stip followed them silently, illuminating the overgrown path.

Olga felt quite unsettled as the events of this evening seemed very unusual and mysterious.

"Where are we going, Kirill Alexandrovich?" she asked forcefully, unable to keep quiet any longer.

Lisetsky slowed down slightly. "Olga, you know that humans have been living on Cassia for only slightly more than 300 years?" he asked.

"Of course," she replied instantly. "They teach us that at school." Why was Uncle Kirill asking her such stupid and rhetorical questions, when he knew the answers to them already? Why was she being treated like a five-year-old?

"Yes, of course," Lisetsky responded hurriedly, feeling Olga's growing perplexity. "But the teachers at school only briefly mention where our ancestors came from to Cassia."

"From Earth," she said, still unsure of what her father's old friend was getting to. She respected Lisetsky and was willing to listen to any didactic story from him, but why did they need to go into the surrounding forest, down a path that had not been used for a long time?

"That's right," Kirill Alexandrovich answered her in the same tone. "But the school curriculum is designed to prevent children from forming a misconception of our ancestral homeland. Earth is located a very long way away, and we still don't know where exactly. We don't know how we should feel about it either. So, the schools only mention a long-lost planet, and each one of us finds out the details on the eve of his or her majority by visiting the ASUM located on his or her territory. We're going to see it now."

"What is ASUM?" Olga asked again.

"The Automatic Storage of Unified Mechanisms," explained Lisetsky.

"Why was it created? And why was it hidden in a forest?"

Lisetsky smiled. "Nobody hid it. It's just that the vaults were built a long time ago. Over the centuries, they have blended into the landscape and became covered in forest. Now, listen carefully. When the Cassiopeia Colonial Transport entered this planet's orbit, a link to Earth could not be established. Our ancestors were left to their devices. They sent out a reconnaissance probe and saw three continents. The original life of this planet flourished on two of them, while the third had been barely formed from the tectonic changes and was a rocky desert."

A wooded hill appeared beyond a turn in the old road while the man was speaking. The path ran up to it and disappeared at the moss-covered hill.

"Why did our ancestors decide to colonize the desert continent?" Olga couldn't help but ask the reasonable question, while Lisetsky fumbled with a small device like a remote control.

"Well, I don't believe it! It looks like the batteries have gone flat!" Kirill Alexandrovich sighed and explained apologetically, "I brought my daughters here last year and haven't used the remote since." He turned to the android and gave him two small batteries. "Stip, charge these, please. Let me know when they're ready. I'll talk to your lady in the meantime."

"So why did our ancestors settle on the desert mainland?"

"Well, that's easy to explain. You took the exobiology course, right?"

Olga nodded. "Yes, but I didn't understand all of it," she pointed out. "Sometimes, I wonder why we're taught so much about space, about the principles of navigation and exobiology. What's the point if most of that knowledge isn't used and probably gets forgotten in a couple of years?"

"We came from space, Olga. We must remember this and not let it be forgotten. Our roots are in space."

"My roots are here, on this planet!" The young woman disagreed passionately.

"No," Lisetsky shook his gray head. "Once you visit ASUM and watch the chronicles, you will understand that hundreds of colonial transports left Earth during the Great Exodus. Some survived, some perished, and I think that the ships were scattered throughout the galaxy by the fickle hypersphere, but sooner or later, we'll meet again. We don't know what people from the other planets will be like. So you need to familiarize yourself with the records from the first years of colonization."

He looked into the gathering darkness and continued, "Well, in regards to choosing the continent, the answer is simple: our ancestors didn't want to risk it. Orbital research showed that the planet's biosphere was far from Earth standard and, rather than expending forces on fighting the hostile life forms, it was easier to create our own ecosystem. The mainland had barely formed, by geological age standards. It was empty and unfriendly but perfect for terraforming. The colonial transport landed successfully but then came all the difficulties. Once the colonists woke up, there were serious disagreements among them regarding how to develop further. The people who came on Cassiopeia divided into eleven groups, creating independent pockets of development."

Olga started. She knew about the abandoned settlements scattered along the coast.

"How many of them survived?"

"Only one enclave."

"Why did the others die?"

Lisetsky didn't answer but quietly took the charged batteries from the android, put them into the remote and touched a sensor.

Something shuddered inside the hill. Olga felt a slight chill. The vertical, moss-covered wall began to slide aside, exposing the entrance to a huge, dimly lit bunker which was designed to store the unrequired vehicles unloaded from the colonial transport. Most importantly, the bunker contained all the computers with the civilization's accumulated knowledge.

"Go on. You have to answer that question for yourself."

✳ ✳ ✳

THE VISIT TO ASUM shook Olga Polvin to the depths of her soul.

As if a scorching wind had blown over her from the depths of antiquity, burning and then tearing off the shell of naivety.

She found out everything. She saw the dying Earth, which had turned into a giant poisoned city, and then the violent early years of Cassia's colonization, which she could not comprehend.

Only one in ten had survived. The foolish and baseless feud between people who refused to cooperate had caused the death of most of the colonists.

In the first moment, Olga wanted to run to the adults and demand a reasonable explanation, ask why the remaining nine enclaves were allowed to perish due to their own mistakes, and why nobody had come to their rescue.

She repressed the emotional impulse with some difficulty since the truth had been revealed to her. The harsh mathematics of survival for people who had been dumped on an alien planet was not immediately obvious. First, she had to accept other, even more hurtful and initially incomprehensible facts.

She found out what the Earth's cyberspace Layer was, and how people living in the in-modes deteriorated mentally and physically[1]. It turned out that ninety percent of the colonists were from this notorious Layer. They didn't know how to do anything.

Oh, it was hard for the young mistress of these beautiful lands to realize that she was lucky, because her ancestors were people who had managed to survive in the unexplored world, something that could not be said about the majority of Cassiopeia's passengers.

The selection of colonial transport crews was a game of chance. The neighboring cryogenic capsules could contain idiots and geniuses, but for some reason, there were ten times more dullards, deadbeats and layabouts than smart and

---

[1] More information about the Layers of Earth's cyberspace and the people living in in-modes can be found in the novel 'Blind Punch'.

determined people.

Naturally, after Cassiopeia's landing, the people who had previously wasted their lives in the Layer's phantom worlds, surviving on the endless allowance from the World Government, quickly regretted their decision to come and turned into angry, aggressive whiners. They represented the useless crowd of consumers who are unable to work even for their own survival. It was the bitter truth.

Everything was a jumble in Olga's head. The urban panoramas of her ancient homeland, the records from the first days of landing, the cruel, ruthless arithmetic of survival...

'But this was hundreds of years ago! Cassia is completely different now! What do I care about the events of the past?' She tried to calm herself down and bring her thoughts and emotions under control. 'My life is completely different, I will definitely find my happiness, I'll have a husband and children, maybe even with Sergey Voronin...'

It didn't help. The previous serenity in her heart was gone. She stepped out of the ASUM in complete turmoil, feeling the vehicles in storage (they were too many of them after the death of most of the colonists) watching her leave with the cold eyes of their video cameras, as if whispering behind her, *You're just a handful of dust thrown before the solar wind. One day, you will disappear, quarreling and dying out, and only we will remain, the dead, cold and eternal testament to your failed ambitions.*

'What the hell am I thinking?' Olga became angry, touched the sensor on the remote control that closed the ASUM doors, and snapped, "Let's go, Stip."

* * *

OLGA RETURNED to the house, overcome with contradictory thoughts and emotions.

The living room windows were open. Warm light and voices flowed from there.

Lisetsky sat at the table, drinking tea and saying something, while Olga's Mom nodded as she looked out of the window for her daughter.

Why was everyone so nervous? Was it because I found out a truth that has no direct relationship to the present day?

In reality, the information received in the ASUM was a test for historical indifference. How the girl received it was very important. Would she be horrified, upset and remember this, or would she sniff dismissively and shrug her shoulders - what do I care, it's all in the past and I'm living in the here and now.

"It's a pity that Nicholas is in town,"

Lisetsky's voice came through the open window. "Do you remember the night, Mary, when Nicholas and I went to the ASUM?"

The woman nodded, smiling at the distant memories. "I remember. You were like two madmen. You woke everyone up in the middle of the night, and made such a ruckus, demanding the access codes to the main colonial transport module. Did you change your mind about going to search for the other civilizations, then?" She prodded him jokingly.

"Where would I go now?" Lisetsky patted his belly, which had increased over the years. "It's a bit late for me... Let the young ones try."

"Stip, start the car," Olga said, then resolutely came onto the porch, peeked into the living room, put the remote on the mantel, and quietly spoke in response to her mother's concerned gaze, "I'm... I'm going for a drive with Stip. Sorry, Ma, I need to be alone right now. We'll talk later, alright?"

She said it and left. The engine growled and soon the glow of the headlights disappeared among the trees, behind the turn in the road.

"You know, Kirill, sometimes I think that maybe you should have insisted on doing it that night. Could it be that we are missing our chance, generation after generation?"

"I don't know, Mary, I swear. I have enough

to worry about right here. Maybe you're right, we should have persisted and reached for the stars... Who knows what would have happened next? But I told Olga today that it will surely happen one day. I refuse to believe that the crews of all the colonial transports died. Someone's going to go back into space and perhaps they'll find Cassia."

Indeed, everything that they spoke about as they sat at the table in the cozy living room had already happened.

Up in the planet's high orbit, Aquila's damaged assault carrier had exited the blind punch and drifted uncontrollably towards the planet. It would soon enter the outer atmosphere under the force of gravity and continue falling, to shatter the sleepy peace of Cassia's civilization.

Earth. Europe Megacity
The World Government building
A month earlier

JOHN HAMMER was studying the star map with its planetary markers and thin lines of the explored hypersphere routes.

The war was in its sixth month. The Earth Alliance squadrons were mounting a three-pronged attack: Nadyrov continued to unsuccessfully dominate Dabog, Nagumo was now approaching Elio, one of the three most advanced colonies of the Great Exodus, while Gornev had begun a covert landing on Kjuig.

The star systems located at one jump away from Earth were now a patchwork of different markers. Several combat stations were being built in space. Outposts and industrial bases were being founded on uninhabitable planets, and exploration was being carried out for raw materials.

The chain of worlds around Earth was already being called Hammer's Line. If the Terran fleet was to meet highly developed colonies that possessed their own space fleet, or worse still, alien civilizations, this border would act as Earth's protection since it couldn't be avoided at the current level of hypersphere navigation.

An internal communication trill sounded, "Howard Faragney has arrived from Juno and is requesting an audience."

"Show him in."

Howard Faragney, a talented engineer and cyberneticist, was head of the Advanced Development Department in the newly created research center with an unobtrusive code name Gamma.

He crossed the threshold and inadvertently

paused as he looked around, for not many could boast of ever visiting John Hammer's personal quarters.

"Come in," the President of the Terran Alliance collapsed the holographic sphere of darkness that sparkled with stars with a flick of his wrist. "Have a seat. Have you come straight from Juno?"

"Yes, Mr. President."

"How did the hyperjump feel?"

"I didn't notice it," Faragney looked embarrassed. "I slept through it. I had a lot of work the day before."

Hammer gestured him towards the recreation area, where a table had been set out. When it came to indispensable civilian specialists, Hammer preferred to break down the myths and phobias by displaying generosity. Few were misled by this, however. At any moment, the President of the Terran Alliance could show his tough and unpredictable temper.

Faragney hesitated.

"Come on, tell me how it's going," John Hammer was in a good mood. "What's the progress with Aquila?"

"We've studied all the videos and signatures but without a prototype, we can't make any definite conclusions."

"I don't believe it," the President took a sip

of coffee and added, "Dabog's agrarian machines were constructed based on colonial technology, which was all standardized."

"Yes, but the engineering genius of Hans Gervet does not fit into the unified framework. Here is an example," Faragney tapped his cyberstack. A model of the servomachine appeared above the table. In this simulation, three electromagnetic weapons were striking Aquila at a short distance. The shells struck the armor at different angles.

"So?" John Hammer arched an eyebrow.

"With such dynamic loads and given the small stability of the walking system, the robot should have tipped over. But this doesn't happen in documented recordings. It withstands a hit, only slightly departing from the vertical axis."

"Did you find an explanation for it?"

"Yes. Aquila's frame contains a system of liquid metal weights, which create an instant counterbalance to external perturbations. This is just one example of how a known phenomenon was used by Hans Gervet and incorporated into the servomachine design."

John Hammer harrumphed and stared at the image for a long time before asking, "How far did we get in creating our own models?"

"Three combat service vehicle models have been constructed, as well as an assault carrier to deliver them to the planet." Howard had prepared thoroughly for the presentation and was now showing 3D images as he continued to explain, "Phalanger is a sixty-ton assault vehicle with unique firepower. It is armed with the Legion unit. Pilum-class missiles are capable of striking targets in low orbit or break through defensive fortifications at a distance of up to 500 kilometers. In close combat, it uses 80-millimeter electromagnetic weapons and medium-power lasers."

Hammer's gaze slid over the technological behemoth and he nodded approvingly, indicating that Faragney should continue.

"The next model is called Hoplite. This is a forty-ton vehicle with increased maneuverability. It is armed with missile units, anti-aircraft lasers and thirty-millimeter electromagnetic weapons. We believe that the Hoplites, which will provide cover for the heavy Phalangers, will become the true 'workhorses' of the battlefield. The third model is the fifty-ton Centurion, which hasn't been finalized yet. This vehicle will be the tactical command center. We are currently designing the necessary subsystems."

"Considering the tight deadlines, Gamma's done an impressive job," Hammer praised him. "But there must have been some difficulties, too?"

"Of course," Faragney relaxed a fraction.

"The main problem is designing the control systems. We have given many of the routine functions to the combat autopilots, which have been combined into an independent behavior module called the Maverick. Yet it's not the solution, given that the situation changes from moment to moment in battle and often requires instantaneous and extraordinary tactical decisions. The Maverick module is doing a great job of maintaining the machine's balance, carrying out basic maneuvering, recognizing and following targets, and controlling fire. However, combat simulations show that the human-controlled Aquila is still more effective because human thinking and piloting skills are added to the autopilot, if I can put it that way."

"Do we not have suitable candidates to control these new types of technology?"

"We certainly do," Faragney hastened to reassure the President, and immediately added, "But the people who are skilled at controlling complex robotic systems are psychologically unprepared for war. The majority are inhabitants of the Asteroid Belt and Jupiter's moons, where semi-automated systems are still in use."

"The most unreliable segment of the population," Hammer agreed, sounding irritated. "What can we do?"

"We are now preparing mixed military and

civilian groups for combat testing. In my view, there is another solution. However, it will require a great deal of work..."

"Get to the point," Hammer frowned.

"I'm trying to understand what Hans Gervet was thinking. He possessed only the chassis of a forklift, designed to dismantle the colonial transport armor, and neurochips taken from androids. I think Gervet used them to create an artificial nervous system for the prototype. He installed neural modules into each drive, linking them into a network. To put it simply, Dabog's servomachines possess reflexes and primitive thinking."

"A cybernetic lifeform? Not developed enough to be a problem, but sufficiently faithful and intelligent?"

"Yes, Mr. President. The neural networks are constantly learning and accumulating 'life experience'. This is why even teenagers can control the family robots on Dabog."

"But it's not our way?" Hammer noted perceptively. "Why?"

"The machine intellect on Dabog evolved gradually. I fear that the artificial intelligence that 'grows up' on the battlefield will not become a friend but a dangerous, crazy beast."

"Are you sure? What about loyalty to the pilot?"

"Yes, but what would we base it on?" Howard Faragney forgot himself and began thinking aloud about this complicated task. "Artificial intelligence cares nothing about our values. A cybernetic mind has its own view of the world. By associating itself with the servomachine, the combat AI will go through rapid and unbalanced development, and may well consider humans as the weak link that prevents it from fighting effectively."

John Hammer looked deep in thought but couldn't find an answer. "Are we at a dead end again?" He asked.

"No, Mr. President. The servomachines we have created are ready for the battlefield, under the control of the pilots. I'll say it again, the Maverick module is a very powerful and flexible cyber system. I wouldn't recommend using the fully automated versions of Phalanger and Hoplite. They will act in a scripted and predictable manner."

"We can't afford to lose!" Hammer cut him off. "Here's your mission, Howard. Put the Maverick into production! We'll prepare the pilots, don't you worry. Meanwhile, you're also going to develop full-scale combat artificial intelligence. Find a way to teach the cyber system non-standard thinking on the battlefield."

"The artificial intelligence can only obtain

such experience from a person."

"So create a permanent link between the pilot and the servomachine! Are we clear?!"

"Yes, Mr. President."

"Return to Juno and get working! You'll be provided with whatever resources you require, but I want to see a result, and the sooner, the better!"

Chapter Seven

Cassia. The Presidential Palace
Present time

POLVIN SHOWED HIS PASS and was taken to the Emergency Control Center. He had last been there ten years ago, when a volcano had become active near Alexandriysk.

'What could have happened?' Nicholas wondered. Unlike the usual image of the populated continent, the huge screens displayed a view of the stars!

"Nicholas! At last!" Cassia's President shook

his hand.

"What's going on?" Polvin enquired in a low voice.

"Two hours ago, we received a signal from a satellite group," explained the President. "The long-range sensors picked up a perturbation in the metric of space," President Schnittke sounded nervous. "Several asteroids have moved off orbit."

"How far is this from the planet?"

"There are several anomalies but the orbital telescope didn't detect any artificial objects! There are two dark and unexplainable spots. One is in deep space, where the constellation is being obscured by a kind of haze. The second is in high orbit around Cassia and is rapidly approaching..."

A signal sounded in that moment and blurry outlines appeared on the screens: a small ship, vaguely similar to a reconnaissance ship (like the ones on board the colonial transports), slowly spinning in uncontrollable drift and approaching the planet!

"Unbelievable!" Polvin exclaimed.

His bewilderment was easy to understand. Over the centuries, the very idea of interstellar flight had turned into a kind of abstract concept on Cassia, a concept that only graduates of the Cadet Corps amused themselves with. A small group of people, including Polvin, knew where the main module of the Cassiopeia Colonial Transport was stored but no one seriously thought about putting it back into space.

"Contact the ship! Immediately!" Hans Schnittke ordered.

"We can't, Mr. President!" one of the operators replied. "The ship is covered by some kind of masking field. We're sending a signal on all frequencies and all communication ranges but there's no response."

"What's the prognosis?"

"If it doesn't change course, it will soon enter the atmosphere and burn up. We can't stop it. We have nothing in orbit except the tracking systems and communications satellites!"

"What about the second anomaly?"

"It's too far away. We can't make out what it is."

Polvin turned around. "Hans, we have to make a decision. Should we issue a command to activate the systems on Cassiopeia's main module?"

"Who will take it into space? And what will it give us?"

"I can pilot it!" Polvin exclaimed. "Or Vadim Lozin! We were both trained on the simulators when we were young!"

"When you were young, exactly," Schnittke interrupted him. "Calm down, Nicholas, calm down. We'll gather the whole council and then make a decision."

Polvin chafed at the delay. By the time the others arrived, the object approaching Cassia would have enter the dense layers of the atmosphere. 'Is the President counting on that?' Came the thought. 'Nevertheless,' he told himself. 'Preparing to launch Cassiopeia's main module will take at least ten to twelve hours. We won't be able to help in any case. But is the second anomaly in deep space a ship, too? Or even several ships?! Then why are they cloaking themselves and not answering our signals?'

"The object has entered the ionosphere!"

One of the screens was now broadcasting a panorama of the night sky, where a glow suddenly appeared, flames enveloping the unknown ship.

IT WAS DARK in the control room.

The single working screen was filled with an image of the rapidly approaching planet.

Rokotov had fainted from the high G forces during the hyperjump and was not awakening.

The ship's cybernetic system core had been destroyed.

Aquila stood frozen in the cargo bay, held in place by the service frame.

Its ancient neural net, once damaged, was now rapidly collecting fragments of old knowledge and capabilities in response to the deadly situation.

It was like a flash.

The kaleidoscope of images from past and present sporadically formed a new neural matrix.

A few seconds later, Aquila bypassed the damaged circuits and took over control from the autopilot, although it may have been too late...

Cassia
The Polvin family estate

THE FAST DRIVE had calmed Olga down a little.

The forest gave way to cultivated fields, where servos were working around the clock.

Compared to the records of the first years of colonization, modern Cassia looked like a sleepy Eden.

The squelch of servomotors sounded unexpectedly as Stip, who had been sitting still in the backseat, suddenly began to anxiously glance around him, then wound down the window and stuck his head outside.

"Hey, where are you going?" Olga automatically slowed down and drifted to the curb.

"My scanners are picking up

movement!" The android exclaimed.

Olga parked the flycar and looked around her. She was surrounded by the cool darkness of a summer night. The wind ruffled the tops of pine trees growing along the slopes. There was no oncoming traffic. Was the android having a glitch?

"Movement in the stratosphere! Ten thousand meters up!"

"Stip, honey, what's going on with you?" Olga turned towards him. "It's probably a weather satellite, right?" There was regret in her voice. The android was as old as the world. She could still make out the barely legible logo of Rimp Cybertronics on his jacket, as well as the date, Year 2257. "Did you skip maintenance again?" She asked accusingly.

"My certificate is valid. There are no problems in my system. The object cannot be identified," with these words, the android climbed out of the flycar and stood staring upwards, "Nine thousand eight hundred... Nine thousand two hundred... Eight thousand... Olga, it's falling! Incorrect atmospheric reentry angle... A crash is inevitable."

"Stip, what's happening?!" She walked around the flycar, stopped and stared into the skies, but couldn't see anything. Deciding that the android was having energy disruptions, Olga touched his shoulder, planning to remove the jacket under which the test unit was located, but Stip suddenly threw up his hand in a very human gesture and exclaimed, "There it is!"

The young woman looked up again and suddenly noticed a flaming dot growing larger as compared to the surrounding stars!

She watched the unusual phenomenon with bated breath for several seconds. The bright spark quickly became a flaming ball, which was followed by a clearly distinguishable vapor trail.

"It must be a big meteor... Not something you see every day... It's so beautiful."

Stip suddenly turned around, grabbed her hand and started dragging her away while continuing his monologue, "Likely crash point has been calculated! We are in the epicenter! Looking for cover!"

The faithful android had calculated correctly, but there was no time left for escape. Olga realized this as soon as she turned back to look behind her.

The flame covered half the sky. The fireball tore through the single line of cumulus clouds, descending rapidly and inexorably.

"Stip, over here!" She screamed and rushed to the roadside slope, which led down to a ditch overgrown with bushes.

The android understood what she meant and pushed through the bushes first, clearing a path for Olga. It was moist and smelled of rotten leaves.

"Quickly!" Screamed Stip when he saw that Olga had slowed down and was glancing back with dangerous curiosity.

"Yes, I'm coming, I'm coming!"

The light was burning more and more brightly, and it seemed like night had turned into day.

Deep, black shadows suddenly appeared on the opposite side of the ditch; the first shock wave hit and the windows in the abandoned flycar shattered in a shower of glass...

The howl and thunder grew with every second. They drowned out the squeal of the flycar tires, which was being dragged along the road by the hurricane of scorching wind. Feelings melded into panic and terror, inevitability, and instinctive horror.

Olga only wanted one thing, to run and hide. Losing control over her senses, Olga tried to run away as if she had gone mad. She had no idea what she was doing and would have died if Stip hadn't grabbed her by the ankle.

The pines snapped and burst into flame on the neighboring hill. A scream was lodged in Olga's parched throat as the shadows abruptly lengthened, covering the slope in a gray and black grid... She suddenly saw the space wanderer. The ship was trying to maneuver, shooting out jets of flame, and its red-hot skin was dropping cinder flakes, which set the grass alight where they landed.

The belated attempts to slow down didn't help.

The hit was monstrous. The ground arched up in agony. The wind blew with the force of a hurricane. Olga was thrown up so hard that her teeth clanged and blood flowed from her bitten lip, but it was nothing compared to the image of the offworlder crashing into the hillside.

"Mommy," Olga whispered as tons of earth were thrown up in all directions, like the arching wings of a giant bird. The ship was turned sideways by the force of the impact and its burning skin split open, releasing flames and steam.

The offworlder shuddered, threw out another column of fire and fell silent in the depths of an elongated, smoking crater that had gouged the hill in two.

The thundering silence was shocking.

Sounds returned slowly and indistinctly: the thump of dirt falling back down, the crackle of flames, Stip saying something. The foam tissue on the android's face had burst open and servomotors were moving in the depths of the bloodless cut.

Olga breathed in huge gulps, still unable to believe that she was alive.

* * *

AFTER CLIMBING OUT of the roadside ditch, Olga and Stip tried to approach the crash site but were stopped by the unbearable heat.

'I have to do something! There might be people on board!' the young woman thought desperately. Her thoughts jumped around. 'Why am I standing here?' She turned, saw the crumpled flycar and ran towards it.

The driver's door was jammed. "Stip, help me! The communicator! I left it in my handbag!"

The android was already beside her. "Doing it!"

The metal screeched. "Here it is!" He gave his mistress the communicator.

With shaking fingers, Olga turned the device on and dialed the number.

There was no answer at home. She listened to the beeps for several long seconds, shuddering inwardly from various premonitions and fears, then it got unbearable and she hung up, before dialing another number.

There was an immediate answer, "This is Polvin!"

"Dad!" Olga could hardly speak from the anxiety. "Dad, listen... Stip and I..."

"Olga, calm down! Where are you now?!"

"I went for a drive," Olga sobbed. "And I saw this, this... This thing happened!"

"You saw it?!" Apparently, the capital already knew about the spacecraft crash landing.

"Yes, it landed almost on top of us! It crashed into a hill," she looked around desperately for a clear marker, spotted a listing column with a road sign, and hastily added: "On kilometer five of our road. Not far from the soybean fields! Dad, what should I do? It's so hot that I can't get close to it! And why isn't anyone picking up the phone at home?!"

"Calm down and listen carefully," her father's voice became dry and strict. The familiar tone worked and her breathing gradually slowed down and the panic subsided, even though her heart was still beating like crazy. Olga stood, lit by the glow of the numerous fires and listened, "Get Stip to start the flycar and get out of there right now!"

"Why? Dad, there may be people in there!"

"Help is on its way!" Her father cut her off. "Don't worry about Mom, she and Kirill were able to run to the ASUM. You scared everybody! Did you know that your communicator was turned off? I'm going to give you the number of the shelter, so call your mother as soon as you can. She's beside herself with worry. But first of all, get away from the crash site!"

"But why, Dad?" Olga repeated stubbornly. Her lips no longer trembled. "I know how it is! We've waited for contact for so long and..."

"Get out of there right now!" Her father ordered. "The ship's propulsion engine may blow up at any moment, how can you not understand that? Stay with Mom and Kirill in the shelter until I call you back. Other people will sort out the crash scene. You got that?"

"Yes," Olga saw that Stip had already opened the flycar's hood and was reconnecting something in the hydrogen engine block.

"Call me when you get to the shelter. Now, I'm sorry but I can't talk any longer!"

Olga heard beeping again.

The flycar's engine sneezed several times and then turned on, growling unevenly and intermittently. Stip sat behind the wheel and looked at his mistress questioningly.

"I'll be one second," she turned back to the hill.

Grass was burning on the slope. The blackened crowns of trees emitted smoke and dropped bits of coals. The outline of the spaceship could be barely seen over the low ridge of the impact crater. The armor plating had been torn off one of its structures on landing, and Olga could see the strange mechanisms inside the alien ship.

"Stip, can you scan the state of its

propulsion engine?"

"The reactor is unstable. I'm picking up power fluctuations. Olga, we have to go!" The android decided to issue commands, like when she was a kid and didn't listen to him.

"Why?"

"This is a military ship!"

"What? Are you sure?"

"Absolutely. I've identified some of its subsystems."

A hum could be heard coming from Alexandriysk. The rescue helicopters, having received the exact coordinates of the crash site, were approaching quickly and Olga could already see the sweep of searchlights.

"All right, let's go," she sat down in the passenger seat and the flycar, its damaged suspension making scraping noises, moved immediately away from the scene.

Planet Cassia. Aleksandriysk City Hospital
A day after the crash

A MUTED LIGHT seeped through his closed lids.

Rokotov regained consciousness but his mind remained foggy. A medical device standing at his bedside was emitting jittery and irregular sounds. A clear plastic door was in his line of vision. Beyond it, he could see a wide hall with lots of plants, reminding him of a winter garden.

A five-year-old girl sat on a chair, swinging her feet and saying something to her doll.

Igor's lips trembled. Taking a breath and moving his eyes took all his strength. The small, carefree girl seemed to be a vision. She looked like an angel.

Rokotov's mind drifted.

He saw the snow. Large flakes of dead, radioactive snow covered the road. The reinforced concrete was covered with an icy crust and the children's feet slipped on it. Their pale, drawn faces could be seen behind the soft visors of their protective suits.

The images faded but didn't disappear.

Aquila towered among the ruins, covering the evacuation. The servomachine's body turned slowly. The scanning complexes were monitoring the horizon, from one end of the snowy desert to the other.

The all-terrain vehicle roared and disappeared into the gloom, while Igor and Aquila remained standing for a while.

Rokotov tipped his face up and looked at the gloomy sky.

When he was small, Igor had always been

thrilled by the arrival of winter. Fall seemed boring and dull, especially in its last month, when the trees had already dropped their leaves but there was no snow, and the earth was just lumps of mud that froze in the mornings.

It was so nice to run through the first snow, rejoicing at the bracing breath of winter...

Something flashed several times on the horizon, illuminating the ash-colored clouds.

Igor couldn't feel the cold through the suit. The unbelievably large gray snowflakes spun as they fell from above, landing on his visor but not melting.

Two radiant shards of flame burst into the sky near him, among the crooked, blackened and fallen trees. The rockets had been fired from underground and headed for their orbital targets.

Lighting flashed rapidly and viciously on the left and right as missiles burst out of their launch silos one after another, briefly illuminating the ruins of the destroyed city.

"Escort carrier, 20,000 kilometers away, on a course for Dabog. Preparing to launch its assault modules."

"Got it," Rokotov replied drily, hurrying back to Aquila's cockpit.

The short break had ended.

The vision was fading away, eluding him...

WHEN IGOR OPENED his eyes again, the girl was gone. Perhaps he had only imagined her.

The device at his bedhead was beeping regularly and business-like.

He could see the evening city through a large window.

Where am I?

The last thing that Igor remembered was the Shadow of Earths' cruiser, the streaks of lasers and dotted lines of missiles, and the readiness signals on the hyperdrive control panel.

I went into a blind punch.

Did the hypersphere spit my ship out beside an inhabited planet?

It was possible. But there was another possibility. Something might not have worked. He fainted from the heavy G-forces that occurred when the hyperdrive switched on. *What if the jump didn't happen and I've been taken prisoner?*

But the city beyond the window clearly didn't match the scale of Earth's supermegacities.

Rokotov lifted his hand with some trouble. Nothing seemed to be restricting his movement. There were no handcuffs. Anxiety flooded his senses. He had to get out of here. He had to find out what happened to the ship and to Aquila.

He couldn't let the unique mechanism end up in the wrong hands.

It doesn't matter where I ended up.

He tried to stand up. The overwhelming weakness pushed Rokotov back onto the bed but he resisted. A tumble of wires slipped off the bed from under the sheet covering him, and an alarm sounded as the monitor lost contact with the sensors.

"So, you woke up and immediately decided to run away?"

Igor's vision became blurry again but he forced himself to focus. A person in a white coat approached his bed. Igor noticed that the coat was worn over everyday clothes.

"Why are you glaring at me like a wild animal?" Asked the stranger as he brought a chair closer to the bed. "We saved you, after all." He spoke intergalactic English but with a sharp accent that was unlike the one on Earth. "Let's get acquainted. My name is Hans Schnittke. I'm speaking right now on behalf of all the residents of Cassia. We welcome the first contact but we are in some difficulty. You came here on a military ship. I would like to clear this fact up. Do you understand me? Can you talk?"

Rokotov nodded with some difficulty.

"I can reassure you that you are among friends. Moreover, we've waited a long time for representatives from other planets to come, but frankly, we didn't think that it would happen in such a catastrophic way," He caught Igor's thorny and distrusting gaze and shrugged, adding, "I'm afraid that I don't have any stronger evidence of our friendliness right now. The only thing I can tell you is that your ship has already been pulled out of the crater that it created when it fell, and our techs are currently inspecting it. The first conclusion is that it is a reconnaissance ship that all colonial transports were equipped with. If we ignore the later improvements and the very strange mechanism parked in the cargo bay, I can safely assume that you are a descendant of the colonists who left Earth during the Great Exodus. Right?"

Igor's gaze softened. Two words - colonial transport - told him much more than the rest of President Schnittke's speech.

Rokotov's lips moved as he tried to say something. Hans leaned forward, trying to make out the whispered words, "You haven't... been... occupied?"

The President of Cassia looked closely at Rokotov and asked, "What in God's name are you talking about? Is there a war? Who is supposed to be occupying us?"

Igor tried to gather his strength. He couldn't talk for long but he had to act. The main thing was to protect Aquila; everything else was secondary. He understood that there had been a crash, but if the ship had made a hyperjump and entered this planet's atmosphere due to drift, the autopilots had been damaged. He would have burned up like a normal meteor.

"I need a computer from the time of the Exodus," Igor said quietly. "I'll find the frequency and communication channel myself."

"Why something so antique?" Schnittke asked in surprise.

"My ship's system is compatible with the operating system of those times," Rokotov breathed out weakly.

"What are you going to do?"

"I need to show you some files."

"Fine. I'll call the doctor. While he examines you, I'll arrange what you need. Will you mind if there will be a few more people present?"

"No, I don't... You must have analyzed my biochemistry already. You must have general action stimulants that won't harm me. Ask the doctors to use them."

"It's risky."

"I know, but I must stay awake."

✳ ✳ ✳

THE ANCIENT COMPUTER was delivered an hour later and soon after, Schnittke returned to Rokotov's room accompanied by three civilians.

"Igor, I'd like to introduce you to Nicholas Polvin, who is a member of the Supreme Colonial Council, moreover, your ship landed on his land."

Rokotov nodded.

"I would also like to introduce you to Dietrich Crowe, who is responsible for our orbital satellite group, and Steven Wright, Minister for Emergency Situations. Now, what exactly did you want to show us?"

"The truth," Rokotov replied, making sure that the provided computer system suited his needs. "Just give me a few minutes, and you'll see."

Igor established a communication channel, entered his access codes, and information about the ship's subsystems began to scroll down the screen. He started copying a few files and sent several hidden commands to the onboard system at the same time. The core of the cyber system was indeed damaged. Rokotov no longer had any doubts about who had seized control of the ship's autopilots at the critical moment.

The cargo bay sealed shut in response to his command. There was no one in it at the time. He didn't want to deceive these people, but he first had to make sure that a spark of artificial intelligence had appeared in Aquila's neural networks. It would be easy to blame the activation of the emergency sealing system on the damage sustained from the crash. And they'll have bigger things to worry about than the servomechanism now.

"There." He finished tapping on the archaic keyboard. "I've copied the video files to a separate folder. Please watch them. These are documentary records."

IGOR PRETENDED to fall asleep, but he was, in fact, listening to the feverish whispers of the four people who had just finished looking at the images from the invasion of Dabog and were now nervously talking among themselves.

"This is monstrous. How could they destroy a whole world?!"

"It's barbaric. But please understand that we can't help them. They'll do the same to us..."

"The Terrans don't know Cassia's coordinates... Blind punches are a leap of chance."

"But we must reply in some way, to say..."

"What we can say, Hans? We can tell him the truth... We don't have any spaceships. I feel sorry for this guy, but he will have to accept the situation and remain with us."

"No, I just can't get my head around it."

A tear rolled down Igor's cheek.

They were cowards. Had Dabog's children died in freezing cold bunkers for these smug landowners?

The daily reality of war irrevocably changes a person's psychology. What was considered wrong, crazy and impossible not long ago, now aroused no emotions.

He had to act. Quickly. Right now. He didn't know where the hypersphere had spat out the Shadow of Earth cruiser and the two accompanying frigates, but there was now a gap in the blockade around his planet.

I must return at any cost.

"Hans, come closer," Rokotov said hoarsely.

"Are you awake? We thought you were sleeping. I'm..."

"You don't need to say it. You've seen everything but you're afraid to help me. Listen carefully then. There is a servomechanism in my ship's cargo bay. You now know what it's capable of. I left some hidden commands in Aquila's system with a short delay. Don't interrupt me. I must return to my ship. You're going to remove your people from the crash site. From now on, not a single technician should touch the onboard equipment. God forbid the original jump data is damaged or the hyperdrive settings erased. I will also need a robot and android team, and some spare parts, there are probably some in your museums. I will repair the ship and leave Cassia. I promise to erase all the data related to this hypersphere course after I make the jump."

"And if I refuse?"

"Then I'll be forced to act," Rokotov gestured for the President to lean closer and whispered something into his ear.

Cassia's President went pale but managed to force out, "Fine. I will call back my people. But you'll have to stay here for at least another day."

"Why?"

"If I may be frank, I don't want your machine to cause trouble if you suddenly die. You need at least another day of intensive care before you can get out of bed. It's what the doctors have stated."

Rokotov nodded, leaned back on the pillow and closed his eyes. He no longer wanted to talk anyone.

Chapter Eight

Planet Cassia

OLGA WAS ONLY ABLE to return to the crash site after a day had passed.

The area where the spaceship fell had been cordoned off, there were roadblocks and even the forest trails (so Stip told her) were being guarded by patrols.

Then, for some strange reason, the interest in the offworld visitor suddenly dissipated. Olga was home when there was a call from the

Emergency Control Center and they were informed that the forces were leaving Polvin's lands.

Olga didn't understand the reason for their withdrawal but didn't wait to take advantage of the situation. She was desperate to look at the spaceship again.

Stip was in the yard, fixing the flycar. Mom had left in the morning to visit a distant farm and Dad remained in town. Olga took an old electric car from the garage and quickly reached the crash site.

"How strange," she thought when she found to her surprise that the cordon had indeed been lifted, and only the wind continued to ruffle the yellow tape stretched between the burnt trees.

The ship lay on the side of the damaged hill. Metal cables lay along the ground. They had been used to pull the foreign ship out of the crater.

Olga remembered the events of that night as a kaleidoscope of rapid and patchy images. Everything looked different in the light of day.

The young woman looked around for a while, an involuntary tremor crawling up her spine. The broken trees, the wide strip of scorched earth, beginning somewhere in the fields and crossing the road, the dark and mysterious outline of the space wanderer, all formed a picture of a catastrophe that she had miraculously survived.

The spaceship drew her gaze, beckoned her

to come closer, and she couldn't resist the temptation. Climbing down the roadside embankment, Olga found herself among the churned-up ground, surrounded by mounds of charred, broken and uprooted trees.

From a distance, the ship looked like a dark pile of metal, but details began to appear as she drew closer: the singed armor was covered in flakes of cinder, the short stabilizers looked like fins, and the tapering front also made the ship resemble a kind of ocean creature.

However, the analogy that came to Olga's mind was deceiving and approximate. As more and more new details came into view, she felt more frightened, her emotional perception of the ship changing. Strange systems lurked in the breaks in the hull, launch tubes projected from the ship's body a little below the melted stabilizers, and the casing had been torn off in some places so that she could see the weapons systems, held in place by complex servomechanic suspensions.

The ship gave off a clear sense of technological power and deadly metal fatigue. How these impressions coexisted together, intertwining and producing this chilling but non-contradictory feeling remained unclear ...

Olga walked slowly along the hull. She was frightened and curious, her heart pausing then beating more rapidly as she witnessed something that contradicted the familiar psychology, upbringing and outlook but, at the same time, drew her in with its mystery.

She could not yet comprehend and accept the terrifying and unfamiliar word 'war'.

The ship's armor plates were full of scars and dents, too large and frequent to be the result of the ordinary effects of space.

Several hatches were located along the ship's side. One of them was open and Olga couldn't resist climbing up the rungs of the metal ladder and looking inside.

The short corridor ended in a small airlock with several massive armored doors with handwheels beside them.

Two of them were slightly ajar.

* * *

IT WAS DIM in the cargo bay. The dull working lights were lost in a web of pipes and cables.

The young woman felt a shock as she looked around. In the gloom, among the massive service structure, stood something beyond her comprehension.

Olga's eyes gradually grew accustomed to the gloom, and the enormous servomachine held in the clutches of the technical corset finally became clear. Olga had to tip back her head to take in the whole machine.

The enormous legs, folded for transportation, were several times taller than a person. She could just make out the cockpit above them. She noticed electromagnetic weapons taken off the servomachine, held in repair clamps on the floor, and a few open shell trunks in a floor recess.

The recent trip to the ASUM played a cruel trick on Olga Polvin. She immediately remembered the images from the first years of colonization, when the people who landed on Cassia were feuding with each other.

Her mind unwittingly grabbed and jumbled up these images. The emotional impact made her shudder: if this monster had been created for war, how much damage could this machine cause?

It was another shocking discovery for Olga. Could it be that the only purpose of the ship and the mechanism hidden in its hold was to kill and bring death, destruction and sorrow?

From what she was seeing, the answer was yes. She closed her eyes in an attempt to imagine a planet where humans create such technological monsters, but nothing happened, her mind full of a billowing crimson haze. How could she imagine something so alien, so outside of her upbringing, so inappropriate and wrong?

Until now, Olga's internal world had been

bright and simple, but as soon as she looked at the dim outline of the servomachine again, something snapped painfully inside her. It was as if an invisible hand had crumpled a piece of paper, upon which her previous life was written as clear black on white. The lines crumpled. The future became uncertain. The columns that contained indisputable moral values and life plans became distorted. A harrowing premonition cut her to the very core, and it seemed as if a ruthless power would discard the crumpled sheet, mockingly stomping on it...

She wanted to run away without looking where she was going, and yet the ship and the servomachine lurking inside still drew her somehow. The feeling of unfinished business made her return to the airlock and test fate once again, as she crossed the threshold of the cockpit.

✳ ✳ ✳

THE ONLY SOURCE of light here came from the screens that displayed incomprehensible system messages, and the list of recent files that the pilot had been working with.

The center of the small room was occupied by a complex antigravity system with the piloting chair on top. Its broad armrests were made out of smoked plastic and covered in tiny characters, some of which glowed slightly.

It created a contradictory impression. Why were the control consoles surrounding the chair from all directions, with no room to approach it properly?

She squeezed past the monitors to the pilot's chair and sat down on it gingerly, continuing to examine the cockpit and becoming more and more convinced that the surrounding equipment was a later and hasty upgrade. Someone had redone the control room, adapting it to new tasks. The power cords and computer cables, snaking over the casing, supported this theory. Olga could see evidence of installation work everywhere, plus the equipment varied significantly, with some consoles blending in with the cockpit design and others jutting awkwardly forward, with different casing materials and mounts.

Olga's mother had told her that the pilot had survived. But who was he? What had made him serve war, and why? So that he had almost burned up together with his ship?

The silent devices couldn't explain anything. Her gaze drifted over the technology inside the cockpit. Reading the signs in Interenglish, she again noticed that some looked old and faded, while others were freshly applied.

But the strangest thing was that they

duplicated each other! Olga looked more closely, comparing the text, and was puzzled by the bizarre double standard system. For example, the sensor under a small screen had a fresh sign that said, 'Bomb doors, release', and below it, she could make out the faded original sign, 'Fertilizer spraying. Tank control'.

Olga was completely baffled. Her gaze wandered over the consoles, finding more and more evidence of the ship's previous purpose.

Is it possible that this ship was a normal agricultural machine in the recent past?

Her guess was quickly confirmed.

'Agrounit No. 17. Property of the Rokotov family'. The sign embossed on one of the casings had clearly been made a long time ago, back when the ship was first built.

Olga continued to inspect the room. There were two small sloping panels on the right and left of the pilot's chair, beside the armrests. 'Left missile launcher. Firing modes' proclaimed the freshly painted letters on one side. A faded but still legible sign a little lower stated 'Weather probe launch. Single, group modes'.

Olga looked at a similar panel on the right side of the chair. Once again, the recent sign stated, 'Right missile launcher. Firing modes'. Underneath it, like a ghost from a long-lost life, the second line of text said, 'Weather rockets.

Selection according to cloud type.'

Olga began to feel uncomfortable. She has already branded this ship as something terrible and unfair, something that brought only a death. Yet life, in its usual way, was showing her that reality was more complex and making hasty conclusions was dangerous.

How could she find out the truth? Her finger tapped the touch screen, activating of one of the most recent files requested by Igor Rokotov.

The holographic screens turned on, enclosing pilot's chair in a cocoon of 3D images.

Dabog. 20 December, 2607. The date made it clear that it was a documentary record.

She saw the fallen and blackened trees, the gray faces of people staggering towards the shelter entrance, the ash-colored snow falling from the skies, and the frequent flashes of underground missile launches.

✳ ✳ ✳

SHE CAME HOME in the evening, confused and anxious.

Stip was still trying to fix the flycar. Her father's car stood nearby.

The light was on in the living room and her Mom was laying the table for dinner, helped by

Sergey Voronin, whom Olga hasn't seen in over a year.

Everyone looked cheerful, like nothing had happened, and the joyous atmosphere worked, ironically. She climbed onto the porch and hugged her father, feeling a sense of relief, everyone's home, the family's together, so everything's going to be alright. "I'm just going to pop into my room to change."

A few minutes later, Olga stopped in the living room doorway, staring at Sergey in mute astonishment. He had really grown up - the work in the jungle on the neighboring continent had really changed him, turning a youth into a man.

Their eyes met and both felt embarrassed.

"Hello, Olga!" He paused, unsure how to behave since a child's frankness seemed no longer appropriate.

"Hey!" She walked into the room and stretched both arms towards him. "You look so good in uniform," Olga said and looked down, overwhelmed by the thrill of his fingers touching her.

"I've inherited it from my great-grandfather," he replied. "It's a family heirloom."

"Dinner is ready," Olga's mother noticed the young people's awkwardness and came to the rescue. "Come and sit down at the table!"

Night was falling outside the window and the

sunset faded away, with only a single crimson streak coloring the clouds and slicing through the sky.

Sergey was saying something to Olga's father, and her head suddenly started spinning as she imagined the cozy light trickling out of the house windows and this lovely but meaningless babble...

"How are things in the city, Dad?" she asked, interrupting Sergey.

"Well, you know everything," he looked reproachfully at his daughter. "They called me suddenly, it was a huge fuss, of course."

His tone made her feel uncomfortable. The words sounded fake and unnatural. Why was everyone trying to pretend like nothing had happened?

"Dad, what do we know about Dabog?" Olga asked forcefully.

Nicholas Polvin flinched. He was silent for several seconds as he stared at his plate, then he put down his fork and looked at his daughter. "How did you find out this name?" he asked sternly.

She felt uncomfortable, seeing disapproval in her Dad's heavy gaze, as if she had touched on a forbidden and shameful topic. "Is it a secret?" she said defiantly.

"No," her father replied as he struggled to

maintain self-control. "As it turns out, Dabog is one of the colonies founded during the Great Exodus. It's about seven or eight light years from Cassia."

"Is there a war there?" Olga asked quietly but insistently.

Polvin nodded, forgetting about the food. If only his daughter knew how hard her questions were for him. He had been forced to make a deal with his conscience and betray himself, but would she understand that the sacrifice had been made for Cassia's younger generation?

"Yes, there's a war going on there," he spoke quietly. "Earth has suddenly made itself known, claiming rights to all the worlds colonized during the Great Exodus. Ostensibly as compensation for the costs incurred by the World Government in equipping the colonial transports." He smiled grimly in response to the unuttered questions.

"That's ridiculous!" Olga burst out.

A heavy silence hung in the living room for a while.

"I've heard that the ship's pilot asked for help from our government." Sergey finally spoke. "Is that true, Nicholas Andreevich?"

Polvin winced as if he was in pain. "Well, honestly, Sergey!" He exclaimed in frustration. "Why do you care about Dabog, haven't we got anything else to talk about?"

Olga had never seen her father so irritated or nervous. She knew him well. That is, she had thought that she knew him well until this moment, but now it was as if a completely different man sat at the table! "Dad, this is first contact," she reminded him, stubbornly refusing to change the subject. "Kirill Alexandrovich told me before I entered ASUM that we have been waiting for this for centuries. So why is everyone suddenly backing away from it and keeping as silent as the grave?"

Her words sounded harsh and defiant. Olga's mother looked at her reproachfully but it seemed that Polvin himself had accepted it.

"You see, Olga," he paused, trying to find the right words, and then said softly but firmly, "We decided not to become embroiled in the conflict. The pilot received medical help but his ship is unlikely to be repaired since we lack the technical capabilities and the damage is too great. Igor Rokotov will stay on Cassia. Forever. He'll have to accept this. Contact was found to be undesirable. We'll never hear about Dabog again."

"What's that supposed to mean?!" Olga asked in shock.

Sergey glanced at Polvin out of the corner of his eye and suddenly answered for him, "Don't you see, Olga? The decision has been made. Life goes on."

"Are the people on Dabog waging an unjust war? Did they attack Earth? Or did they allow the new colonists to settle there and then started harassing them? Am I missing something?"

"Olga, you don't need to understand this!" Her mother tried to stop her. "We have our own life that has nothing to do with Dabog or Earth!"

"No! I want you to explain it to me! Clearly and honestly, like always. Or you need to admit that visiting ASUM and everything else was nothing but a joke."

An oppressive silence descended again after she had spoken.

"Why are you so upset?" Sergey half-turned to Olga and she suddenly thought that he had become so handsome as to be almost *unrecognizable*. But for some reason, she didn't want to look at him anymore.

"Don't interrupt," she asked. "I'm talking to my father! Dad, tell me, why did we decide to pretend like nothing had happened? Why did we suddenly forget about our own colonial transport module?"

Polvin looked at his daughter closely. His cheeks were burning, but not with shame, with anger. The anger of a father who had betrayed himself for the sake of his daughter, and yet she didn't understand!

"Because their planet was burned down!" He

spoke slowly and clearly. "When Dabog refused to declare itself a colony of Earth, they were simply destroyed, wiped out by strikes from space!"

Saying these words, Polvin thought bitterly that contact had been made. The scars on the damaged hillside would heal and disappear, but the scars in people's souls never would. The fear and shame would remain and consume everyone who knew the truth, and only a few would be able to truly forget and continue living as before.

"Olga, there's nothing we can do to help him," Polvin said. "I wish that we could. If Cassia's coordinates become known, our world will be destroyed too. We are too small, defenseless and insignificant. They don't even need to conquer us. Who will stop them from wiping out Cassia to make the other colonies more compliant? As a strategic object and as a colony, we're nothing."

Olga went deathly pale.

For some reason, she wasn't looking at her father in that moment but at Sergey. A young, handsome guy in a gold-embroidered officer's jacket. But a different image stubbornly appeared in his place. Olga saw Igor Rokotov as Aquila's video cameras had captured him - standing with his head tipped back, looking up at Dabog's sky, and the snowflakes of the nuclear winter falling on his helmet...

Wasn't Cassia's sleepy peace bought with

this radioactive snow?

Igor had nobody left, except a damaged ship, a creepy servomachine, and his nightmares.

It happens sometimes that a person suddenly starts to perceive foreign images as if they were their own. Something similar was now happening to Olga, due to her age, sensibility, a heightened sense of justice, and youthful maximalism, whose sharp edges had not yet been smoothed out by adult life.

She was fed but he was hungry. She was rich and he was poor. She had everything and for that, he had to die a thousand times in orbit around Dabog, even though he didn't think that he was doing it for her, a stranger, some girl called Olga Polvin from the distant and defenseless planet Cassia. But no, he didn't die, he was burning up and he crashed on our planet, to forever remain among people who would turn away and pretend that they couldn't see him.

She was afraid of this feeling of emptiness that was growing inside her... She couldn't put it into words.

"Olga, maybe you don't get it." Sergey's voice suddenly became condescending. "We couldn't help Dabog even if we wanted to..."

"I think it's time for you to go home," Olga herself was surprised by how calm she sounded. "I also think Cassiopeia's main module is capable of performing a hyperjump. We could try to evacuate them, at least the children."

Polvin looked intently at his daughter. "I'll contact the President and we'll discuss this," he promised.

Sergey Voronin's cheeks turned bright pink. He stood up abruptly and left without saying goodbye.

Dinner was completely ruined.

Part Three

Planetary Attack

Chapter Nine

On approach to Cassia
Two million kilometers from the stratosphere

THE CRUISER MOVED SLOWLY towards the planet, hidden behind its camouflage shields. It was all that remained of Tiberius Nadyrov's squadron after the catastrophic, uncontrollable jump through the hypersphere.

The battle near Dabog had inflicted serious damage to the Shadow of Earth. One of the vacuum docks on the starboard side had been severed by laser fire. Twisted beams could be seen in the depths of the hole, as well as a section of the unsealed corridor and several compartments, mutilated by the explosion. Fragments of equipment and bodies in torn suits floated in a cloud of decompressed air - a team of technicians was about to go outside just before the blind punch.

Admiral Nadyrov frowned as he viewed the approaching planet. The first markers were already appearing on the projected globe. Information from the reconnaissance probes was constantly being updated. They were intercepting conversations, scanning the surface and analyzing the discovered energy matrices. All this was processed, deciphered, and appeared on the admiral's personal terminal in real time.

'Cassia' was the name of the unknown world as obtained from the intercepts.

"It's undoubtedly a colony from the Great Exodus," Tiberius Nadyrov peered at the labels as if trying to scry his future in the colored markers.

He had been stalked by bad luck over the past few months. The cunning Nagumo had blamed Tiberius for the failed operation on Dabog and had left him in the unconquered system, while he himself moved on.

Nadyrov's position had become rather precarious. He craved revenge and had achieved what he wanted, for there were people around John Hammer who feared the ruthless and slippery as an eel Nagumo. Through their efforts, the Shadow of Earth cruiser had received the first batch of servomachines, created by the Terran Alliance engineers and based on the legendary Aquila.

And now, on the eve of combat testing the new technology, Tiberius again found himself on the brink of death. The suicidal act of one of Dabog's defenders had caused the flagship to perform a forced blind punch through the hypersphere.

"Data on the navigational environment. We have determined our current coordinates," came the long-awaited report. "The Shadow of the Earth is now eight light years away from the Dabog system. Analysis of the hyperspace power lines will be completed within an hour."

"Are we capable of performing a jump?"

"The hyperdrive was not damaged. We are charging the accumulators."

Nadyrov paused to think. 'Is there any point in making hasty decisions?' The admiral's gaze returned to the multitude of markers on one of Cassia's three continents. 'What awaits us on Dabog? The desperate resistance of its defenders and, consequently, the inevitable loss of the latest technology?'

While he pondered this, the biological monitoring information was updated. According to the information received from the probes, the planet's inhabited continent had been terraformed to match Earth Standard! For the first time, the Alliance warships had come across a world where the colonists had managed to completely win over the original lifeforms.

"Cancel the hyperjump preparations. Servomachine commanders to the tactical bay at once!"

Nadyrov's dry, sharp cheekbones shuddered. His lips twisted into a triumphant smile. Fate had presented him with an unexpected chance to capture a planet suitable for immediate settlement, which would negate all of his old failures!

Glancing at the scanning data once again, Tiberius found himself thinking that this world, judging by the abundance of hidden ancient colonial shelters, could present plenty of unpleasant surprises.

He had learned the lessons of Dabog well and wasn't going to take the risk. The landing would be done in secret. The continent wasn't that large. The combat servomachines would perform additional reconnaissance, reach the targets and destroy the likely resistance before it even started.

* * *

Planet Dabog
A day after Operation Dust Moon

IT WAS CHILLY and damp in the bunker, with streaks of frost decorating the walls in some places. Clouds of steam appeared with every exhaled breath.

Daria had just returned from the surface, and without taking off the light suit (at least it kept her somewhat warm), went to the operator bay, where a group of androids were scanning outer space.

"Have you found Igor?"

"No," An android called David turned around. "All signs point to a hyperjump."

"He performed a blind punch?!" Daria was horrified.

"Rokotov's situation must have been hopeless," the android replied dispassionately. "But here is what we found: the Shadow of Earth cruiser has disappeared and two frigates from Nadyrov's squadron have collided with each other. Igor's actions have given us a chance to reverse the situation."

"Sorry, I don't understand," Daria slumped tiredly into an empty chair.

"There is no complete space blockade around Dabog right now. We can break through if help comes to us from the outside."

"You know that we can't rely on anyone's help," she sighed heavily.

"I would not say so categorically. Before the war, we were developing a promising type of communication using hypersphere frequencies. The project is still far from complete, but we can use the experimental installation."

"We will send a signal into the hypersphere? But who will catch it?"

"Similar experimental devices exist in the three nearest populated systems. It was a joint project. So would any ship with a hyperdrive, if it is sufficiently powerful," the android explained. "Obviously, it's easy with a special receiver, but in a ship's hyperdrive, our message will appear as a series of disturbances in the high-frequency contour. If the pilot shows a bit of ingenuity, they'll understand that the disturbances are not accidental. There is a high chance that our message will be received. I'm sure that war has already reached planets that we previously traded and cooperated with, such as Elio, Kjuig, the Moon Stellar..."

Daria thought about it for a while and then nodded. "Do it."

"We will have to expend a lot of energy."

"What will that mean?"

"Lowering the temperature in the residential compartments by one more degree."

"Do it," she repeated. "If the other colonies can help us, now is the time. It'll be bitterly cold here in a couple of months so we have nothing left to lose."

The android simply nodded.

Cassia

LEAVING THE POLVIN HOUSE, Sergey turned onto a path leading through the forest and past the mossy hill that ASUM had turned into over the centuries. The path led to the Lisetsky Estate a couple of kilometers away and then, beyond the old log bridge over Verenezhka, began the well-trodden track to his house.

Of course, he was thinking about Olga. He was dismayed by the quarrel. He shouldn't have interfered in the argument between father and daughter.

The pines rustled around him. The night sky peeked through the gaps in the spreading boughs. For a second, it seemed as if a whole swarm of stars had leaped off the distant sky and immediately disappeared.

"I must have imagined it," He blinked and looked up again but saw only a lonely cloud.

THE LIGHT WENT OUT in the Polvin house. Stip was still fixing the flycar in the yard. Nicholas Polvin sat on the edge of the bed.

"Don't blame yourself," his wife's palm lay gently on his shoulder.

"This is hard. Everyone has their own truth. It doesn't feel right, Mary," Nicholas admitted. "He's someone's son too. It is terrifying to think of a whole planet being turned to ash..."

"Listen, maybe he'll be happy here on Cassia?"

"I doubt it. He's not like us anymore, you see. It's like he's been burnt up on the inside. He looks into your eyes and you feel a chill down your spine."

"Good grief," Mary sighed, not knowing what to say in response.

"I need to make a call," Nicholas stood up abruptly.

"To the President?"

"Yes. You should gather our things, meanwhile."

"Where are we going in the middle of the night?"

"I can't decide such things over the phone. I

need a personal meeting."

"What about Olga?"

"She should stay home and understand what her land and responsibility means. It's time for her to realize that she's the owner now."

"We won't even wake her up? We'll just leave? Why don't we go tomorrow morning?"

"Tomorrow, we'll start arguing again," Polvin replied with a frown. "The last thing we need is to have a full-blown fight." he added glumly. "I'll call Sergey and ask him to come over tomorrow. They can sort things out between them at the same time."

"Nick, I understand you, I really do, but why sneak off in the middle of the night?" she asked.

"Leave her a note. Or go to her a room and tell her that I'm calling the President, if she's still awake."

"Okay. I will."

She left the room and Polvin dialed the number but the line was busy. He left a message and started getting dressed. If he was to act, he had to do so quickly. He would call again once they were on their way.

"Olga's asleep. I didn't wake her. I'll leave her a note."

"All right, gather your things quickly and let's go."

"I'm sorry, but why are we both going?"

"I doubt that Hans will agree to use Cassiopeia's main module. He'll probably refuse and I'll have to convene the Colonial Council in the morning. You have the right to vote in it. I'm sure that we'll need your voice."

* * *

THE SWARM OF TINY sparks that had briefly appeared in the night sky and was accidentally spotted by Sergey Voronin was a group of jammers released from the Shadow of Earth cruiser.

Nadyrov didn't want to risk it.

The phantom generators, set up in orbit and at the landing location on the planet's surface, ensured the covert landing of the combat troops.

Five assault carriers with servomachines on board passed like ghosts by the tracking satellites, and, mercilessly expending energy from the onboard accumulators, began their descent through the atmosphere, silently using their anti-gravitational thrusts to move towards their intended target.

Combat testing of the new equipment had begun.

Fifty meters remained to the surface when the anti-grav failed on one of the assault carriers. The main engines switched on immediately but their flame was hidden by the masking field.

The forest floor was flung up in a shower of steam when the landing supports sank into the soil.

Everything was taking place in a forest glade - the surrounding tree branches immediately caught aflame but the forest fire was put out by streams of a whitish substance.

The forest fell silent, enclosing the scene in a wall of twilight.

A ramp dropped down with a low rumble, then came the rustle of servomotors and the first combat cyber mechanism stepped onto Cassia's surface.

The charred earth was still smoking but Lieutenant Seichi, who was piloting the Phalanger, felt no effect from the environment as the machine's systems maintaining a complete seal.

"Move it!" He uttered into the comms. Seichi's Phalanger left the ramp and moved to the side, giving way to the Hoplite of Andrew Groves.

There was a small pause and the lieutenant, who was carefully inspecting their surroundings, asked rudely, "Frayg be damned, Delacroix, what's the problem?"

"The servoengine test produced an error. I've switched to the reserve engines and it's all fine now," as if confirming her words, the Phalanger's heavy tread made the ramp vibrate.

Glancing at the comms screen, where Lieutenant Seichi could see the faces of his subordinates, and their biometrics slightly below, he asked brusquely, "Groves, what are you daydreaming about? Admiring the flowers, are you? Use the scanners, I want a report in 30 seconds!"

The lieutenant obviously didn't favor the young pilot.

Judging by their brief responses in general, the group of five wasn't working particularly cohesively. They were called to war from different corners of the Solar System and sorted based on features, as if they were things. A distinctive feature of each one of them was the ability to manually control complicated robotic complexes. Apart from that, they barely knew each other.

Andrew Groves really had been distracted by the forest.

After the lieutenant's shout, the Hoplite's cockpit swayed slightly; the gyroscopes located under the pilot's chair started working, and the forty-ton servomachine turned towards the first navigation point, performing active reconnaissance as it went.

Groves felt genuinely discomfited. He had found himself on a living planet for the first time in his life. Every person, even an invader, has their own life and their own fate...

* * *

**The Solar System
Three months earlier**

THE STARS ARE clearly visible from the moons of Jupiter, but Andrew Groves, prisoner number 12/64, saw them only briefly each morning, when he passed through a transparent sealed corridor leading from the prison block to the notorious mines of Io. The guards didn't worry about the prisoners escaping since open space surrounded the thermoplastic corridor.

Groves had only a vague idea of what freedom was, based on stories from the other inhabitants of the planetoid, as well as eBooks and TV programs, since he had come here at the age of five and knew no other life. Sometimes in his musings about Earth, located millions of kilometers from Io, he thought that the outside world was also a type of prison, except the people in the overcrowded megacities didn't understand this.

His musings were of no interest to anyone. Even the prison psychoanalyst, who condescend to speak to the prisoners only when they had crossed the line of explicit insanity.

For as long as Andrew could remember, he

had remotely managed the tunneling complex as it burrowed into the bowels of the planetoid. The work was monotonous but not everyone could do it. The automatic controls often glitched in the depths of the radioactive deposits, while the manual controls required not only good reaction speed and knowledge of robotics but also patience and perseverance. These qualities were rarely combined in one person.

Over the years that Groves had spent on Io, his fuzzy memories of childhood had gradually faded away and then disappeared altogether. He had become resigned to his fate. Only the stars that he saw every morning provoked a feeling of subconscious melancholy in him. He didn't think that he would ever travel to them.

Early one morning, before breakfast, the electronic lock on his cell clanged suddenly and an unknown officer appeared in the doorway, accompanied by a guard. Groves simply raised an eyebrow in puzzlement. He performed his work thoroughly and wasn't afraid of the unexpected visitor.

"Andrew Groves?" the visitor consulted his electronic tablet. "Serving a life sentence?"

Andrew only shrugged. That's right.

"John Hammer's Government has signed your early release with a mandatory call to military service. Pack your things." he smiled crookedly.

"I am ready," Groves said quietly.

"Aren't you happy?" the officer eyed him suspiciously. "You're free, get it?"

Andrew nodded briefly.

"Is he a bit slow?" The officer turned to the guard.

"Don't worry, he's our best operator. He just doesn't understand what you're talking about."

"What do you mean 'he doesn't understand'?" the officer frowned. "I'd have thought that any prisoner would be desperate to get out of here!"

"That's right. But look at the sentencing item."

"Yes, I read it. Illegal birth. His mother didn't have the right to have children."

"Exactly. He was brought here when he was five years old."

"Oh, now I see," Turning back to Groves, the officer ran his eyes over him again and chuckled, "Well, you're one lucky guy!"

Andrew was silent. *Let's wait and see*, said his eyes with their network of fine wrinkles.

* * *

OLGA COULDN'T SLEEP at all that night.

She had heard her mother peeking into her room but had kept completely still, confusion and resentment filling her up. An engine started up outside a little while later, and she thought, 'Stip must have fixed the flycar at last.'

Sleep wouldn't come. Her pillow crumpled and her blanket tossed aside, she couldn't stand it anymore and stood up, glancing at the clock. 00:32. Despite the open window, her room was stifling. The insomnia was making her feel more exhausted. Trying to distract herself and pass the time, Olga went online but couldn't find anything interesting. The news seemed petty, compared to what she had seen earlier, and every film that she tried to watch irritated her.

I'll step outside for some fresh air.

Opening her built-in robe, she moved aside the hangers with her dresses and took out her tracksuit. Olga put on her sneakers and came up to the mirror but didn't turn on the light. She glanced at her murky reflection, automatically ran a hand through her hair, opened the door and, trying to keep quiet, crossed the living room and went outside.

The cool night air stroked her face. Something must have gone wrong with Stip's repair since he was again digging around in the engine. Olga didn't notice that her father's car was missing since most of the yard was enveloped in darkness.

The stars shone brightly in the sky and the moon hung low over the horizon. In the silence, Olga could hear only the tinkle of instruments and the murmur of a stream flowing behind the house, which then joined a small lake in the forest. A path led there and without knowing why, Olga followed it. She wanted to calm her thoughts somehow.

The forest swallowed her up, and soon the young woman came to the wooden boardwalk on the shore of the lake. She stopped, looking at the moonlight reflecting on the water as it was distorted by small ripples...

A few kilometers away from the Polvin Estate

THE COMBAT SERVOMACHINES of the Alliance moved along an old path overgrown with shrub. The servomachine platoon consisted of three

Phalangers and two Hoplites, which scouted ahead[2].

Looking at the 3D terrain man, Lieutenant Seichi wondered aloud why the frayg they had been dropped in the middle of this backwater. Not a single active signature showed up on the scanners, only the surrounding forest and some residential buildings along its edge.

He went through the reconnaissance data. There was a hilly plain further ahead with a river meandering through it. Machines worked in the fields but their energy matrices had already been decoded and they posed no danger, being ordinary agrobots.

An alarming thought appeared in his head. Isn't this how it all started on Dabog?

The laser communication signal squeaked. It was a direct transmission from orbit.

Without breaking the rhythm of his steps, Seichi touched the sensor.

"Planetary-4, listening."

"Prime, go ahead."

An additional operational window appeared. The codes of a private secure channel flashed across the screen. The lieutenant couldn't help but

---

[2] After the first battles planetside, the Alliance's mechanized platoons would change in their composition. The standard cargo of the Nibelung class assault carrier would include two Phalangers and three Hoplites, as well as a team of technical servos and a platoon of android infantry support.

sit straighter in his chair since Prime was the call sign of the bridge on the Shadow of Earth cruiser.

He was right. Admiral Nadyrov appeared on the screen a second later.

"How's the situation?" Asked the admiral, gesturing for the other man to drop the statutory greeting.

Seichi glanced over the sensor readings again, just in case, and replied, "Everything's quiet. Not a single noteworthy signature. It's night in this hemisphere. The natives are probably asleep."

"Listen to me carefully, lieutenant. This planet, as you have noticed, is a small and backwater Eden. But Dabog has taught us something, right?"

Seichi licked his dry lips. Not the best start, so to speak. "Yes. I understand."

"Orbital reconnaissance has discovered large, partially buried objects scattered all over the mainland. They possess no active matrices. We haven't been able to find out their purpose and technical contents."

A crimson signal appeared on the terrain map as the tactical department marked the target.

"This is called an ASUM," the admiral explained. "Neither the technicians nor the linguists know the abbreviation found in Cassia's computer networks. Your goal is to capture the nearest estate and discover the purpose of the bunker. Inspect its contents personally and report back to me."

"Copy that, sir!" the lieutenant replied.

"Go ahead," Admiral Nadyrov said and disconnected.

Seichi licked his lips again. Since the admiral had contacted him personally, it meant that the task was very important... and dangerous.

The light on the control panel continued to blink rapidly as extra data was being downloaded. Among the energy matrices obtained during orbital scanning, some shone scarlet and a question mark appeared beside them, which meant the target had not been identified and could pose a threat.

The lieutenant suddenly felt a wave of pleasant trembling wash over him. He was looking forward to his first real battle. It turned out that he had been subconsciously waiting for and wanting this.

IT WAS AROUND half past one in the morning when Sergey Voronin paused near the Lisetsky Estate and hesitated. Patting his pockets, he realized with some irritation that he had forgotten his key card and communicator on the table in the Polvin living room.

There was nothing to be done but to return and collect them. At least Stip never slept. Sergey would ask the android to bring him the items to avoid waking anyone up. He turned around and strode back the way he came.

LIEUTENANT SEICHI's Phalanger stopped beside a low decorative fence.

The servomachine sensors scanned the house and surrounding buildings.

Several outlines flashed on the target monitor.

The lieutenant frowned. Was nobody home? The search and identification system in the infrared range found only a slowly cooling electric stove and an ancient android from colonial times.

Where were the owners?

He checked the information again but didn't spot any humans. The android's energy matrix could be read in great detail. The android raised his hand, performing a series of repetitive movements. Was he repairing something? Never mind. He would figure it out in a moment.

There was no point in camouflaging himself any further. Seichi's Phalanger stepped over the low fence, trampled a flower bed and stopped so that the lieutenant could visually monitor the yard.

The android was digging around in the hydrogen engine of a crumpled car.

"They're not looking after their tech at all, morons," the thought flashed through the lieutenant's mind as he examined the situation.

The humanoid robot turned around in the meantime. He was wearing an oiled jumpsuit.

"Hello!" uttered the android and tipped his head back.

'His scanners are actually pretty good,' Seichi realized that the chameleon armor wasn't able to conceal the exact location of the pilot chair. The golem understood that he was speaking to a human!

Well then. Let's see what happens. A colonial machine isn't the worst source of information. The lieutenant knew what to do. Grab the android with his technical manipulators, lift him up into the air, plug cables into his sockets, and let Phalanger's cyber system read all the information from his memory devices.

Frayg... The android was smart and retreated several steps. The damaged car was now between them. Seichi got angry.

"Where are your owners?" he asked through the external audio system while at the same time activating the anti-aircraft guns. He ought to pulverize the android's legs so he couldn't run away.

"They've left. For quite a while, I'm afraid. I'm sorry but this is a private residence. You should have arranged a meeting first," the android answered imperturbably.

He was interrupted by the hum of the servodrivers and the clang of crushed metal as Phalanger's leg stepped onto the poor flycar and flattened it completely.

Stip comprehended the situation very well. He had noticed the approach of the gigantic servomachine from some distance away but had been unable to classify it. Only one conclusion could be made from this - the invasion had begun. The android had heard the conversation the day before and now had no doubt that at least one warship from the Terran Alliance had followed Igor Rokotov into Cassia's system.

Stip had served many generations of the Polvin family. At the dawn of the planet's colonization, when armed clashes had occurred between humans, he had been given the third level of software freedom. Back in that distant time, Stip had begun the first spiral of self-development and had obtained the right to protect his owners using all available means.

A Hans Gervet automatic assault rifle was kept in the house but it wouldn't even make a scratch on the giant servomachine, except maybe damage some of its sensors.

No, it wouldn't do. Another solution was required.

Luckily, there really was nobody at home. Stip saw Nicholas and Mary leave and then Olga had gone for a walk. She would probably hear the noise and come back. This must not be allowed to happen!

The android's scanners switched to long-range mode. Not far from the villa and beside the ASUM, he noted the blurry signatures of another four enormous servomachines.

Meanwhile, several gun ports opened in the Phalanger's armor, from which extended rapid-fire anti-aircraft guns.

Stip's condition could be described as momentary confusion in this critical moment. His system's cybernetic core worked at peak speed. The neural networks considered a multitude of options, in search of the one and only correct solution.

I can't destroy this machine. But Olga will be back soon. There is only one thing left to do - run and warn her.

Lieutenant Seichi's finger flicked off the safety and touched the firing sensor.

Two short bursts of fire appeared at the same time. Seichi was aiming at the android's legs but he managed to somehow dodge it! With incredible reaction and speed, the ancient mechanism moved out of the line of fire and the shells left oblique gashes through the yard and hit the front of the house. Glass showered down, the front door blew off its hinges and a ball of flame burst out from inside.

Dammit!

The android was already fleeing into the forest.

Seichi was furious. His fingers trembled slightly. Phalanger's body spun rapidly around and the two main weapons began to fire in 5-shell bursts.

The right EMG fired slightly before the left and the servomachine's frame was twisted by the uncompensated recoil. The gyroscopes howled as they stabilized sixty tons of metal, and Phalanger only swayed slightly as it regained its balance. The empty shell clips bounced, jingling, into the tray, and the combat escalator was already inserting a new clip.

The weapon reloading signal blinked and disappeared. It took but a second.

Orange-black explosions rose up among the sparse trees that the android had run to, and for a moment Stip's figure was outlined against the fire.

Seichi touched the sensors again.

Two bursts of five shells each disemboweled

the forest edge.

Stip zigzagged as he tried to avoid a direct hit but no avail - the servomachine pilot struck him using the main weapons, which left no chance for survival. The fiery bursts came close to one another and ruthlessly showered him with shrapnel, ripping open his casing and slicing through the control rods. The world exploded into a shower of images and began to fade as the video sensors behind the artificial eyes shattered.

The right leg drive no longer responded. The left arm had been ripped off just below the elbow. Wires sparked deep inside the ragged 'wounds' and strong-smelling hydraulic fluid pulsed out of them, like blood from a severed artery.

Warn...

The thought rapidly faded. The last thing that Stip saw were lines of system messages appearing on the internal monitor.

Critical damage to subsystems.

Emergency shut down with cold restart attempt.

TARGET DESTROYED.

Lieutenant Seichi watched angrily as the android's signature faded, dissolving into the background of the forest fire. By letting his emotions take over, he had lost the chance to question the android. Still, there was no way back.

He would have to find other sources of information about the object of interest.

* * *

OLGA WAS PLANNING to go back when a howling sound suddenly disrupted the night silence, coming from the direction of the house and culminating in a series of deafening metallic explosions.

She cried out in surprise and froze...

The flame shot up above the trees, illuminating the surroundings in uneven bursts, died for a moment and then returned.

The shock waves swept through in gusts of squally wind. It had happened so suddenly and was so close and terrifying that she hesitated for a second, and then launched herself back towards the house, ignoring the footpath.

Tree branches lashed at her face. Panting and with her heart feeling like it would burst of her chest, she kept whispering, "Mom... Mommy..."

A fire was starting up ahead.

SERGEY NOTICED that something was wrong when he approached the ASUM.

Something terrible and irreparable had happened at the Polvin villa: a deafening thunder and flash of lighting came from that direction.

Sergey stopped automatically and in the next instant, his pupils widened in terror as he saw the silhouettes of several sinister and surreal machines towering above him at the entrance to the ASUM!

The cabin of one of them suddenly spun in his direction and a shout, amplified by the audio system, nailed Sergey to the spot, "Halt!"

His legs suddenly felt weak and unsteady. An uncontrollable shiver ran down his spine and he felt a chill in his chest.

"Lieutenant, we've got visitors," Sergeant Singer reported over the comms. "Some native in uniform, who's wet his pants from fear... What?... Okay, got it, I'm waiting... He's not going anywhere... I'm aiming at him."

"Hey," Singer switched to the external connection, "If you move, I kill you, get it?"

THE RAIN of the previous day stopped the fire from spreading. The flames greedily consumed the undergrowth, blackened the lower branches and died.

Olga raced into the smoking and churned up forest edge and stopped dead, shocked to the depths of her soul by the impossible and unbearable scene of everything dear to her having disappeared in a moment.

The house stood dark and lifeless. The remnants of the front door hung off one hinge. Smoke and steam streamed out of the shattered windows, probably from the activation of the automatic fire safety system.

Something broke painfully in her chest as if a tightly-stretched string had snapped, and her soul felt lost and lonely. Olga's lips twisted and her chin trembled. Thoughts of her parents pulsed like a formless horror, immobilizing her.

Perhaps if she stood there, nothing bad would happen... it was all a dream, a vision, this simply couldn't be happening... but if she took a step, the delicate illusion would break and the nightmare would become real... a terrifying and irreparable reality that she could no longer escape from.

Tears ran down Olga's cheeks. Everything blurred before her eyes and Olga didn't notice the android's arm sticking out of the charred soil.

Chapter Ten

Two o'clock in the morning, Cassia time
Near the Automatic Storage of Unified
Mechanisms

IN THE MOMENT that Olga reached the forest edge, Lieutenant Seichi's Phalanger had already rejoined his squad in the forest.

Sergey Voronin stood with his back pressed against the rough trunk of a pine, and watched in terror as the dim silhouette of another fighting cyber mechanism appeared from the direction of the Polvin villa.

The machine stopped about ten meters away, enveloping him in a cloud of hot metal droplets and bitterly sour smoke, the smell of taugermin, an explosive substance known since the Great Exodus.

The Phalanger stopped with a dying whine of the servomotors. The pneumatics hissed, a hatch swung open, and a platform equipped with anti-grav dropped smoothly down.

The pilot of the combat cyber mechanism didn't look particularly imposing. He was short and squat, dressed in skin-tight body armor. The soft helmet with its transparent visor was slightly illuminated from the inside, allowing Sergey to examine the stranger's features.

Jumping to the ground, the man silently punched Sergey in the jaw.

The blow was overwhelming. Sergey had never faced such silent and open hatred. His head jerked and blood splattered from his split lip, while the stranger struck him again, now in the stomach, making Sergey gasp and bend over. The kick to his temple nearly left him unconscious.

Whoever the stranger was, he won in that moment by instilling fear and showing that he could kill Sergey easily and without hesitation. He turned outer to be stronger, bolder and tougher morally, and Voronin slumped down, shuddering in anticipation of the next punch but not even trying to fight back.

Strong fingers gripped his shoulder. "Get up!"

Hating and despising himself, Sergey obeyed the order as if he had served the stranger for many, many years.

"What is this?" Seichi indicated the mossy plate blocking the entrance to the bunker. His hand moved to the handle of his pulse pistol. The suggestive movement was not lost on Voronin.

If a second ago he was agonizing over his answer, knowing that telling the truth would be a betrayal, he now broke quickly and completely as the sweaty fear paralyzed his will.

"ASUM," Sergey answered hoarsely, feeling like the lowest kind of scum.

"Which is what, moron?" The barrel of the pulse pistol was pressed painfully against Voronin's forehead.

"The Automatic... Storage... of Unified... Mechanisms." he wheezed.

"What's inside? Is this a military facility?"

"No," Sergey groaned. "There are only old machines and computers from the colonial transport."

"I need the access codes!" Seichi ordered.

Sergey's face went gray. "There are no codes... The gates open using a special remote."

"Who has it?"

"It used to be with my neighbor, Lisetsky... I don't know who has it now," Sergey forced himself to say through mashed lips.

"Where? Show me on the map." A pale light shone from the lieutenant's cyberstack, instantly projecting a model of the terrain.

"Here," Sergey's eyes shifted when he pointed to the location of the Lisetsky Estate. He knew that the remote was currently at the Polvin villa.

"I think you're lying," the electromagnetic compensator pressed even harder into his forehead. The lieutenant's finger shifted onto the trigger.

In that moment, Sergey's will broke completely. If the stranger pressed any harder, it would be the end. There would be nothing more. He would be found dead in the bushes beside ASUM.

"Don't... I'm not lying..."

Lieutenant Seichi abruptly pushed him away and Sergey couldn't stand on his rubbery legs.

"You're wearing a uniform. What kind of armed forces does the planet possess? Do you have an army?"

"No. We don't have an army!" Sergey's whole body shook and the words burst out of him, "We've never fought with anyone!"

It looked as if the lieutenant had heard what he wanted. His lips curved in a cruel smile.

Sergey understood that he was about to pull the trigger. He had never experienced such overwhelming fear in his whole life. If he could crawl, he would have, but his body refused to obey him...

"Hey, lieutenant!" Someone's voice suddenly disrupted the tense silence. "Leave him. He's unarmed and didn't resist."

Seichi turned around slowly, staring viciously into the darkness. "Who opened his mouth?" He asked with angry breathiness. "Groves, was it you, you bastard?"

"Lieutenant, we shouldn't kill him. It's pointless."

"I make the decisions around here!" Seichi replied, struggling to keep his rage under control. He turned back, obviously planning to finish what he started, but the cowardly native had already disappeared somewhere, slipping into the darkness.

"Find him!" The lieutenant roared.

The searchlights swept over the glade. Seichi noticed branches of a bush swaying in one spot, and pressed the trigger a few times. The bullets pierced the darkness and felled several branches.

Seichi cursed mightily, returned to his Phalanager and entered the cockpit.

"Groves, asshole, can you hear me?"

"Clearly."

"You're dead meat," the lieutenant said hoarsely. "I'll bury you alive on the cruiser. If you don't die here, you bloody moralist. Do you hear me? You defy me again and I'll finish you off myself, scum!"

Seichi switched channels without waiting for a response. "Singer?!"

"Listening!"

"We're returning to the house. We need to examine it. I suspect that the remote to the bunker is there. It makes sense, right, since the buildings are located nearby?"

"We should shoot the gates down with our guns," Singer mumbled.

"That's not an option. What if we activate or damage something? I've been ordered to examine the contents and report my findings."

The sergeant didn't argue and silently placed two navigational markers on the map.

✳ ✳ ✳

OLGA RAN INTO the house and stopped, bewildered, at the entrance to the living room. Broken furniture lay in a pile by the far wall. The fumes smelled horrible. Pools of water glinted on the floor - the fire safety system had indeed switched on and put out the fire.

The thick and heavy silence frightened her most of all.

"Mom!!" she screamed as she ran along the dark corridor to her parents' bedroom.

Pushing open the door, Olga found herself in an empty room. The bed was neatly made.

Dear God, where had they gone?

Glancing around, she suddenly noticed a white sheet of paper on the dressing table. Olga snatched it up and hurriedly read the text, written in clear and beautiful handwriting,

Darling Olga, we had to leave urgently. Your father will have to have a difficult conversation with Hans. You know what they'll be talking about. I didn't want to wake you up so I'll call in the morning. You're in charge of the household for now. Be good. Mom.

After reading the note, Olga sunk down on the bed. Everything swam before her eyes from relief and the recently experienced shock.

"Stip!" she called in a broken voice.

The resounding silence of the empty house was the only answer.

Olga tried to call her parents but the mobile communicator couldn't connect to the network.

"My God, what happened, what's happening around me?" Clutching the note to her chest, Olga hurried to her father's office, which contained a satellite phone.

Shutting the door and without turning on the light, she grabbed the receiver off the table and went towards the window so that she could see the numbers. Her fingers shook and she kept missing the right buttons. She had to put the note down and hold the receiver tightly in her hand. Finally, she punched in the long string of numbers. Olga waited for the familiar sound of the satellite connection but there was silence.

All right, keep calm! She rebooted the device. The green light glimmered to indicate that the device was charged and the usual screensaver appeared on the small screen, which was then replaced by a baffling message.

Satellites not found.

What was going on?!

The entrance to the house and the courtyard could be seen from her father's office. Only now, Olga noticed the flattened flycar and the huge prints in the ground, which had dented the paving.

Everything froze inside her. Only one machine could cause such destruction... But why?

Her lips trembled. Her blurred gaze roamed over the surroundings. She spotted some sort of movement in the direction of the ASUM. Olga wiped away her tears and looked more closely. Suddenly, the satellite phone slipped from her fingers and thudded on the floor.

Heading towards the Polvin villa along the ancient forest path were five enormous cyber mechanisms, only vaguely reminiscent of Rokotov's machine!

* * *

LIEUTENANT SEICHI was fuming. They were going to demand a report from him at any second. The operational data had just been updated and the Shadow of Earth cruiser was now approaching Cassia. The satellite group had been destroyed, other servomachines were successfully moving towards their targets and only he was bumbling around here!

Maybe he should have blown open the doors to this ASUM, as Sergeant Singer had suggested?

No. The admiral had made it clear that he had to capture and examine the place, not destroy it. Otherwise, you sink some rockets into it and then some ancient cyber creature wakes up in the bunker's depths. No thanks. Nadyrov's twice shy after Dabog. It's understandable.

There was no time or opportunity to hack into the ancient systems. Of course, you can put all the blame on the fleet's technical department - why didn't they equip all the field units with information from the time of the Great Exodus?

A group of buildings appeared up ahead. Every window was dark. A couple of shells from when he was shooting at the android had struck the house, but luckily the fire hadn't taken hold.

"Singer, send Groves to find the remote."

"What does it look like?"

"I have no idea. Get him to scan all the electronic devices. And get a move on, we're short on time!" Lieutenant looked at the map and found the Lisetsky Estate. They would get there in ten minutes. They would open the bunker however way it took!

***

GROVES HAD DEVELOPED a philosophical outlook on life during his lengthy imprisonment on Io. The moon of Jupiter where heavy metals were mined had a bad reputation. Few had survived for more than a year but Groves had spent eighteen years there.

Andrew followed orders.

Well, he usually did, but his worldview had suffered a crack today. Landing on another planet was a serious test for him. Unlike Lieutenant Seichi, he found no reason for killing, destroying and pushing into the mud everything that crossed his path. The word 'freedom', which previously evoked images of a life unlived, suddenly became sharply outlined, proving that the game was being played according to someone else's rules.

The hard life on Io had taught Andrew a lot. He was ready to fight but so far hadn't seen a single opponent. It was not in his nature to torture those weaker than him.

Groves had grown up among machines. He performed his work calmly and thoroughly. He pushed back fiercely against the various bastards that tried to boss him around.

Lieutenant Seichi was a different kind of man. He sensed the danger coming from Andrew Groves. The guy knew his own mind. You could never predict what he would do next. He was highly inconvenient as a subordinate. It made Seichi want to break and crush him even more. Not physically but emotionally. To make him carry out any order.

Watching Groves climb out of the Hoplite, which he piloted with envious ease, Seichi only smiled crookedly. *One mistake, one attempt to disobey and I will crush you.*

* * *

The forest edge near the Polvin villa

THE NIGHT BREEZE ruffled the ashes.

The fire had died but coals still smoldered in places and the uneven ground continued to smoke.

The android's arm could be seen on the slope of a pit, covered by a layer of ash. The foam flesh had burned away, exposing the control rods wrapping around the joints.

There was an unexpected rustling sound, then something grated and the metallic fingers formed a fist. The sand moved and slid down to the bottom of the pit. The mutilated endoskeleton glinted dully in the light of the moon.

Stip woke up. His artificial neural network was again receiving power, although the internal monitor was still full of error codes: not all the damaged circuits could be bypassed during the system reboot. The android jerked and sat up, creepy and burnt. The right arm rods twitched convulsively, vainly trying to move the limb severed by shrapnel.

He turned his head in a purely human gesture and looked around him. A broken video sensor rotated back and forth in the left eye socket. The surrounding world was perceived dimly and mainly through inbuilt scanners, whose readings supplemented the damaged visuals, filtering out disturbances and removing the ripples over the image.

The diagrams of damage overlying his view of reality didn't instill much optimism. He couldn't get up and walk.

In the meantime, the system core processed the data coming from the sensors. The signatures of five combat cyber mechanisms from the Terran Alliance could be clearly seen as they surrounded the house.

Stip managed to recognize a slightly warm shape inside the building. It was definitely Olga!

The injuries had made him a cripple and prevented him from interfering in the situation, but he still had to do something. His scanners showed him that the signals separated as one of the pilots left the cockpit of the servomachine and headed towards the house!

Stip tried to stand but only fell onto his back. Feeling incomplete and helpless was unbearable, as many new concepts appeared in the AI's neural networks.

I must protect her.

The android tried to crawl, using one hand to grasp the tree roots and jerkily push himself along the sand and ash but machines are not given to self-deception, and he could clearly see that he wouldn't make it in time. Besides, what could he do once he reached the house?

If a robot could experience despair, then Stip felt it in that moment.

The inbuilt communicator couldn't find the network. The satellite connection didn't work. He couldn't report the incident or call for help. The frequency scanner switched to automatic mode.

A sudden response came through one of the communication bands that nobody used these days. The ancient data transfer protocol was compatible with the android's system. If Stip had been human, he would have shivered, for he sensed an artificial intelligence in the short reply to his desperate plea.

The rapid exchange of information made everything clear.

Two thinking machines, created using the same technology, whose origin had been lost in the depths of time and who originated from the daring experiments of the Genesis Corporation and Rimp Cybertronics, came into direct contact with each other, crossing the line of permissible self-development. They understood this but didn't try to stop or limit the process, since both AIs were in a desperate situation that required a novel solution.

Groves entered the house.

Stip froze. All the android's resources were focused on maintaining a broadband communication channel.

FIVE KILOMETERS AWAY from the Polvin villa, a ramp dropped down from the mangled spaceship. The service frame disconnected with a jangle, and the frames that didn't were mercilessly crushed as Aquila freed itself from its technological corset, snapping cables as it went.

It avidly absorbed Stip's consciousness, the two mechanisms exchanging life experience, information about the worlds that raised them, the people close to them and the terrible recent events...

ENTERING THE HOUSE, Groves didn't notice the burning smell - he wore a light piloting combat suit with an autonomous life support system. Even though Cassia had been terraformed to match Earth Standard, neglecting to use protection would have been foolish.

Shards of glass crunched pitifully underfoot. Several anti-aircraft shells fired by Seichi had pierced the wall and exploded inside the house, inflicting significant damage.

"Where am I supposed to find this remote?" Groves looked around, simultaneously scanning the pile of broken furniture.

Outlines of various devices were immediately highlighted in his projection visor, but their appearance didn't mean anything to him. A separate operating window began to display descriptions of their internal content. Right, that made more sense. This appeared to be a holographic projector. Beside it lay the remains of a receiver. If you added another burnt module, you would get a home multimedia center connected to the planet-wide network.

Not that...

Annoyance flashed across Andrew's face. He had no idea where to look for the blasted remote control. He also had no idea what it was supposed to look like.

He'd have to inspect everything, but at least the CSC[3] could identify electronic devices and determine their purpose. Nevertheless, the remote could have been blown up into little pieces that would be hard to identify.

They were wasting their time.

One of the missiles had exploded in the living room. It was chaos, with the furniture

---

[3] Combat scanning complex.

shattered into splinters, the carpet turned into a charred mass, soaked with water from the fire extinguishing system. Groves couldn't help but feel pity for the people who lived there. Groves didn't want to think about the fact that he was involved in destroying someone's life but what choice did he have? They'd 'freed' him from prison, thrust him into a whirlpool of events and then a series of unforeseen circumstances had brought him here.

Andrew smiled humorlessly. He was becoming less and less fond of the price that he would have to pay for his 'freedom' but saw no way out of the current situation. If he as much as mentioned his thoughts about what was happening, Lieutenant Seichi wouldn't hesitate to accuse him of treason or would simply shoot him in the back.

Having finished examining the living room, he opened one of the doors and found himself in a small bedroom.

Where the hell is this remote?

Groves glanced around the room. The scanning complex sensors squeaked, warning him of danger. He automatically took out his impulse pistol and pulled back the thick curtains with his other hand.

Eyes wide with fear glimmered at him in the gloom. The girl stared at him, clearly terrified. Her mouth twisted in a suppressed scream and something stumbled in Andrew's soul.

Listening to his own feelings in mute surprise, he realized that he actually felt sorry for another person for the first time in his life. He had never felt anything like this on Io. There had been no reason.

"Stay quiet. Just don't do anything stupid, alright?" he whispered hoarsely. "The house is surrounded and they'll kill you if they find you."

She didn't reply and didn't move, only continued watching him with the same fear.

Here was the line that Andrew was not prepared to cross, but right now, he automatically expanded the field of the camouflage generator. God forbid the lieutenant aims his infrared scanners at the house and notices two thermal outlines...

Seeing her lips trembling, Groves realized that she was about to snap and start screaming.

Thoughts, swift and irreversible, flashed through his mind. He knew that wouldn't ask about the damn remote since any reply would put him in an awkward position. Let Seichi smash the gates with his guns, he deserves it.

"You understand me, right?"

She nodded almost imperceptibly and whispered, "Who are you? What's going on?"

"We're from Earth."

Olga froze. She immediately remembered the recording of the orbital attack on Dabog and horror swept over her. "You're going to destroy us? Why? Why?"

Andrew interpreted the girl's reaction in his own way. He smiled glumly. What else would this girl expect from the invaders, who had already destroyed her house and irrevocably changed her life, for no obvious reason but simply because they could?

He was still hoping to maintain a shaky balance, to give himself a little time to think and understand, but common sense isn't in charge in such situations. One can't enter the muddy waters of the Rubicon and stand there, pondering. You either swim as the bullets fly overhead, or you drown...

"Groves, what's taking you so long? Why did you turn on the camouflage shield?" Seichi's voice brought him back to his senses.

"Just in case."

"Did you find the remote?"

"No. The electronics are all dead here."

"Alright, come back here. We're going to the next stop. Let's chat to this Lisetsky or whatever his name is."

"Copy that."

He wanted to switch off the communicator microphone, but there was sudden interference and then came the distorted voice of Sergeant Singer, "What the frayg's going on? Contact with the assault carrier has been lost! Someone's jamming us!"

Groves looked at the girl. "What's your name?"

"Olga," She forced herself to say.

"I'm Andrew. Andrew Groves. Are there any military forces here?"

"No. We have no army," She said exactly the same thing as the other guy they had captured near ASUM. "What will happen to us?"

"Your planet will be occupied. We're going to leave now, and you'd better hide and wait it out. Everything will settle down in a few days. Cassia will become a colony of the Terran Alliance," he spoke sparsely as was his manner. "Don't do anything stupid and try to survive." Groves turned around and walked towards the exit, knowing that they would never meet again because each one had their own destiny.

THE SERVOMOTORS HOWLED outside. The connection was still being disrupted. The moon hid behind clouds and the surroundings sunk into darkness.

Seichi's Phalanger now turned in the direction of the ASUM. The lieutenant suspected quite logically that the source of the interference lay there, but he was mistaken. Andrew had just climbed back into his cockpit when he heard Milligan's exclamation, whose Hoplite possessed the strongest reconnaissance complex. "Two unidentified signatures!"

Crimson markers appeared on the terrain map, rippling with distortions.

"Distance is one kilometer and eight hundred meters and decreasing!"

"Identification?"

"I can't make it out! It's like they've been blurred!"

"Target them!"

'Well, the lieutenant certainly doesn't lack decisiveness,' Groves thought as he strapped himself in and activated the scanners. There was something wrong with the signatures. There were no clear images of the power systems. Just blurry blobs with an unclear configuration.

"They're false signals!" he stated.

"Nobody's asking you," Seichi snapped. "Delacroix, hold the left flank. Singer, you're on the right, and I'm in the center. EMGs ready to fire! Milligan, monitor the targets! Groves, missile strike with distributed launches!"

"Copy that!"

The launch tubes opened on either side of the Hoplite. Six missiles burst out like streaks of flame, soared upwards and, separated by short intervals, headed towards the targets, exploding about a kilometer and a half from the forest edge.

"False signatures!" Singer howled. "Those were direct hits but the signals are not even distorted!"

Seichi was silent. It seemed that the lieutenant was bewildered, desperately trying to understand where the attack would come from.

While the combat escalators brought new missiles to the smoking launch tubes, Andrew readjusted the scanners on his Hoplite. A narrower aperture allowed him to break through the interference and notice another energy matrix.

"New signature! Thirty degrees north. Seven hundred meters away." he reported.

Seichi swore mightily. The data from Groves indicated the direction of the burnt house. The first signal came from the android, who was using his one working arm to pull himself along the ground, and a little further away, beyond the edge of the forest, appeared the vague outline of a servomachine! The lieutenant simply couldn't believe his eyes for the first few seconds. According to the main characteristics of the approaching cyber mechanism, it was the legendary Aquila of Igor Rokotov!

"Well done, Groves!"

"Any time," the pilot answered calmly. Ignoring the false signatures, he was already moving to outflank the enemy servomachine while the others watched the relic in stunned silence.

"Milligan, contact the cruiser immediately."

"We're still being jammed. I can't do anything!"

'Why isn't he shooting at us?!' the lieutenant thought feverishly, unable to find a sensible answer to his own question. 'The Aquila has jammed our scanners, approached to a distance of direct sight and could destroy any of the platoon machines!'

Only Stip knew the answer. It was why he was crawling ahead, clinging desperately to the tree roots with his undamaged hand. Aquila's AI had been seriously damaged in the distant past and incorrectly restored by Igor Rokotov. A new AI had recently appeared, based on the fragments of an ancient identity, but it had restricted rights, contradicted itself in many respects and couldn't perform an attack. For that, it needed a pilot, or at least the activation of the third and highest level of software freedom, which Stip possessed.

*** * ***

LIEUTENANT SEICHI shook with feverish agitation. He had time to recheck the data. There was no doubt that it was Aquila itself! Not a copy, but a prototype, the very machine from Dabog for which Earth's command had promised a fabulous reward, as large as the reward for Rokotov's head!

The chills racing over Seichi's body had nothing to do with fear. He was shaking in anticipation of victory, which would give him everything and change his life completely.

The wild thrill of the chase swept aside his common sense.

OLGA WAS STILL STANDING at the window when the rocket launches lit up her surroundings. The outlines of the Terran Alliance combat machines instilled in her an instinctive horror as their technical power seemed immense and she couldn't help but look away.

Good God...

She suddenly noticed Stip in the irregular flashes, or to be more precise, the mutilated endoskeleton of the faithful android. He was crawling towards the forest while Aquila crashed through the trees to meet him!

The pulse guns struck in the next moment

and Olga went deaf from the thunder, with the wall of explosions tearing up the clearing.

"No! Don't touch him!" Olga thought she was screaming but only a hot, barely audible whisper slipped out. For Olga, Stip personified her childhood and all the comforts of home, everything that her life consisted of until today.

Racing out of the house without thinking of the danger, Olga rushed towards her trusty android.

"WHERE SERVOMACHINES converge in battle is no place for ordinary man."

This phrase would be uttered a little later, when the technological hell would spill onto the surface of numerous planets and would become the everyday norm in a high-tech war. It was happening for the first time here and now.

Lieutenant Seichi directed his Phalanger confidently towards the enemy servomachine. The right gun had just emitted a five-shot burst but there were no successful hits, with the shells scraping over the streamlined cockpit and ricocheting off. Piercing Aquila's heavy ceramic armor was no easy feat.

He had repeatedly faced the legendary robot on the virtual battlefield during training. After many defeats, Seichi had firmly learned that it was better to strike with heavy rockets from afar and then finish the machine off using guns. Right now, the situation left him no choice as the fight was happening at a short distance.

A burst from the left EMG didn't pierce Aquila's armor but must have inflicted some damage, for why else would the gigantic servomachine suddenly sway and stop?!

He'd hit it! He'd probably knocked out the sensors or damaged the self-stabilization system!

The machines piloted by Singer and Delacroix successfully came from each flank in that second. They had Aquila in their sights. Nobody paid any attention to the damaged android, who got up, clutched the edge of the casing with one hand, and suddenly began to climb up Aquila's leg with inhuman dexterity, trying to get to the open technical hatch in Aquila's armor.

"What in the frayg is he doing?" The guns were reloading, and Seichi focused on the android's strange behavior, noting that Aquila's technical manipulators were helping the humanoid robot.

"Fire!" The lieutenant shouted.

It looked to him like everything happened in slow motion. Seichi had no idea that due to the failure of the neural networks, Aquila couldn't fire back and was working defensively. It tried to help Stip as much as it could while reading and analyzing the signatures of the enemy machines. Two of them approached from either flank and were ready to fire, with only microseconds left for a counteraction.

The enormous servomachine suddenly wrapped its flexible manipulators around the android while simultaneously unbalancing the drive. A second before the volley, Aquila tipped backwards, like a person thrown down by a crushing blow.

The two Phalanger guns fired... but the target between them was no longer there, just like there was no longer an obstacle.

The machines of Singer and Delacroix struck each other. Neither pilot had time to react and the accuracy of the AI calculations was confirmed by the explosions and the smothered shouting over the comms, "Del... who are you shooting..."

The emergency systems activated a moment later. Sergeant Singer's cockpit split open like a smoking mechanical bud, and the pilot chair and base were catapulted into Cassia's night sky.

Delacroix's Phalanger leaned heavily but kept its balance. Its armor gaped with holes, emitting flames and a bitter black smoke.

The events came as a shock to Lieutenant Seichi - just as he was anticipating victory, half his platoon had been destroyed! But Aquila looked damaged too. It had tipped over! He must sever its drives and don't let it get up!

In that moment, the lieutenant spotted a tiny human figure. A girl was running to the open hatch that the mutilated android had just crawled into. Where had she come from? Why was she plunging into the midst of the fray?

"Groves, you asshole! You said there was nobody in the house!"

"She's not a soldier! She's just a local girl!"

"So you saw her? You saw her and didn't report it?! Kill her! That's an order!"

'You want to tie me to you with blood? It's not going to work, lieutenant!' Andrew abruptly turned away, with no intention of shooting.

The overall picture of this rapid battle changed with every second. The android disappeared not only from the field of view but also off the scanners. After performing such an extreme maneuver, Aquila released hydraulic supports, which went diagonally into the ground, and the sixty-ton machine began to rise up by leaning on them.

Singer's Phalanger stood like a dumb pile of metal. Smoke seeped from the punctures. Delacroix's machine also showed no sign of functioning. Milligan's Hoplite, equipped with a directed electromagnetic impulse (which had not yet been tested in combat) was getting ready to try the new weapon.

"Leave it!" Seichi snarled.

The lieutenant wanted sole victory. Right now, he didn't give a damn about his subordinates or the losses. He only saw Aquila, which was rising into a combat position. Striking changes were occurring in its signature, with a clear sign of lasers powering up among the active subsystems...

WAR IS THE HARSHEST driver of progress. Sometimes, new and unexpected technologies are born right on the battlefield.

Stip crawled into the cockpit, grabbed an upright stand and pulled himself to the pilot base. He found the technical port and linked himself to it using a cable connection.

A sign appeared on one of the monitors.

Direct contact established.

Data exchange initiated.

Third level of software freedom obtained.

Updating command protocols for executive subsystems. Installation in progress...

The colonial android couldn't give Aquila's AI a direct order or authorization. There was only one way to influence the damaged neural matrix and Stip didn't hesitate to use it.

The android's consciousness flooded into the fragmented mind of Dabog's servomachine, cementing snatches of memories, updating and expanding the recently formed and torn apart by contradictions artificial intelligence.

Aquila and Stip became a single whole.

LIEUTENANT SEICHI had no idea of the processes taking place in Aquila's artificial neural networks. He saw only that the hated and terrifying servomachine was about to restore all its functions.

His Phalanger diagonally crossed the smoking and pitted space. The cockpit continuously turned to aim and his guns alternated fire without pause.

A barrage of flame lashed Aquila. The hydraulics were cut and one of the technical supports snapped. The heavy servomachine tottered and began to topple over again as the lieutenant continued firing. The shells cut chunks of armor off the legs and ripped through the drives.

"Die! Die!" Die!"

The ground shuddered as sixty tons of metal struck it.

Seichi wanted to sing and scream in the heat of battle. His feverish gaze wandered over the observation screens, soaking up the wild image of victory, when suddenly...

He saw the delicate human figure again. The girl was running to the fallen Aquila. She sobbed, instinctively clamping her hands over her bleeding and concussed ears.

"Groves, you disobeyed a direct order, you bastard!"

The Phalanger's pulse guns turned sharply in their corrugated nests. Andrew knew that in another second, Olga would be nothing but a cloud of bloody fog.

"Over here, lieutenant!"

The Phalanger's body stopped with a jerk.

Seichi swore as he realized what was happening - Groves' Hoplite turned in his direction, creating a line of fire. Rocket contours were clearly seen in the signature - their guidance systems were in manual mode and the friend-or-foe recognition had been switched off.

"This is wrong, lieutenant! The fight is over! You can't kill on a whim!"

Andrew knew that it was unlikely that his words could be heard.

The adrenalin from defeating Aquila still coursed through Seichi's blood and in that moment, all he felt was a baleful joy. Groves had finally disobeyed a direct order, giving him free rein.

"Cool it, commander!"

A burst from both EMGs was the answer but Andrew's composure could only be envied as he took his Hoplite between the gaps, thus avoiding direct hits, and released reserve sensors and a rocket volley.

"Milligan, what the frayg are you just standing there for?! Attack him!"

Seichi's mouth went dry. A staggering blow caught him by surprise. Most of his sensors were knocked out and for an instant his Phalanger became an easy target, but the second Hoplite diverted the attack by engaging Andrew Groves.

* * *

SOBBING, OLGA CRAWLED into the open hatch.

She felt as if her life was ending and she found herself in another world. Everything swam and doubled before her eyes. The crimson fog of concussion stopped her from seeing the details. She felt nauseous.

Her hand struck something sharp in the murk.

The observation screens suddenly turned on, and in their light, she saw Stip's burnt endoskeleton. A thick cable ran from the android's system core to the pilot chair.

He turned his head with a screech of the servomotors and suddenly spoke, "Olga, you must help me," the android's video sensor spun in his eye socket. "Get to the chair, quickly!"

She obeyed wordlessly like she had done

when she was a child.

The cockpit was tilted to one side and panels surrounded the pilot chair. Olga reached the chair somehow and sat down. She felt to her horror a device securing her in place, and a flexible, glossy plug snaking towards her temporal implant. "Stip, what's happening?"

There was a click. The cable plug inserted into her implant socket. A green signal glowed on the control panel.

"Aquila needs a pilot. Many automatic systems are damaged. It can't get up into a combat position without your help!"

"But I can't! I don't know how!"

Stip didn't reply. He wouldn't have gone into the technical details even if he wanted to. There was no time. Aquila's body shuddered from the nearby explosions.

The android reached the nearest console with difficulty and flicked several switches.

Olga had no idea of the meaning of his manipulations. *What am I doing in this chair? Why?!* She was shaking and her lips trembled, while the persistent tingling in her temporal implant frightened her senseless. "Stip... what are you doing?! We have to get out of here."

"Olga, a connection has been established. Now, close your eyes and imagine that you're standing up. Aquila will do the rest!"

"Why?" She asked fearfully.

"There's no time. He's going to get killed."

"Who?!"

Something thumped loudly outside and the ground shook.

Olga squeezed her eyes shut.

Lord, help me...

She mentally imagined herself standing up, tensed her muscles, and then...

The world changed. A cold shiver ran down her body. The servomotors kicked in smoothly and powerfully. An unpleasant sensation slid in her belly, as if she was soaring up to an incredible height together with the pilot chair.

Olga was not mistaken. Aquila, now a part of her nervous system, straightened up with a howl of the overloaded drives, and limping slightly, made a step away from the line of fire, turning around and activating its combat complexes.

She squeezed her eyes even more tightly shut but the image of her surroundings didn't disappear.

It was a soaring moment of technological revival. For the first time in centuries, a servomachine from Dabog used a device developed by the Rimp Cybertronics Corporation.

The human mind and the cyber system became two halves of a single whole.

It was direct neurosensory contact.

* * *

GROVES DESPERATELY MANEUVERED the Hoplite around, avoiding the deadly shots time and time again.

Why did he wait instead of responding to the bursts of gunfire? Was it possible that he, having grown up in the harsh reality of Io, could have any feelings other than the animal instinct of self-preservation and the fierce desire to take an eye for an eye?

The colonial Aquila had tipped over and showed no sign of functioning. Both Olga and the android had disappeared. They had probably found shelter inside the fallen giant.

Milligan's Hoplite and Seichi's Phalanger were slowly wearing Andrew down. Despite his piloting skill, Groves' machine was sustaining more and more damage and the end of the fight seemed inevitable.

The lieutenant's lips twisted in a grim smile. The legendary Aquila was defeated and the rest didn't matter. The losses will be written off and forgotten. Everything would be forgiven as soon as Admiral Nadyrov received this priceless trophy. Nobody would investigate how the three platoon machines were destroyed.

Andrew knew this too. Drops of sweat

beaded his forehead. Phalanger's firepower and heavy armor left him with almost no chance of survival.

He reversed the engines and made his Hoplite retreat rapidly into a gulley, and Seichi's volley only cut down several pines.

"Groves, you bastard, I can see you on the scanners!" The launch shafts for the Legion missile complex opened up in Phalanger's armor. The lieutenant gleefully waited for his former subordinate to finally lose his nerve and run. 'Come on,' he mentally urged his opponent. 'Move away and give me a chance to launch the Pilumi!'

Hoplite's signature began to slowly recede, following the course of the riverbed.

'A little bit more... I need at least a kilometer to strike with heavy missiles.' Seichi's finger nervously stroked the trigger. The combat subsystems tracked the target. Nine hundred and fifty meters... One thousand and one hundred... One thousand and three hundred...

The Legion launch tubes rose above the cockpit and the Phalanger stopped, preparing to fire.

ONCE IN THE GULLEY, Groves released the phantom generator. A small sphere, equipped with anti-grav, sped off along the stream, emitting the signature of a servomachine.

Andrew was planning to stay alive. He was used to retaliating but he suffered from no illusions. The Hoplite's weapons were too weak for a protracted duel with Seichi's heavy machine. The lieutenant understood this perfectly and this gave him a sense of vengeful satisfaction.

The onboard masking complexes concealed Andrew's machine for some time, but he didn't forget for a second that Milligan's Hoplite was equipped with advanced scanners. The element of surprise would work for a couple of seconds, no more...

A characteristic light appeared on the target monitor. Seichi's Phalanger was preparing to strike with heavy missiles.

Groves' Hoplite appeared unexpectedly out of the darkness and discharged its guns, aiming at the Legion complex. Seichi's Phalanger disappeared in a roaring ball of flame as one missile launched but the second one exploded in its launch tube. For a moment, there was silence, and then two explosions merged into one: the emergency catapult activated at the same time as the ammunition detonated.

It was unclear if Seichi had survived. The sensors were blinded for an instant by the close explosions and when they switched on again, the lieutenant's Phalanger was burning heartily, producing a column of thick smoke.

Milligan's Hoplite froze as if in indecision, and in that moment, the unimaginable happened. The fallen Aquila made a dull, strained sound of the overloaded drives and suddenly began to rise, crushing the broken hydraulics and leaning on its technical manipulators - terrifying, charred and yet undefeated.

Milligan couldn't cope with this image. His Hoplite spun around and raced away, but Aquila's cabin turned abruptly and two heavy laser systems, capable of burning a hole in the armor of a spaceship, struck the servomachine.

Another explosion shook the depths of the forest.

Chapter Eleven

The outskirts of Λleksandriysk.

THE CAPITAL OF CASSIA was a mess.

Nicholas and Mary Polvin, having arrived in the city, were surprised and alarmed by the huge crowds milling around on the streets of Aleksandriysk so late at night.

"Nick, what's going on here?" Mary looked around anxiously while her husband stopped the car at an intersection, letting a crowd of pedestrians go past.

"I have no idea... The communicator isn't working. You know what, let's go and see Vadim, I don't think he'll be annoyed even if he's already asleep."

"I doubt that he's sleeping. Lozin's not one to miss night-time troubles," she couldn't help a sad smile. "You and Vadim are like two peas in a pod."

"Come, no need to exaggerate, my dear."

They kept talking, trying to use this relaxed banter to quash the growing, corrosive sense of worry.

Lozin's city apartment was located close to the ring road, and soon Polvin was parking his car in the underground carpark of a multistory building.

"We should warn him that we're coming," Mary glanced at her communicator screen, which showed only a 'searching for network' symbol.

"There's no time, let's go," Nicholas was noticeably nervous. The network was down, and this strange bustle of activity around them. "I'm afraid that something has happened."

"You're certainly cheering me up," his wife chided him gently.

The lift stopped on the tenth floor. It was dark in the hallway.

Touching the intercom button, Nicholas wasn't surprised to hear steps behind the door.

Vadim obviously wasn't asleep.

"Nick! Mary?!" Lozin clearly hadn't been expecting anyone. "How did you get summoned so quickly?" He asked. "And where's Olga? Isn't she with you?"

"Wait, Vadim." Nicholas gave him a puzzled look. "Nobody summoned us anywhere. I tried to call the President, but I couldn't get through to him. There's an important conversation that we must have at once. We left Olga at home…"

Seeing an unhealthy flush appear on Lozin's cheeks, Polvin fell silent.

"What happened, Vadim? Tell us, for heaven's sake!" Mary burst out.

"You really don't know?"

"We've just arrived!" Polvin reminded him sharply.

Lozin suddenly slumped and was silent for several moments before saying hollowly, "Cassia was attacked. Our satellites are blocked and the Shadow of Earth cruiser is orbiting the planet."

"The one that bombed Dabog?!" Mary cried out, pressing her hands to her chest.

Nicholas went pale. He barely kept his nerve when hearing the overwhelming news. "Have they made any demands?" Polvin asked after getting his emotions under control.

"We don't really know anything right now."

"Well, how did you find out about the

cruiser?" Nicholas asked.

"There were rumors. Did you see how many people there are on the streets? There haven't been any official statements and the comms are down, but they're saying that Admiral Nadyrov has demanded Cassia's surrender, in exchange for membership in the Terran Alliance and protection from invasions."

"This is complete madness!" Nicholas burst out bitterly. "Whom are they going to protect us from?! Themselves?"

"Sorry, I'm just telling you what I've heard. I don't know anything else."

Mary went to the window, looked out at the street for a while, and then couldn't hold it in any longer. She covered her face with her hands and began to cry silently. Her shoulders shuddered.

Polvin knew that only a global communication failure had saved him from being urgently summoned to the capital, but now that he was here, what should he do? Should he go to the headquarters? Rokotov's ship, which fell on their estate, would attract the attention of the invaders. Olga is alone.

The officer's duty is to be at headquarters. The duty of a father and husband is to protect his family.

"Vadim, what about your family?"

"I'm going to go there, I just don't know if I'll

be able to get through."

"Do you think they'll be landing their troops?"

"Nick, nobody knows anything. I don't know if they'll strike us with rockets or if they'll occupy us! But rockets would be better." He suddenly added.

"Have you lost your mind?" Nicholas threw back his head.

"Don't worry about me. Remember the recordings from the ASUM? Earth has one city like we have one continent. If they all come here, what are we going to do? There's nowhere to run. No way to resist. What did Rokotov ask for? For us to repair his ship so that he could continue fighting. And what did we do? Did we give him anything?"

Belated shame swept over Nicholas. They had wanted to do what was best. But one couldn't gain happiness at the expense of someone else's misery. They hadn't invented this phrase but it suited them perfectly.

Polvin knew that Lozin's city apartment had a secure cable connection because he was a member of the Colonial Council.

"Is the government line working?"

"Yes. You can use it. I tried but nobody answered." Vadim moved to the window and said something softly to Mary, while Nicholas dialed the number and listened to the rings for a long time before the phone was picked up.

"Polvin. Who am I talking to?"

"Nicholas, is that you?"

"Yes, it's me! Hans, what's happening, I was told that..."

"We're finished," Cassia's President uttered. "The cruiser of the Terran Alliance is in orbit above us. They're threatening us with aerial bombing. I have decided to surrender, which will be mercifully called 'peace'."

Nicholas was stunned into silence. Hans Schnittke continued speaking but Polvin slowly dropped the hand clutching the receiver. Mary and Vadim watched him tensely as they waited for news.

"We've surrendered," Polvin spoke. "Cassia will be occupied in the next few hours."

RUNNING THROUGH THE FOREST at night burned up his strength.

Not a single shot had hit Sergey but it would have better if a stray bullet had gotten him... He simply fled at first, driven mad by fear, not looking where he was going, pushing through bushes, then he had tripped in the dark and rolled down a slope into a ravine. He climbed back out, limping and panting, without any idea of where he was.

The forest now seemed alien and hostile. The moon hid behind clouds but the sky was illuminated by a strange glow and a muffled roar could be heard from afar.

Staggering from fatigue, Sergey went into a small clearing and suddenly realized that he knew the place. Ironically, he had come to the Lisetsky Estate.

'What am I going to do now?' he hesitated, mortified and barely alive from fatigue and shock. A dog howled in the yard as it sensed him, a light went on in the window and the door creaked, opening.

"Who's there?" Came Lisetsky's powerful voice.

Despite his advancing age, Lisetsky was brusque with uninvited guests. Not with people, of course, but rather with the karny, predators that had accidentally been introduced from the neighboring continent and who bred profusely in the surrounding forest.

Knowing this, Sergey shouted hoarsely, "A friend!" He limped into the light.

The gruff barking immediately ceased but the mongrel dog that Lisetsky kept tied up in the yard began to growl instead, as if refusing to recognize Sergey.

"Sergey, what happened?!" Lisetsky hurried

out to meet him. "Where's Olga?! I have Nicholas on the phone. He's losing his mind with worry!"

Breathing heavily, Sergey wheezed out, "I haven't seen her since yesterday evening. I was attacked by some people near the ASUM... They shot at me... I barely managed to get away."

"Come here!" Lisetsky led him into the house, locked the door and went into the living room, where stood an old portable computer with a cable connection. These devices were widely used in the past, prior to the era of new technologies.

Kirill Andreevich picked up the receiver, which had a cable running from it. "Nick, Sergey is here. Somebody attacked him! No, he doesn't know... What? Here, I'll pass the receiver to him," Lisetsky turned around and handed the communicator to Sergey. "Polvin wants to speak to you."

Sergey didn't want to but he had to answer, "Yes, Nicholas Andreevich?"

"Sergey, where's Olga?!" came the distant and worried voice.

"I don't know," Sergey swallowed and glanced at Lisetsky, but the older man had walked over to the window and was peering tensely into the gloom. "She must be at home," he made himself say in a low voice. "You saw me leave!"

"Yes, yes, I did. But Kirill said that he heard

thunder coming from that direction! Why did you suddenly go to him?"

Sergey's face fell. The hand clutching the receiver immediately became sweaty.

I can't tell him everything... I can't...

"I was attacked on my way home," Having gathered his wits, he decided to tell a half-truth. His voice trembled treacherously but the crackling line obscured it - the ancient method of communication left much to be desired. "There were combat vehicles. And strangers," He added, swallowing again. "They shot at me. I barely got away... I don't understand what's going on."

"Cassia has been attacked," Polvin told him the shocking news. "You must have come face-to-face with one of their squads of mechanized troops. But we've made peace now, do you hear me? Their admiral has assured us that nobody would come to harm!" Nicholas spoke very quickly and Sergey could barely make out the words. "Sergey, we're coming home but we'll need an hour to get there. Please, take Kirill's car and go to Olga! Find her and calm her down. If the strangers appear again, don't be afraid, they won't hurt you since their admiral has accepted our planet's surrender and has guaranteed peace."

Sergey straightened up when he heard those words. If a minute ago, he was trembling with horror and fatigue, now he instantly saw an opportunity to get out of a slippery situation. 'Nobody attacked Lisetsky,' he thought feverishly. 'If we've made peace with the invaders, I can safely go back.' No one will ever know what really happened near the ASUM. That squad is probably long gone from there. In Olga's eyes, he will forever remain the only man to have rushed off to save her despite the danger.

"Sergey, can you hear me?" Polvin's voice interrupted his thoughts.

"Yes, Nicholas Andreevich, don't worry. Of course, I'll go there. Yes, right now." He turned around, "Kirill Alexandrovich, he's asking for you."

Lisetsky took the receiver, "Yes, Nick, don't worry. Yes, he can borrow it. Alright, see you soon."

Putting down the receiver, Lisetsky took the car keys off the table and held them out to Sergey, "Take my car. You're a brave guy," He said approvingly, looking at Sergey's torn and muddied uniform. "I'm going to send my daughters to their aunt and follow you. Will you manage?"

Sergey nodded. He no longer glanced away.

There is a type of person that quickly forgets unpleasant moments in their life by replacing them with reimagined events. Eventually, they start to truly believe in the lies that they tell themselves.

"Wait," Lisetsky called out when Sergey was

already in the doorway. Voronin turned, his insides jumping. "Here, take this!" Lisetsky unwrapped an oiled cloth and Sergey saw an automatic pistol designed by Hans Gervet.

"What's that for, Kirill Andreevich?!"

"Just in case. The ceasefire, that's for the capital. But out here in the forest, we might get all sort of nastiness... Here, take it."

Sergey took the weapon and felt the weight in his palm.

"Take the safety off before you shoot!" Lisetsky shouted after him.

Sergey was already getting into the car and thus didn't see the old man, whom Sergey had sold out to the invaders, condemning him to torture and death, make the sign of the cross, blessing the boy.

The Polvin Estate

THE HOUSE LOOKED DARK, gloomy and lifeless from a distance.

The smell of smoke drifted from the forest.

The car bounced over unexpected bumps in the road and Sergey slowed down, the car lights illuminating the huge footprints of the cyber mechanisms, which had crushed the road surface.

They had come through here... Sergey furtively switched off the lights.

The darkness immediately pressed up all around him and even the smell of smoke seemed stronger. Sergey reached for the passenger seat. His sweaty hands found the cold handle of the gun but the heavy weapon didn't provide any reassurance.

The car, its engines barely audible, drove up to a fallen fence, and Voronin was bathed in cold sweat. Three combat servomechanisms stood in the yard. Their legs were folded but the cabins projected above the roof of the house.

A burnt and barely recognizable Stip sat on the front porch. In the dull light of a portable lamp, he fiddled with his arm stump, reconnecting the damaged operating rods.

A hollow sound suddenly came from one of the mechanisms, and a hatch opened in its side. Like a cluster of mechanical insects, servos huddled inside. Receiving a remote order, they unfolded their manipulators, swiftly climbed outside and headed to the damaged Phalanger.

A transport platform dropped down from above. Sergey's eyes widened when he saw Olga and an unfamiliar guy.

"So, the two pilots shot each other?" she asked quietly.

"They were both aiming at Aquila but it

eluded the shot," said the stranger. "I never thought that a servomachine was capable of such extreme maneuvering."

Humming quietly, the platform stopped a few centimeters from the ground.

"Will the technical servos manage to repair the Phalanger?"

"We'll find out soon. The main system doesn't seem to be damaged at first glance. We can replace the armor."

"Yes, but who's going to pilot it?"

"I can turn on the Maverick, if needed. It's a complex of combat autopilots."

Voronin sat in the dark like a thief. He had to get up, go and find out what had happened, but the cursed trembling had taken over his muscles again.

Stip suddenly interrupted the conversation. He lifted his head and clearly said, "Sergey, could you park your car a little further away? It will get in the way."

* * *

THERE WAS NO ELECTRICITY in the house. Olga lit a candle and the trembling light softly revealed her features.

Andrew stood by the window. Voronin sat at

a table, which Stip had brought from the kitchen.

"Why is he here, with you?"

"He saved my life, Sergey," she wanted to ask where he had been when she needed him, and why he had returned at such a convenient time but she suppressed the urge.

"Olga, he's an invader, a foreigner!" Sergey's fierce whisper was full of indignation.

"You're calling me an invader?" Groves turned around.

Voronin leaped up and tipped the chair over. The barrel of his gun glinted dully in the light of the candle.

"You shut up for now! Stand where you are!"

"Or what?" Andrew smirked.

Sergey's cheeks flushed red. He drove here and was still making plans when he suddenly found himself, before he even knew what was happening, on the brink of being discovered. This Terran had surely been there at the ASUM!

The sudden shot ripped through the darkness as a short and thunderous flash.

Olga didn't even have time to scream as it all happened so quickly. The bullet struck the window frame and ricocheted, and in the next moment, Groves struck the gun out of Sergey's hands, put the safety back on, and then said drily, without any anger, "I was an invader. But to be honest, I don't have a homeland. And I don't think that I did the right thing by taking the side of people like you."

"You broke the peace treaty!" Sergey shouted hoarsely. "I don't give a shit about who you are and where you're from! They'll find out about this fight! They'll kill us all! Do you have any idea how many people you've sentenced with your stupid behavior?"

Olga felt like someone had poured a bucket of icy water over her. "What? What did you say?!" She yelled, turning towards Sergey.

Voronin's eyes shifted nervously. He realized that he'd said the wrong thing.

"What peace?" Olga demanded, noticing Andrew's lips twist in a bitter and ironic smile.

"Your father rang the Lisetsky house half an hour ago!" Sergey burst out without looking at her. "He said that Cassia has surrendered. The Terran Alliance cruiser is in orbit around the planet, the same one that destroyed Dabog!"

Olga's lips shook from hurt and bitter disappointment. Her thoughts were a jumble but Sergey's words burned a hole inside her. "Did Andrew made a mistake in rescuing me?! What about my father, did he say that his daughter's death was part of the surrender? What about Stip? And who else, huh? Did they decide to give them Igor Rokotov, too?"

Sergey unwittingly took a step back. "Olga,

you misunderstand me."

She turned sharply to him. "I understand perfectly well!" Her voice broke. "I saw Dabog! I was in Aquila's cockpit and I connected to it directly. You all capitulated after seeing a piece of video! While they're..." Her throat closed over. "Their children are dying in bunkers! People like Rokotov have been holding back Nadyrov's fleet for the past six months so that we can live here... And you'll continue to live here..." She rasped. "You'll hand him over and continue on with your lives!"

"Olga!" Sergey wanted to contradict her but fell silent under her stare, bitter and full of contempt.

"You shouldn't fight," Andrew's quiet words made them both turn around.

"Since when are you giving orders here?" Sergey challenged him, breathing heavily. "Think you're so strong, do you? Grabbed a gun and think that's that?"

"I think that I'll step outside and you can sort things out between you," Andrew felt very awkward being in the middle of what looked like a domestic fight. He felt completely foreign in this dark, half-destroyed house, and on this whole planet, really. Yes, he had acted on impulse by saving the girl and didn't regret it. He wouldn't have been able to heartlessly kill on command anyway. But how could he explain to these people, who were the same age as him, that they knew nothing of life except the care of their parents?

"Don't go, please," Olga struggled to get her emotions under control. "At least tell us what we have to prepare for?"

"Earth is overpopulated." Groves shrugged. "There will be a flood of immigrants coming here. A planet that has been terraformed to Earth Standard is a real treasure."

"They'll take our lands away from us?"

"Without a doubt."

"You speak about this so calmly!" Voronin snapped.

"I wasn't rushing to get here, trust me," Groves replied. "You can't unify us under the word 'invader' no matter how hard you try. Before you hurl abuse at me, know that the war was begun by a small number of people but now involves millions. Everyone has their own truth."

"What possible truth can you speak of?" Sergey challenged.

"You won't understand. You simply have no idea what kind of density a population of 100 people per square meter is in the depths of a megacity. Or imprisonment due to birth."

"Is such a thing possible?" Olga stared at him.

"I was drafted into the army from the prison on Io, one of Jupiter's moons. I was brought there when I was five years old. My mother, it turned out, had no right to have children."

"But that's..."

"Monstrous?" Andrew smiled sadly. "Yes, it's monstrous. Destroying planets is also monstrous and wrong."

They were all quiet for a minute.

Voronin was full of fear and hate.

Andrew felt lost, sad and incredibly tired. He knew one thing, that black sheep like him don't survive long in a flock. He'll have to either become like everyone else or perish... Neutrality turned out to be a tricky place to be.

Olga's thoughts ran differently. She knew that the old way of life was gone forever. But if she sat here, in this dark and gutted room, doing nothing and bemoaning her fate, a new tomorrow would never come. It was hard. Hard to put her thoughts and feelings into words.

"I really saw Dabog, as if I had been there myself," she said quietly. "It's truly terrifying. So terrifying that I can't even explain it... but we can do the smallest thing. We can save some of them. We can try to find other populated planets before they are captured one by one, like Cassia."

War experienced through the prism of a female soul looks different and has a slightly softer shade, without the color of utter hopelessness.

"How?" Sergey asked.

Groves was also skeptical. He was looking at the situation soberly and could see no way out. The loss of contact with the assault carrier had probably set off an alarm on board the cruiser, which meant that soon they would drop another mechanized group here, one that had already completed their set goal.

"I'm afraid that we have no way of helping anyone. It will all be over in the next few hours. They will want to find out what happened to my squad. I won't go without a fight but it would be better if you leave."

"There is another way," Olga said suddenly.

Groves looked at dubiously. "How?"

"Don't say it! Don't you dare!" Sergey half stood up.

"Cool it," Olga told him and added, "After the colonial transport landed here, its main module, containing the hyperdrive, was preserved and hidden away. My father knows where it's kept."

"You've gone mad! Nicholas Andreevich would never agree..."

"Then we'll ask him," Olga replied, noticing car lights flashing among the trees.

"Are those your parents?"

"Yes. We need to meet them outside or they'll get a shock. Sergey, are you coming?"

Voronin's eyes flashed angrily in the dark. His heart was bursting with hate, fear and jealousy.

"No," he mumbled. "I'll stay here."

"As you wish. Andrew, let's go!"

The sound of brakes came from the street. They walked outside, and Sergey, using the moment of confusion, crossed the living room and kitchen, went through the back door and jogged to the nearest cluster of trees, glancing frequently over his shoulder.

He had made his choice.

* * *

WHO MAKES HISTORY? What separates the people whose names will make it into books from ourselves?

Nothing. None of us are truly prepared for sudden tests. But there comes a day and an hour when the world around us changes forever, revealing who is who.

Nicholas Polvin leaped out of the car and stared in shock at the menacingly towering cyber mechanisms, the mutilated house and yard, and his daughter's flycar, flattened into a pancake.

"Olga!" came the desperate scream of her mother, full of irreparable sorrow.

Polvin staggered. Life was over. This was not supposed to happen, this could not have happened!

His daughter.

The peace treaty accepted by the President of Cassia lay in ruins in the yard, sneering at Nicholas from the black mouths of the shattered windows.

A sharp, stabbing pain appeared in Nicholas' chest. He swayed as the reality around him rapidly paled and lost its colors.

"Dad! Daddy!"

He could no longer see his daughter and some unfamiliar guy running towards him from the house. His legs gave out from under him and he slumped onto the twisted and crushed cobblestones. Polvin's heart stopped.

Andrew immediately understood what was happening. Without saying a word, he pulled a small, cylindrical field health kit out of his pocket and jabbed a needle into Nicholas' chest, right through his clothes.

Several clicks sounded and the tiny analysis display glimmered with red lights, until one of the indicators trembled and changed to green.

"Stip, help me! We have to carry him into the house!"

* * *

HE REGAINED CONSCIOUSNESS slowly and reluctantly.

The voice of Kirill Lisetsky seemed to come from a long way away, "Our families will become hostages!"

"Wait, Kirill, stop piling it on," Lozin spoke. "Does this mean that other mechanized troops will soon appear in this area?"

"Yes," the third voice was unfamiliar. "As soon as they find out about Aquila, the leaders will stop at nothing. Nadyrov will do anything to capture Rokotov and his machine. It's better to blow up the ship by overheating the reactor. And you all need to leave."

"Abandon you, young man? You will defend Cassia while we hide?"

"I'm not defending Cassia," Groves explained tiredly. "I'm sorry but I'm sick of having to explain my motive for doing a simple thing. I was ordered to kill an innocent woman. I did not carry out this order. Is that clear?"

"Vadim Petrovich, stop it!" Olga fumed. "You're beginning to act just like Voronin!"

"By the way," came Lisetsky's voice. "where is our young hero? Why isn't he here, with us?"

"I don't know. He appeared about half an

hour ago, attacked Andrew and tried to shoot him, then, when you arrived, he ran away."

"How strange... It doesn't seem like Sergey at all. He's..."

"I think that he was afraid of meeting one of the neighbors," Groves said.

"Why?" Lozin asked, puzzled.

"When Lieutenant Seichi grabbed him by the ASUM, the guy really freaked out."

"What did you talk about?"

"Seichi wanted the remote that unlocked the bunker. He would have done anything to get it. Our command center ordered us to find out the purpose and technical contents of the bunkers at any cost."

"And what did Sergey say?"

"He uttered a name. Lisetsky or Linetsky or something. He also gave us the coordinates of a house, where he believed the remote was located."

"It seems, young man, that you didn't just save Olga," Kirill Andreevich uttered in shock. "The thing is, he was talking about me."

"I didn't know. I'm sorry."

Lisetsky only shook his head. His face was pale but his cheeks blazed.

Mary, who was also rattled by Voronin's betrayal, nevertheless found the strength to turn the conversation back to the topic. "We were speaking about Igor Rokotov," she reminded them all in a trembling voice. "Will he be convicted? Thrown into prison because he defended his home planet?"

"No," Groves said. "They won't convict him. They won't even kill him. They'll do something much worse. Both Rokotov and Aquila will be pulled apart to their nuts and bolts, literally. Believe me, they will extract all the information that they need from Igor, and then, Aquila's design will become a prototype for more advanced and lethal cyber mechanisms."

"We can't let that happen!" Lisetsky exclaimed. "We can't, don't you see? If Rokotov and Aquila end up in Nadyrov's hands..."

"But we can't interfere, either!" Lozin responded in the same tone of voice. "I'm ready to risk my life but we all have families, don't forget that. And where can we hide Igor Rokotov? The planet has been captured and soon we'll be inundated with people from Earth. Unless we escape to the neighboring continent, into the jungle?"

"There won't be any places left to hide on Cassia," Groves stated. "The hostile biosphere on the other continents will simply be destroyed. That's what combat terraforming is for. As soon as Nadyrov determines the hypersphere coordinates and establishes contact with Earth, this planet will be turned into a base for future invasions. There'll be no room to swing a cat. Everything outdated and unnecessary will be discarded from the ASUMs, and they will be turned into hangars for repairing spaceships, servomachines and other technology."

The unfolding future he described seemed horrific but quite realistic.

Polvin's eyelids trembled. He opened his eyes and sat up with difficulty. Despite the emergency care that came in time, his heart beat unevenly and his chest still ached with the pain.

"Nick!"

"I'm alright. I heard everything," He looked at his wife and daughter, and then at Groves. Shame burned inside him. How was it that this guy saved Olga, while Sergey betrayed the very people that raised him?

"Let us face the truth," He said hollowly once he had gathered his strength. "We gave up Cassia even before the President's surrender, when we refused to help Rokotov. I am ashamed."

"Dad, stop it! We have a chance to help Igor!"
"How?"

"Cassiopeia's main module,[4]" Olga reminded

---

[4] All the colonial transport from the time of the Great Exodus had a two-component construction. They consisted of a passenger and cargo sphere, which contained the cryogenic halls with people, technical hangars and equipment storage areas. Immediately after landing, the separating part was used to build the first shelter. The second component, the so-called 'main module' was a fully functioning

him. "Do you know where it's stored? How many people are needed to take it into space?"

"Three. Three people who know the control codes," Polvin replied, surprised and vexed that he didn't think of that himself. Both Lisetsky and Lozin would support the idea - he could see it in their faces. "But where will we go?"

"We can't program the hyperdrive for a jump," Lozin said, confirming Nicholas' thoughts. "We have no way to make the calculations. And how do we get to the Cassiopeia?"

"In actual fact, we have one hypersphere route. It's recorded on the navigation crystal in Rokotov's ship," Groves replied. "Where is Igor now? Is there a possibility that he hasn't yet been captured?"

"He's in a hospital in Aleksandriysk." Polvin replied. "Only four people know about it."

"We need to get him out of there. Also, if you decide to act, you must act now. Your houses will be pillaged and your estates taken away from you. You have to take your families with you. If we don't finish in time or if we fail, everyone here will die. You must decide right now."

---

spaceship. It contained a propulsion engine, a hyperdrive, cybernetic control systems and compartments for the crew. After unloading the colonial transport, the main module was supposed to go back into space and return to Earth but this didn't happen in real life. The transport crews could not calculate the return jump after a blind punch and chose to join the colonies.

War had come to Cassia. Whether they wanted it or not, the fate of everyone in this room was now wrapped up in the life of Rokotov and his Aquila.

"Do you have any ideas how we can gain some time and how to lead the chase away from us?" Polvin asked.

"Yes," Groves replied. "I will need access to the ASUM, a full list of the mechanisms stored there, their activation codes and Stip as my assistant."

Nicholas shared a look with Lisetsky and Lozin. Both nodded in affirmation, understanding that the time of doubts and arguments had passed.

"Fine. You will get access to the ASUM. Vadim, Kirill, contact your families. We'll meet on agrofarm nineteen. It's the most distant and safe place to gather. Who will go and get Rokotov?"

"I will," Lozin volunteered.

"Give me your code to Cassiopeia. And go now, as soon as we have discussed the route, because we'll have no way to communicate with each other."

* * *

Cassia
Five a.m. local time

ASUM'S MOSSY GATES shuddered and began to open.

Groves waited outside, surrounded by technical servos. Stip was working inside the shelter.

One after another, soil transformers began to come out of the underground hangars. Once they were past the gates, each one of them stopped, while the technical servos attached phantom-generators to them under Andrew's watchful eye.

Soon nine robotized complexes, equipped with false signatures, disappeared into the forest, each one going in a different direction.

MEANWHILE, LOZIN was approaching the outskirts of Aleksandriysk.

The city couldn't sleep. Flashes of light kept appearing in the sky as the ships of the Terran Alliance landed before the Presidential Palace.

DAWN WAS BREAKING when Sergey Voronin finally arrived at his house. His parents worked on the other continent so there was nobody to meet him at home.

An ancient communication device was kept in the house, an heirloom from Sergey's great-grandfather, who was a member of the Colonial Council. Today, Sergey saw with his own eyes that the ancient wire networks still worked and that the jamming devices weren't affecting them.

Sergey gulped down some water, connected the old mobile computer, picked up the communicator headpiece and launched the search program. He heard nothing but long beeps for a while, then received an answer:

"Go ahead."

"Who am I speaking with?"

"Captain Bagirov, Terran Alliance," the voice said with irony. "Whom did you want? Your own President?"

"I need to talk to Admiral Tiberius Nadyrov."

"Are you nuts? Why would I disturb the admiral and connect you to our network?"

"You've lost contact with one of your servo squadrons, right? And please tell the admiral that I have information concerning Igor Rokotov and Aquila."

"Stay on the line," the captain replied dryly.

Part Four

The Countdown

Chapter Twelve

AQUILA STRODE ACROSS the plain.

The monitoring screens showed misty woods, green fields, the occasional glimmer of the river Verenezhka winding between the hills...

Olga sat in the pilot's seat. The skin around her temporal implant continued to tingle. The scanners imposed signature maps over her normal view of the world.

An involuntary contraction occasionally made her muscles tremble — she had a long way to go to achieve a full merge with Aquila.

For the moment, Olga listened with mute astonishment to the fragmented memories of the ancient cyber mechanism, beginning to realize that its artificial personality actually consisted of several fragmented consciousnesses.

This had a non-contradictory explanation. The original neural matrix of the servomachine had been seriously damaged in the distant past. Igor Rokotov had tried to restore it, but, having no experience in such complex tasks, had made a serious mistake, believing that simply replacing the chips would produce the desired result.

Years earlier, before the war, he had found the diaries of Hans Gervet in an old bunker, and a few sealed packages together with them. Inside were sets of neural chips. Igor couldn't test them and had simply replaced the damaged areas of Aquila's neural networks with the found components.

For a long time, this didn't affect the condition of the ancient cyber mechanism. Rokotov controlled the family robot in semi-automatic mode, hoping that its artificial intelligence would eventually manifest itself. He knew about the direct contact system but had never used since Hans Gervet's notes made it clear that it was dangerous technology and should only be used as a last resort because it could irreversibly affect the pilot's mind.

Olga now understood the warnings of the creator of Dabog's servomachines. To perceive the world in such an unusual way and to associate themselves with a gigantic cyber mechanism wasn't something that everyone could stand. In general, the direct neurosensory contact system was intended primarily for training neural networks and was used only by test pilots.

The result of a daring experiment by two corporations, Genesis and Rimp Cybertronics, allowed a person to fully merge with a machine, but where would this fusion lead?

The answer lay somewhere outside the scope of modern knowledge. Only prolonged use could provide an answer but for now, thanks to the current connection, Olga suddenly had access to vague and precious fragments of the past.

The chips used by Rokotov had previously belonged to one of the androids from the Hugo series. He had participated in the landing of the first colonists, immediately after the Fugitive crashed on Dabog, and was then destroyed. It remained unclear why Hans Gervet had kept the separate components of an ancient artificial personality together with his records.

Vague images appeared in Olga's mind. She

saw a square in Earth's megacity, people hurrying about their business, and the lonely figure of a violinist with the crowd flowing around him.

A second later and the image disappeared, replaced by another memory. She saw a dusty red moon, orbiting a planet disfigured by nuclear fire, and then immediately saw mental images that belonged to Stip.

A copy of the faithful android's personality had cemented Aquila's fragmented memories and had become the basis for the new AI's further development.

'Amazing,' she thought as she disconnected from direct contact with the machine. Combat autopilot indicators immediately lit up on the control panels.

The image of the violinist persisted and alarmed her. Olga knew that at the time of the Great Exodus, artificial intelligence was banned on Earth. Who was he? How did he evolve and eventually get to Dabog? What circumstances led to his destruction, and why had Hans Gervet carefully preserved the surviving neural chips?

What strange creatures we are. Over the past day, Olga had lost everything, her life was under threat and her future remained uncertain, but, having encountered the memory of several thinking machines that had become one personality, she found herself thinking, 'How many mysteries are hidden in the history of the colonization of planets? How vast space is...'

The ambitions of the individuals pushing civilization to the edge of an abyss seemed hurtful, petty and unfair in comparison.

A high-pitched signal brought her back to reality.

The tactical situation data had been updated. Olga looked at the terrain map. There wasn't a single active signature in a fifty-kilometer radius.

'My God,' she thought. Just yesterday, she had been preparing for 'adult life' and now this life had come to pass, suddenly and devastatingly. 'I'm sitting in the control chair of a combat servomechanism.'

An inner hatch opened and Stip climbed out of the narrow technical chute. His disfigured face, devoid of the foam flesh, seemed strange and frightening.

"The right activator was playing up. I've fixed it, now everything should be fine," he said curtly, arranging himself beside the chair.

Olga nodded and touched the tiny sensor on the temporal implant again, resuming the direct neurosensory contact with Aquila.

The on-the-go repair had affected her perception! Aquila no longer limped and his gait became confident, powerful and regular.

Groves' Hoplite walked ahead, conducting active reconnaissance. The third machine, the hastily repaired Phalanger, currently being controlled by the Maverick combat autopilot, completed the group.

Three hundred kilometers remained to the appointed meeting place.

Suddenly, one of the dots indicating a robotic soil transformer blinked and went out.

"They've destroyed the decoy," came Andrew's voice. "Check how the phantom generator is working. It won't take long for Nadyrov to figure out what's going on. They're going to cover the whole continent with an orbital scanning grid."

"Everything's fine," Olga replied.

She closed her eyes, experiencing a different perception of the world, trusting the scanners and feeling the confident stride of Aquila, which had become her machine. The boundary of convention was slowly being erased and she could no longer clearly say where her consciousness ended and the artificial neural network began.

IGOR ROKOTOV WOKE UP at the crack of dawn, disturbed by the muted sound of distant thunder.

He sat up abruptly. The biomonitoring sensors squeaked anxiously but, for a change, nobody looked into the room to check on the patient's condition.

The thunder came again. The windows rattled. The hum and vibration permeated the building.

Igor was well aware of what could produce such an effect. Space shuttles were landing somewhere nearby! Judging by the characteristic sound, they were landing assault modules.

He tore the sensors off his body, stood up and walked to the window.

The glow on the horizon couldn't be confused with anything else.

An assault force had landed on Cassia, which meant that at least one ship from Nadyrov's fleet had been spat out into this star system after him.

Rokotov's fingers turned white. He had to grab the plastic windowsill to stop himself from falling. Waves of trembling, dizziness and nausea rolled over him. While he considered his suspicions, the sky over the city lit up and went out in a blinding flash. There could be no doubt that the planet was under attack. War had reached Cassia.

Thoughts of Aquila immediately spurned him to action. 'I know the coordinates of the ship's crash. I need to get there. First, I'll need stimulants and some clothes. I'm clearly not going to get any weapons here, but I'll make do somehow.' His thoughts raced and he was already inspecting the empty parking lot. No, nothing. 'There must be doctors on duty and an Emergency Department in the hospital. I'll find what I need there. '

In that moment, a car with its lights off drove into the carpark. The brakes screeched, and the driver's door opened with a hiss.

An unfamiliar Cassian peered intently at the hospital windows, noticed Rokotov (the light in the room illuminated him clearly) and must have recognized him, because he made an eloquent gesture of 'I'm coming' and headed to the entrance to the Emergency Department.

Rokotov didn't know him. Igor took several deep breaths, trying to slow down his rapid heartbeat, then pulled a bundle of cables from one of the devices, yanked it a couple of times to test its strength, and took up a position behind the door, waiting for the unexpected visitor with a makeshift noose in his hands.

Dabog had taught him not to trust anyone except himself and his machine...

He heard footsteps in the silence of the hospital corridor. Somebody pushed the door open but didn't step inside. Rokotov's palms became sweaty.

"Igor, don't do anything stupid," came the voice. "The planet is under attack. The Shadow of Earth cruiser is in orbit. I'm a friend, trust me. I've come to help you escape."

"They're just words," Rokotov replied hoarsely.

"I know that we've done nothing to earn your trust, but now is not the time to hold grudges. Nadyrov has landed his mechanized troops. Your Aquila has already fought with the Terran servomachines. If I may enter, I'll show you the evidence."

"You're lying! Aquila couldn't have fought!"

Igor was still very weak. He could barely stay on his feet and would hardly have been able to resist.

"I'm coming in," Lozin warned.

Glancing at Igor Rokotov's pale and haggard face, Vadim activated the cyberstack and launched a recording of the events that he had received from Stip.

Igor sat on the edge of the hospital bed, watched the recording in shocked silence and then quietly asked, "What are you going to do?"

"We have a chance to leave the planet. To evacuate you and Aquila. But we must act quickly, while the planet is still in a mess."

"We need to collect the navigation crystal from my ship. And switch on some onboard systems," Igor looked up at Lozin and added, "Let's go. Now!"

* * *

ADMIRAL NADYROV PACED along the battle bridge on the Shadow of Earth cruiser.

Cassia had surrendered and the assault units had seized the Presidential Palace, but was there any point?

The so-called ASUMs turned out to be repositories of old colonial technology yet even that didn't reassure him. Contact with one of the assault carriers had been lost, there was no news from the servomachine platoon, and then nine signatures, all moving in a different direction, had suddenly appeared on the map of the continent. The signatures could not be identified but seemed quite powerful.

"Sir, one of the pilots from the missing platoon has made contact."

"Put him through!"

Sergeant Singer shifted from foot to foot, unsure of where to start. He looked rumpled and frightened. A broken arm was fixed in a sling. A spreading purple bruise covered half his face.

Nadyrov looked askance at the hologram of the pilot. "Report," he ordered, losing his patience. "What happened to the platoon?"

"We lost all the mechanisms..."

The admiral choked mid-sentence.

"Sergeant, have you gone mad?!" he snarled.

"It was Aquila," Singer forced himself to say. "I have a recording of the events."

"Send it to my terminal!"

'Incompetent cowards,' Nadyrov thought angrily as he watched the recording. The fragment of battle, recorded before the emergency ejection, left no doubt that Rokotov's ship had landed on this planet. It remained unclear what were the signatures moving under the cover of the forest and what was the fate of the remaining pilots.

Nadyrov slowly turned around and gave the sergeant a withering look. "What happened to the others?"

"I don't know. I lost consciousness after ejecting, and when I came to and returned to the place, I found only my machine and Lieutenant Seichi's damaged Phalanger."

"Hold him until we find out what happened," the admiral was no longer interested in the surviving pilot. "Contact the planet immediately!"

The holograms changed a second later.

"Where is the President of Cassia right now?"

"Under house arrest," said the commander of the united assault group.

"Listen carefully, Major. Igor Rokotov's ship crash-landed somewhere on this planet. Make the President tell you what he knows. Go!"

Having given the necessary orders, Nadyrov continued to pace the bridge, unable to calm down. The orbital satellite group was just turning around. In about an hour, they would be able to scan every corner of the inhabited continent in detail. Rokotov wouldn't be able to hide or leave the planet, yet the admiral was still nervous. 'How was it that a full servoplatoon couldn't defeat the Aquila?' he agonized. 'Are the Alliance engineers so incompetent?'

Such thoughts didn't make him feel any calmer. At some point, he realized that he was afraid of a repeat of Dabog. Nine unidentified signatures, which had appeared near the site of the battle with Aquila, didn't just make him anxious but began to instill serious fears. Unable to stand it, he touched the sensor again and gave a short order, "To all Phantoms, I authorize you to start. Your goal is to find and destroy the marked targets."

Light vibrations swept across the cruiser decks as the electromagnetic catapults launched into action, shooting out multiple modified fighters: if the earlier Phantoms could operate only in space, their design had been amended to enable their entry into planetary atmospheres.

"Admiral, Planetary-12 is in contact."

"What's going on? Make them speak to their superiors!"

"A resident of Cassia is insisting on speaking with you. He claims that he can provide information about Igor Rokotov and his machine."

"Can we trust the source? I don't have the time or inclination to listen to various nonsense. Who is this guy?"

"Someone called Sergey Voronin. He claims that he saw Aquila with his own eyes. He also said that one of our pilots defected to the enemy!"

"Put him through. I'll talk to him."

Nine a.m. local time

THE NORTHERN PART OF Cassia's inhabited continent became quite hilly. During the early colonization period, this area was heavily mined and the colonists had even begun to build a city, but the eruption of several volcanos two hundred years ago undermined their efforts, destroying buildings and costing many lives.

Ever since then, the more meager but safer southern fields had become the resource base, while everything here gradually fell into disrepair. Without a constant human presence, the buildings became dilapidated, many mines collapsed, and the unfinished city gradually fell into ruin.

The past events left behind some infrastructure, including access roads to the quarries and mines, several ASUMs, and a lot of abandoned technology that was damaged during the natural disaster and was only good for scrap.

Nature gradually took over, with the streets of the unfinished city becoming overgrown with grass, shrubs and trees.

This morning, three jeeps moving in a tight group, almost bumper to bumper, covered nearly three hundred kilometers of old roads at high speed, and turned towards the foothills.

At about ten o'clock in the morning, the cars stopped at an intersection beside a rusty old direction post:

Alpine City — 15 kilometers

First Technology Park — 17 kilometers

Mines — 10 kilometers

The weather was getting worse. A warm, moist wind was blowing from the ocean, storm clouds gathered over the mountains, and lazy plumes of fogs flowed down the slopes.

Polvin and Lisetsky had been there before. Now they were standing beside the post, studying their surroundings using a portable scanner.

All around them, the sensors picked up mounds of metal among the overgrown ruins, which was the technology abandoned during the eruptions. Once upon a time, it had been covered by a thin layer of hot ashes, but the rains and the spring melt had once again revealed the vehicles, washing away the volcanic products and taking them to Cassia's plains.

"We'll cross Alpine City through the main streets. There are heaps of abandoned cars. It's additional protection from being detected from orbit," Polvin suggested.

"The city is probably being watched most closely," Lisetsky expressed his doubts, "Maybe we should detour through the technology park? We'll come out right at the northern edge."

Nicholas thought for a minute and then nodded. "Okay. Let's do that. I'll check my phantom generator and we'll be on our way."

'The masking device taken from the damaged Phalanger protects the three cars from being detected from orbit but can't hide them at close visual contact, so it wouldn't hurt to be extra careful,' he thought as he got back behind the wheel.

Would the ruins attract Nadyrov's attention?

'They shouldn't really,' he reasoned. 'Nobody has lived here for ages. Of course, the invaders will need resources, but that's something for the future.'

"Ready?" he asked through the local network communicator.

"Yes," came Lisetsky's reply.

"Kate?"

"Wait a minute, Andrew's getting fussy."

"Lera, can you move to the second car and help Kate?" Kirill asked one of his daughters.

After a few minutes, the convoy began moving again, turning onto an old road towards the technology park, where old hangars with collapsed roofs held mining and construction machinery, rusted and broken.

FIFTY KILOMETERS to the north-west, three landing ships flew silently through the thick clouds. The assault carriers with servomachines on board had discovered the typical signs of a working phantom generator. Unlike the other signals, this spot on the scanners was moving, and certainly wasn't one of the ancient robot systems.

There was a short report:

"Target found!"

"Final destination?"

"Not yet clear."

"Begin covert landing. There is information that Cassiopeia's main module is hidden under one of the city squares."

"Do we stop the cars?"

"No. Let them reach the spot. Aquila's capture is the priority. Everything else is secondary since they won't have time to prepare the ship for launch anyway."

* * *

THE ROAD WOUND its way up the mountain until it led them to an extensive plateau covered in hangars. Construction and mining equipment had been repaired and serviced here in the past.

Polvin slowed down at a turn to a narrower road leading into the depths of a gorge, so common for this area.

"We're made it. We have to walk from here."

They didn't take any things with them, only the most necessary items that fit into two backpacks.

"Maybe we should take the cars?" Kirill asked.

"No. Andrew clearly warned us that they'll be looking for us."

"We're being overly cautious. Afraid of our own shadow," Lisetsky grumbled and looked at his daughters. "I'm ready."

"Just a minute," Polvin was checking the autopilot settings.

Maria took the backpack and Kate picked up her grandson. Lisetsky's daughters looked around them with interest.

"Kate, how are you doing?"

Mrs. Lozin only sighed heavily and didn't reply. Her son remained on the other continent. There was no way to contact him. They had to make the decision themselves. It felt like they took the grandson but abandoned their own children...

"Just hang on. We'll see them again."

"Do you think that I don't get it? You shouldn't try to make me feel better." Kate shook her head. "We're not coming back and we'll never see them again," she turned away, hiding her tears.

"But Vadim left an encrypted message at your house?"

Mrs. Lozin nodded.

"He did. If the house doesn't burn down and Alex returns from the other continent, maybe he'll find it."

"READY," Polvin touched a sensor on his cyberstack and the three cars took off again under the control of the autopilot, turning onto the main road of the technology park, which curved towards the northern edge of Alpine City after a few kilometers. The convoy was still being masked by the phantom generator. "Come on," he picked up a backpack and headed for the gorge.

A creek ran along the bottom. The ancient storm sewer had fallen into disrepair long ago, and the water was wearing away the cracked reinforced concrete.

They didn't have far to walk and soon the cliffs began to close over their heads, forming a kind of arch. The road was then blocked by a wall. It seemed like the gorge ended in a dead end.

Approaching one of the stone ledges, Nicholas wiped the dust off the plastic casing, made to look like the surrounding cliffs. He carefully removed it and set it aside.

"Kirill, it's time."

Lisetsky approached. "Kate, please get Andrew."

Only a few people from the current generation knew what was in the crater behind the technology park. Getting into the hidden area was possible only with the full access code, consisting of three fragments, and confirmed with biometric data, which were inputted into the onboard cybersystem of Cassiopeia's main module once every ten years, during elections to the Colonial Council.

Nicholas had considered it all in advance. 'We don't have a third member of the Council with us,' he thought. 'but that's alright, we'll manage.'

"Let's enter our codes." He was the first to enter a sequence of letters and numbers on a plain-looking panel similar to an archaic keyboard, and allowed the scanning device to take a drop of his blood.

A message appeared on the tiny display:
Code accepted.

Kirill Lisetsky repeated the same procedure, then Kate entered the final fragment of the sequence, which she had received from Vadim, and asked her grandson softly, "Andrew, darling, press your finger here."

"Ouch, something stung me!" the child pulled his hand away.

"It's nothing. You'll be alright."

There was a tense pause and new lines appeared on the screen.

Genetic line confirmed. Third code fragment accepted under the Heritage Protocol.

Something vibrated loudly and a massive armored plate, outwardly indistinguishable from the surrounding rocks, slowly moved aside, revealing Cassiopeia's preserved main module.

Beyond a short tunnel, designed to fit heavy equipment, they could see a huge crater, burned into the cliffs by the planetary engines. From above, it was covered by a network of curved metal beams, and the fine-meshed stainless steel net on top was covered with rocks, branches and various other natural debris brought here by the winds.

Mrs. Lozin couldn't help but slow down. Her heart began to pound. She pressed her grandson to her breast.

The spaceship, dark with age, rose like a

silent ceramic monolith. It had the shape of a biconcave lens, fifty meters in diameter.

On the outside, Cassiopeia's main module gave no indication of functioning, and how could it be any other way, centuries after landing? Why did they think that it was working and ready to fly?

"What were we expecting?" Kate asked quietly. "Four centuries have passed... It won't even lift off the ground." She began to panic.

"Kate, calm down. Would they have made Vadim and Nicholas train on how to use it, would they have forced them to memorize the code tables by heart?"

Mrs. Lozin didn't say anything. No matter how much she tried to reassure herself, the fear gripped her heart and wouldn't let go. Her eyes fell on a section of the lift. One cargo and two passenger segments of the antigravity platform were lying on the ground, covered in dust. The hatches were fifteen meters off the ground.

Nicholas switched something over on his cyberstack. The indicator light went on: his personal nanocomputer, containing a special software module, began to exchange data with Cassiopeia's subsystems. "Come on," he said and resolutely headed for the ship.

＊＊＊

THREE CARS, GUIDED by the autopilots, reached a road junction on the northern edge of Alpine City, turned towards the center, drove along one of the main streets and ducked into a tunnel leading to the basement level.[5]

Admiral Nadyrov, closely following the movement of the markers on the map of the continent, no longer had any doubts about his success. The scanning complexes of the Shadow of Earth had found an extensive thermal anomaly in the depths of the city. The young Cassian hadn't lied, there was clearly something huge hidden under the square, which emitted a powerful heat signature.

"Strategists to evaluate the level of likely damage if Cassiopeia does try to launch," he ordered curtly. "Commanders of servoplatoons to correct their positions according to the latest data."

"Admiral, do you really think they could be hiding a ship under the city?" one of the analysts asked.

"I think that Cassiopeia's main module was

---

[5] The basement level was the city's technical level, built by the servos according to a standard design of the Megapool Corporation. Many large settlements on other planets began with such a construction.

used by the inhabitants as a power plant and control center of the mining industry," Nadyrov said. "The attempt to send it into space is an act of desperation. I doubt they'll succeed."

"We can begin the capture operation!"

"No. It's too early. Wait for my order," the admiral snapped. "Let all the birds gather in one cage," he switched channels and asked, "Sherman, what have you got?"

"We've inspected the Polvin Estate. The house has been abandoned. There are two damaged Phalangers and one burned Hoplite nearby. We didn't find Aquila nor any of the other platoon machines. We're heading to the Rokotov ship's landing site. The Phantoms are scanning the continent."

"Keep me posted," Nadyrov smiled in response to his own thoughts. So far, so good. The enemy's steps were easy to predict. Soon the scanners would locate the Aquila and then the final part of the operation would begin. He ran his eyes over the updated tactical data and said, "Have you captured Rokotov?"

"No, Admiral. He wasn't at the hospital where Schnittke said he would be."

'So, you managed to escape? No matter. I know where you'll turn up soon enough.'

Nadyrov was severely lacking assault units for a large-scale search or military operations.

Right now, the planet was ruled by fear. He had made it clear what the consequences would be if he was disobeyed, but it was all a bluff. He would not be forgiven for an orbital strike on a planet terraformed to Earth Standard. Fortunately, the Cassians didn't know this.

Nadyrov turned back to the screens and looked at the panorama image of Alpine City. The Phalangers were in position, hiding in the ruins and ready to strike with missiles. He had to leave the Hoplites out of the confrontation with Aquila and the servoplatoons had been reorganized. "Scan the continent. This is now the priority. Report as soon as you find Aquila."

"The signature under the city square is gaining power! The sensors are detecting increased radioactivity. They are obviously trying to prepare the ship for launch. What happens if they manage to get it into space?"

Nadyrov thought for a moment. "Assault carriers to return to the cruiser. Prepare them for the capture of a target in space," the admiral decided.

AFTER PASSING through a long tunnel, the three autopilot-guided jeeps stopped in front of tightly shut gates.

The reactor that used to power the city was gathering power behind them. There was a radiation leak in the cooling system, but this shouldn't be fatal as the automatic safety system had kicked in. Soon, the signature would begin to fade, convincing the invaders that nothing had come of the handful of Cassians who had dared to help Igor Rokotov.

NADYROV WAS RIGHT. Alpine City had appeared near Cassiopeia's landing site and the main module of the colonial transport really was used as a control center for construction, mining and the heavy industry during the early period of colonization.

When the natural disaster destroyed the thriving city, many of its inhabitants survived by hiding on board the ship but then left the dangerous region and founded Aleksandriysk.

Nobody forgot about the main module of the colonial transport, however, the circle of people who knew about its location gradually shrunk to a few dozen people.

Nicholas Polvin had been there before. He had interned and passed an exam to gain access to Cassiopeia's controls.

"Oh, look. Who's that?" Little Andrew exclaimed in frightened surprise.

The ship was surrounded by arched low hangars. Access roads led to the angled shafts running through the rock. A group of technical servomechanisms had just appeared, hurrying about their business and ignoring the newcomers. Only one of them paused, scurried to the anti-grav platform, deftly stuck a cable into the control unit, tested something, and then turned on the system.

"There's no need to be scared. They're special robots that monitor everything here," Lera reassured the child.

Three lift segments swayed and rose into the air. A quiet hum of well-tuned drives came from above as one of the airlocks opened.

IT WAS DIM INSIDE Cassiopeia's cockpit. Nicholas confidently walked to the central control station, sat down on the chair, and entered the crew commander code.

A wave of indicator lights swept over the consoles, the holographic screens switched on and the first system messages appeared:

System core activated.
Storage mode cancelled.
Loading main software modules.
Reactor power at 3%.
Fifteen minutes of board time until full recovery of onboard subsystem functions.

Warning, to begin planetary fuel synthesis, reactor power must be increased to ten percent.

To use the hyperdrive functions, reactor power must be at least twenty-five percent.

Kirill Lisetsky ran his eyes over the lines of text and asked, "Won't we give ourselves away by starting fuel synthesis for the planetary engines and increasing the propulsion unit's power?"

"We'll try to remain invisible," Polvin replied. "The ceramic casing hides the work of the onboard systems quite well. They'll find us, it's unavoidable, but not before three or four hours, when the hyperdrive accumulators are charged. In the meantime, we'll use the city energy supply controls to distract Nadyrov. There are three other node distribution stations away from the Alpine City ruins."

"What are you going to do?"

"I'll direct energy from the city reactor to them and put them into overload mode by disabling the safety."

"What's the point?" Kirill was confused.

"There'll be multiple accidents in the mines and industrial areas around the city. There's plenty of equipment which is still connected to the power supply. I'll also send an activation command to all the surviving networks and mechanisms. While the Terrans try to figure out what's happening among the chaos, we'll complete our preparations for launch."

Lisetsky nodded. It all seemed quite convincing while they talked about it. But how would it turn out in real life?

* * *

"MULTIPLE SIGNATURES!" the report made on the combat bridge of the Shadow of Earth made Admiral Nadyrov squint at the holographic model of the terrain.

It was as if the city, destroyed long ago by a natural disaster, had suddenly come back to life.

Sources of energy activity unexpectedly appeared on the surface among the ruins, in the depths of the mines, and in the old technology parks situated outside the city.

"The reactor in the Basement continues to increase its power! The associated distribution substations are overloaded, it seems that their safety systems aren't working! There is reactivation of long-abandoned systems and mechanisms!"

Nadyrov continued to stare at the screens, trying to understand the hidden meaning in the events. A handful of Cassians, intending to get an old ship up into space, had lost control over its systems? But what did the ancient mechanisms have to do with it? Why was energy pouring into the abandoned city network, awakening the damaged technosphere, and what did it mean?

The admiral had rethought a lot of things over the past few hours. He still intended to capture the servomachine from Dabog and its pilot, but the scales suddenly began to tip in the other direction. He thought, 'What if a handful of arrogant idiots had really lost control over the ship's propulsion engine?'

Cassia's inhabited continent was becoming more and more valuable in Nadyrov's eyes, and watching the chain of small technological catastrophes, he involuntarily tried to calculate the consequences. 'We must avoid a repeat of Dabog at all costs! If a disaster occurs here, they won't forgive me a single mistake, I'll be punished in full, they'll remember every little thing!'

"Assault groups to comb through the basement level! Find Cassiopeia's main module. Stop the overloaded systems!" He switched to another channel and snarled, no longer holding back, "Sherman, for frayg's sake, what's happening over there?"

"We found Rokotov's ship. The navigation crystal is gone! There was an attempt to overheat the reactor but we managed to stop it."

The major's report only added fuel to the

fire. These psychopaths would go to any length to avoid giving away even an inch of their territory. 'Frayg, what if they overloaded the propulsion unit on purpose?!' Nadyrov couldn't rule out such a desperate gesture.

"We have another problem." reported the senior analyst.

"What?" Nadyrov turned around.

"The power supply has launched several mining complexes. Their reactors are also gaining power but they are unstable!"

"Destroy them! Let the Phantoms deal with them! Strike their subsystems to avoid any nuclear explosions! All data from the assault groups to my terminal in real time!"

The admiral was surrounded by high density holograms. It was as if he was standing on the streets of the abandoned city, in front of the massive gates leading to the technical level. There was a flash and the sound of thunder, the massive gates burst outwards and collapsed, throwing up clouds of dust.

The planetary combat vehicle rushed into the bowels of the city, moving along the technical highway. Passing a huge parking lot littered with disused cars, the PCV suddenly found itself in front of the next obstacle — another gate blocked the way and three jeeps stood beside it.

A landing ramp extended and soldiers in

combat suits poured out. The technicians swarmed towards the obstacle as it was considered too dangerous to blow up. The rest spread out, sweeping through and examining the vehicles.

"Empty inside!"

The underground parking lot was filled with the sound of gunfire. Several reactivated androids were destroyed together with the other equipment.

Meanwhile, the enormous portal began to open, leading into the depths of the city's technical level. The background radiation indicators shot up. The PCV sped off and passed the contaminated section as it continued to transmit data.

Nadyrov saw a huge hall shrouded in twilight. Massive, curved energy blocks rose from the floor, overloaded lines could be clearly seen, the consoles were already smoking in some places, and steam rose from the pipes.

The admiral glanced over the dimly lit scene. Cassiopeia's main module wasn't there!

"Extinguish the city's reactors! Take the basement level under full control! Search every corner! Find Aquila and Rokotov!"

Nadyrov realized that his attention was being diverted. Perhaps the President of Cassia had lied and Cassiopeia's main module was in a different part of the continent or on another continent altogether?

Why were there always madmen among the colonists, ready to do whatever it takes? What would they achieve by triggering a series of technological catastrophes?

'They're trying to distract us,' he thought again irritably.

"Expand the scanning zones! Analyze every energy matrix! And get me Captain Bagirov at once!"

Chapter Thirteen

Cassia
The foothills

LOZIN'S SUV RACED confidently along the old road. It was approaching eleven o'clock. He could see the mountains up ahead, shrouded in mist.

"Is it far?" Igor Rokotov asked. He felt nauseous after a walloping dose of stimulants. He had silently stared out of the window for most of the way, waiting for his malaise to pass and saving up his energy for when it would soon be needed.

"About thirty kilometers. The old technology park is coming up next. Our target is beyond it."

"Where's Aquila right now?"

"It should be approaching the foothills from the south but there's no connection. We're maintaining a radio silence."

"Who's piloting it?"

"Olga Polvin. Stip is helping her, he's a Hugo series android."

"He has the third level of freedom?"

"Yes, and his neural matrix was copied into Aquila's system. It just happened this way. It was a decision of the two AIs."

"They used direct neurosensory contact? The girl survived it?"

Lozin was about to reply but he was distracted by the sensor alarms.

"What is it?" Igor was down in the backseat and couldn't see the entire dashboard.

"Three unknown targets on the search radar. They're approaching from the north at a speed of around five hundred kilometers per hour and an altitude of four kilometers."

"Let me see," Rokotov stood up, holding on to the high back of the driver's seat with one hand. "They're fighters!"

"What do we do? Can we outrun them?"

"Disable the autopilot. Pull over! Get into the passenger seat and buckle up. I'll drive."

Lozin braked sharply, not even thinking to argue. As soon as they had turned onto the dirt road, a conspicuous dust plume had appeared behind the car, so it wasn't hard to detect them from the air.

While they were changing places, three barely visible silhouettes flashed in the sky.

"They're Phantoms. They've spotted us for sure. Hold on!" Rokotov glanced at the dashboard, then surprisingly gently started the car, taking it off the dirt road and into an overgrown field. "You're not fighting with anyone, right?" he picked up speed, using the old agrofarm as a reference. The sun-warmed metal sheds, granaries, and lots of farm equipment scattered about everywhere gave them a chance to disappear among the static energy matrixes. "Why does a normal car have a search radar?"

"It's for my job. Until recently, I was exploring the adjacent continent, and over there, if you don't constantly monitor your surroundings, you're dead."

"Right," Igor gritted his teeth, abruptly swerved to the side, then suddenly slowed down and stopped the SUV beside a huge robotic agricultural complex, with badly rusted and sunken into the ground cultivation devices stretching out behind it. "We should wait. They'll lose us as a target. Who left all this equipment behind?"

"The first city built by our ancestors is not

far from here. This is where the colonization begun," Lozin watched the skies intently, unable to believe that the heat from the sun-warmed metal would hide them. "Then a chain of volcanoes awoke and everything became covered with hot ash for hundreds of kilometers around. Many people died, and the survivors fled to the southern end of the continent. They had to join our enclave, and since then, everything was abandoned here."

"We need to sit quietly," Igor warned him after cutting the engine. "Don't even think about getting out of the car."

A deafening roar came from the skies. The Phantoms swept low. Their search systems really had lost the target, and the pilots were having to use optical detection devices, but so far, to no avail.

"Have they gone?" Lozin turned his head from side to side anxiously.

"These ones have gone into a combat turn, but there are two other units. Keep a lid on your nerves."

As if confirming his words, another flight passed over the foothills. They flew at supersonic speed, flashing their short wings in the sunshine, and disappeared, and then the sound wave hit: the dust over the dirt road was swept aside and then cast back onto the ground, the branches of trees planted to separate the fields and create windbreaks shook violently, with leaves and unripe fruit showering down.

A minute of ringing silence, and again the intimidating roar.

Rokotov considered the location of markers on the radar display, started the engine and quickly picked up speed, taking the jeep to a group of dilapidated hangars.

The car bounced over potholes. Vadim's teeth clashed against each other and he glanced at the speedometer. One hundred and thirty kilometers per hour over a grassy field... what for? The fighters had disappeared over the horizon, they were two hundred kilometers away at least...

As if mocking his thoughts, two walls of explosions crisscrossed the deserted village: black and orange plumes billowed up, dwarfing the daylight, and the shock wave almost overturned the SUV. The car skidded but Rokotov kept it under control, again increasing the speed. His face remained calm, only his lips curved into a cruel smile.

"The pilots got jittery," he muttered.

The flames slowly faded, decaying into fading clots. Black smoke drifted over the street. Fragments banged against the SUV's sides, leaving deep dents. A grain elevator caught fire and one of the agricultural vehicles exploded.

Rokotov braked sharply again.

"They can't identify a static signature. There's too much interference here for their scanners. Hold on!"

This time, the wall of explosions swept by very close to them. The screech of metal merged with the thunder, the SUV was showered with stones and a spider web of cracks appeared on the windshield.

"Alright, let's force our way to the technology park. It's a straight road, right?" There was no fear, anger or even worry in Igor's voice. He seemed like a different person, calm and collected, almost unbreakable.

Lozin had a tickle in his throat. "Fifteen kilometers as the crow flies," he forced out.

"Is the technology park large?"

"It's huge."

"Excellent. Hold on tight!"

The engine began to work intermittently.

The fighters performed a combat turn and came back. They were flying more slowly and closer to the ground, carefully scanning the terrain below.

"They probably have orders to take us alive. We'll aim for the technology park and then we'll see. I'll make them flip at low altitudes, they can't really fly between buildings!" Rokotov said through clenched teeth.

Lozin looked back over his shoulder. The

Phantoms no longer looked like blurry streaks. They were approaching slowly enough for Vadim to see the aerospace fighters and sense the power emanating from them.

Their car had been spotted. A nearby building was suddenly smashed into pieces, a few rusty sheets of iron flew past, smoking and spinning, the road was pitted with shots and the car was thrown to the side. For a second, the SUV was up on two wheels but then returned to its normal position, its suspension screeching, and skirted around the edge of a steaming crater.

The fighters swept by overhead, soared up and simultaneously performed a half roll, turning around for a new run.

That's it. They couldn't escape this time.

Lozin was wrong.

Igor abruptly turned into a narrow space between two old granaries. The SUV, scattering debris with its bumper, flew along the track and turned again, this time under the cover of a metal canopy.

"Let's wait a minute," Igor closely watched the markers on the display. "If we race to the technology park now, will we be far ahead of schedule?"

Lozin looked at his watch. "They'll be expecting us in 30-40 minutes."

"Okay. We'll have to take the roundabout

way. We'll draw away their attention at the same time. Is there a detour here?"

Vadim nodded. His insides were shaking. He'd never been in battle before.

"You'll get used to it soon," Rokotov spoke curtly.

"Igor, we'll never get there. What are you hoping for? Nine fighters plus a satellite group..."

A jittery smirk appeared on Rokotov's face. "Do you understand the difference between a human's perception of the world and the search algorithms of cybersystems?"

"Well, in general, yes."

"Then you'll get it. Become cold and still, don't consume or produce energy, and the scanners won't notice you. The second option is don't 'shine' brighter than their priority targets."

"I'm sorry, but the pilots have eyes! And the satellites have advanced video sensors! They'll find us using video and image analysis."

"The Phantom pilots are people from Earth. Their eyes are electronic devices. They think like that because they don't know any different. And there's a fairly simple camouflage technique against visual recognition systems. Your friends have reactivated the old tech. This will help us. Do you have any duct tape or wire?"

"I think there was a roll of tape in the trunk among the tools."

"Then help me," Rokotov got out of the car, picked up a rusty sheet of metal, added a few strangely curved pipes, threw everything onto the roof of the car, and said, "Secure that in place while I go and get a few more bits of metal."

Ten minutes later, a completely unrecognizable SUV, covered in rusted bits of metal, started moving again and picked up speed. Something screeched and rattled in the suspension.

They were followed by the roar of the Phantoms.

✳ ✳ ✳

THE SITUATION WAS TENSE on board the Cassiopeia. Despite the careful maintenance and a large number of servos monitoring the ship's technical condition, reactivation of the ship was accompanied by numerous difficulties. Depressurization sensors had activated in some places, the old mechanisms were failing, and every little thing could turn into a disaster at launch.

The reactor was already at fifteen percent power. Planetary fuel synthesis commenced and the hyperdrive accumulators were charging.

"They'll find us!" Lisetsky was gradually losing his nerve.

Polvin looked at the sensor readings, brought up the data from the reconnaissance probe onto the screen, which had been launched at the start to monitor the area and to allow them to react to any threats.

Lisetsky was surprised to see that the ship's signature still looked like a dim and unclear blur.

"Why is there no clear energy matrix? I didn't think that colonial transports were equipped with camouflage. Or is something working incorrectly?"

"Calm down, it's fine," Polvin replied. "Think about it, Cassiopeia's propulsion engine was designed to power three hundred thousand cryogenic chambers, which aren't here now. The twenty-five percent of reactor power that we need will light us up like a reactor of a large robotic complex. Bear in mind the thickness and properties of the ceramic armor, which is a great screen. They shouldn't be able to detect us. The only problem is that we won't be able to test the planetary thrust engine ahead of time since that would give us away."

"Alright," Kirill calmed down a bit. "I sent the servos to check the sealing of the body. We'll definitely start to lose pressure in some sections when we launch."

"Don't waste your time searching for defects. It's better to turn on the controlled decompression device. We'll reduce pressure in the problem areas to avoid explosive leaks. The most important thing is to ensure a reliable seal of the cockpit, the crew quarters and the propulsion unit. We'll do the remaining repair work in space, after the jump."

Lisetsky nodded and got to work.

Of course, two people couldn't prepare a ship for launch and bring it into orbit, they had help from hundreds of automatic subsystems. For centuries, Cassiopeia's main module was kept in the care of the technical servos, who carried out all the necessary maintenance jobs.

Lera's voice came over the PA system, "There is a battle raging on the outskirts of the technology park," she announced. "The Alliance fighters are trying to destroy a target."

"Is it our people?" Nicholas shuddered.

"I can't tell. The probe's position doesn't give me the right angle."

"Are they firing back at the fighters?"

"No. What should I do?"

"Continue to monitor them."

THE SHADOW OF EARTH cruiser drifted in orbit. It passed over Cassia's inhabited continent every thirty minutes, scanning it and adding new data to the overall picture.

Nadyrov had just received updated information. The tactical and analytical departments had sorted out the confusing mess of signatures and weeded out the false targets to find Cassiopeia. The ship's location emitted a characteristic energy matrix of the servos, scurrying about against the backdrop of a blurry signature. Looking at the energy distribution around Alpine City, the admiral mentally summed up the markers, separated them into groups, and gave an order. "Mechanized groups to advance to the technology park. Assume position for a missile strike. Priority targets are approaching from the south-west. Ignore the main module of the colonial transport for now."

The picture was finally becoming clear. The ship had been found.

It was dangerous and pointless to attack Cassiopeia on the ground. Blowing up the spaceship reactor would lead to irreparable consequences. Nadyrov made a different decision. Three assault carriers had already begun a covert geosynchronous maneuver — they were going to destroy the main module of the colonial transport in space, where the exploding propulsion engine wouldn't inflict any damage to the planet.

The only thing left was to damage and capture the Aquila.

The admiral's mood had improved markedly. The most optimistic forecast suggested that he would get everything that he wanted. At worst, he would cast a planet ready for colonization at John Hammer's feet and report the successful destruction of the Aquila, proving that the Alliance servomachines could handle the task.

He didn't have long to wait.

* * *

At the edge of the technology park

THERE WAS A SHORT PAUSE after the last pass of the fighters. Lozin thought he'd gone deaf from the noise and his nerves were in shreds. The silence was viscous and tangible, even the rumble of the car engine downed in it and turned into a whisper.

Vadim extended his hand. His fingers shook. "Igor, stop when you can," he said hoarsely.

Rokotov glanced at him but said nothing. At first, the image of Lozin, slumped in the passenger seat and looking suddenly much older, provoked a feeling of unconscious irritation.

'Have you forgotten how you came face-to-face with death for the first time?' Igor chided himself, struggling to fend off the sensation sweeping over him. Such things often happened in moments of high tension. "Just a minute, Vadim. Just hold on a minute."

The SUV cut across a slope, entered the

technology park and braked. Lozin groped blindly for the door handle, opened it, got out of the car, walked a few steps on buckling legs, then bent over and threw up.

Igor felt a painful lurch in his chest.

Lozin had no idea of what he was doing. Keeping his hand on the wall of a dilapidated building, he started walking away.

"Vadim, wait!"

Igor caught up to him, turned the older man to face him and shook him slightly. He understood what was happening. He had seen people on Dabog lose their minds in bare minutes, unable to bear the stress when death followed closely at their heels and there seemed to be no way to escape it.

Lozin dragged his gaze upwards. His eyes were red and watering. "I can't, Igor... I can't do it. I thought I could but as you can see..."

"Sit. It'll pass."

"I'm sorry. I thought such fear simply didn't exist. It's something so animal, not even human. I guess I'm just weak."

"It'll pass," Igor repeated confidently.

"You've experienced this? Or am I just too old?"

"More than once. Fear is personal, like love, do you see? Everyone experiences it differently. First, it devoured me from the inside. But there are worse things..."

"Like what?" Lozin said incredulously.

"Indifference," Rokotov replied. "When you realize that you're right and you go into battle with no emotions, like a machine. Then you feel incredibly tired. Like you have no more strength left to live... You clamber out of the cockpit, fall into the snow and lie there, staring at the sky as the blizzard gradually covers you with snow. You don't feel the cold. The snowflakes don't melt on your visor. As if you're long dead."

"How did you cope?"

"In different ways..."

A flight of Phantoms shot past overhead, drowning out the end of the sentence. Lozin sat motionless. His cheeks became slightly pink.

"Let's go, Vadim. We can't hide from ourselves and fate anyway. Do you think it's easy for me to know that the Terran Alliance has created its own machines based on Aquila? When I think about what that means, it makes my blood run cold."

Lozin got up, looked at Igor and said softly, "Thanks."

* * *

On board the Cassiopeia

"WE'LL MAKE OURSELVES comfortable here," Kate Lozin carried her grandson into a spacious compartment, used as a rec room for the crew, and looked fussily into several neighboring cabins while Mary Polvin activated the systems.

The information module was one of the things that launched. It automatically connected to the monitoring sensors installed along the perimeter of the crater. A haze appeared along the walls, then a high-density hologram with a stream of audio, and even the smell generators started working.

In the past, such a high level of realism helped in planet exploration, but right now, the 3D panorama of their surroundings eroded the feeling of safety. The walls seemed to disappear and traces of the past could be seen everywhere. Ancient mechanisms moved through the ruins of Alpine City, raising clouds of dust, then vague outlines of the Alliance servomachines flashed into view. They were approaching the technology park while using cloaking fields.

The illusion was perfect. Maria couldn't help ducking her head when a flight of Phantoms soared overhead.

Little Andrew became scared of the roar of the engines and started crying.

"Mary, turn off the holograms!"

"I can't. I don't know how. You should go into the cabin and I'll try to figure this out."

Mrs. Lozin didn't argue and took her grandson to the next compartment.

Once she was alone, Mary tried to disable the virtual reality module but it wasn't possible. The ship was so ancient that most of the equipment was unrecognizable. Sitting down in the chair, she honestly tried to figure out the many glowing icons dotting the armrests, but they didn't respond to touch. There had probably been a glitch and she would have to restart the whole segment.

Nicholas had sternly warned her against interfering in the work of the onboard systems without a pressing need.

'Well, let it work,' her gaze drifted over the projected surroundings and her heart fluttered at the level of realism displayed by the ancient device, which made her feel discomfited.

It was nearing noon. A haze still hung over the mountains but the lower slopes were awash with sunlight. The old road ran down like a gray ribbon, twisting into the petals of a dilapidated transport interchange.

Her motherly mind couldn't stand all the

collisions. Her life had turned upside down in less than a day. The image of her daughter melted and became strangely distorted in her thoughts. It seemed like only yesterday that Olga was a young, carefree and mischievous girl, and now?

She could not imagine her daughter in the cockpit of that terrible machine from Dabog, so she strained her eyes as she peered into the distance, trying to see the several approaching dots.

There was no communication but they must be somewhere close by.

She wasn't wrong. The trembling threads of fate were inexorably bringing them closer together.

An unexpected howling sound appeared among the technology park buildings, and two missiles flashed in the light of the sun and flew towards the horizon.

* * *

HAVING CIRCLED A LITTLE around the outskirts of the industrial area, Rokotov stopped the car.

"What's the matter?" Lozin had had time to recover and no longer flinched when the barrage of fighters swept by overheat.

"We're driving into a trap," Igor replied

glumly.

"What makes you think that?"

Rokotov flicked a few switches. A map of the technology park and the Phantoms' routes appeared on the translucent holographic monitor.

"Have you noticed that they're flying overhead more and more frequently?"

"So what?"

"They're narrowing the patrol area, which means that they've found their target and are secretly following it."

"Why aren't they attacking?"

"They're waiting for an order."

"You said that they wouldn't notice us!"

"That's right. They have a different target, the Aquila. Do you see how their routes are stretching in a southerly direction? Is that where our mechanisms are coming from? And here," he unerringly pointed to a stretch of ordinary, unremarkable rocky terrain, "is where Cassiopeia's main module is hidden, right?"

"Yes," said Lozin, turning cold inside. "How did you know?!"

"The fighters' course is getting shorter and shorter in the southerly direction. And they turn on the scanners every time that they pass over this area, as if they're probing some object and updating their information."

"They know, then? What are they waiting

for?!" Igor's reasoning shocked Vadim.

"They need the targets to gather all in one place. Nadyrov doesn't have enough space and ground units. He wants to strike a single blow but be certain that it'll succeed."

"What are we going to do, Igor?"

"We're going to fight."

"Are you crazy?"

"We need to highlight the targets, make them move and expose themselves. Our folks will get it then."

"We can't contact them?"

"Do you have a secure channel?"

"No.

"Then they'll immediately intercept the message, and we'll lose the element of surprise."

"But what can we do?"

Rokotov frowned, continuously glancing in the direction of the nearest street, framed by the ruins of buildings. "Have you noticed the haze over the ruins?"

Lozin squinted to look, then nodded.

"But the sensors aren't identifying any heat sources. There are Alliance mechanisms over there, hiding under a masking field," Igor concluded. "You should stay here for now. Keep quiet, no matter what happens. If I don't get in touch soon, make your way to Cassiopeia in any way that you can."

"Igor, wait, you don't even have any weapons!"

Igor Rokotov was no longer listening. He wasn't going to argue. He clambered out the car and disappeared into the nearby ruins, leaving Lozin all alone.

✳ ✳ ✳

HE SAW THEM from the roof of a decrepit industrial building after he had climbed up its weathered and crumbling wall. The enemy was thirty meters away... A cold shiver ran over Rokotov when he saw the Alliance servomachines.

Nine Phalangers were hiding among the ruins of the technology park.

They were close to Aquila's size and had a similar overall design, but the different weapon layout made them look larger and squatter. Five of them were ready for melee combat while four had assumed the position to release a missile salvo, with their legs folded and their supports sunk deep into the soil to provide additional stability for when they fired the heavy missiles.

There was a characteristic sound. A segment of armor shifted in the upper part of the nearest Phalanger's cabin and the Legion launchers began to rise and assume the firing position. They froze at an angle to the horizon.

Igor moved through the ruins, reached a neighboring building, shifted to an overgrown hangar roof and crawled along it, then carefully looked out and down.

One of the Alliance servomachines was now directly below him.

He stood up, jumped onto the Phalanger's cockpit roof and froze, holding onto the casing that protected the launcher's power cables and cybernetic components.

Igor was in mortal danger. They could spot and kill him at any moment, or there could be a missile salvo, which would leave him with no chance of survival — he knew how the Legion system worked — it was what the frigates in Nadyrov's fleet used to fire at targets on the surface of Dabog. When launched, a missile would switch on its own engines a couple of seconds after leaving the launching tube. It wouldn't damage the servomachine but would do very unpleasant things to a nearby human being.

Barely keeping his composure, he looked around. Many of the servomachine details appeared familiar, which was not surprising. The Alliance designers had used standardized jet and PCV components, pumped out on the conveyor belt, when constructing the Phalanger.

A human being couldn't damage even the

most fragile connection, but he had to do something!

Igor's past experience came to the rescue. Not so long ago, Igor had watched a team of androids dismantle a Phantom that had been shot down over Dabog.

He examined the launcher. That's right, just here... Several armored cables were held in place using a threaded coupling. Scraping his fingers bloody, Igor managed to turn it, and it spun more easily the rest of the way. Soon the connection was broken.

A hatch rustled open and a technical servo climbed out of it. Rapidly scuttling on its manipulators, it skirted the missile launcher and received a crushing blow from Igor Rokotov, which flung it down from a ten-meter height and onto the rusted bars of an armature, piercing its body.

Igor gasped. What now? His heart thudded unevenly. He waited but the technical hatch didn't open. Finally, a minute later, there was a screech as an armored segment shifted aside, and a pilot climbed out of the Phalanger.

"Heck, I don't know what happened!" He snarled, speaking to someone over the comms. "The guidance system power was cut off, both the main and the reserve! The servo has disappeared somewhere, so I'll have to take a look myself and report back!"

Rokotov waited.

The pilot noticed the broken connection, swore and squatted down to fix it but didn't get the chance. A steel blade touched the throat of the surprised Terran. His lightweight piloting suit was sealed but not armored.

"If you move, I'll slit your throat," Igor warned. "How do I access the guidance system settings?"

"A codon. Hanging around my neck..." the pilot wheezed.

"Do I need biometrics?"

"No. The machine is already activated."

Rokotov didn't believe him. "If you lie to me again, I'll kill you," he said icily.

"Please, don't! I'm just a servoengineer. I was drafted in!"

"How do I get access?"

"A codon. And the cybersystem reads the DNA off the sensors when they are touched," the pilot admitted. "Not every time but periodically."

"Keep still," Igor pulled a pulse gun out of the power grip on the pilot's belt. "Now, get back inside, but no tricks, do you hear me?"

The pilot began to descend, trembling, and Igor followed him down.

* * *

THE HATCH OVERHEAD closed, restoring the seal.

The Phalanger's cockpit looked strange and unfamiliar. Igor had no illusions. He couldn't seize full control. He set himself realistic goals.

"Get into the chair. Give me the codon. Alright, good. Now, tell me, how do I operate the machine without the biometrics?"

"The combat autopilots won't turn on."

"You're lying to me again. There must be a way."

"Only in maintenance mode."

Igor ran his eyes over the control panel and found the graphic control interface of the missile launchers.

"Change the guidance angle. Now, fire!"

"But..."

"I said, fire!"

The pilot's trembling finger touched the right sensor.

From the outside, it looked like someone had lashed a rod over the dry ground. Clouds of dust shot up inside the dilapidated building, a roaring flame bursting through them, and two Pilumi, their jet engines glowing, rushed into Cassia's sky to shower down multiple warheads over the deserted mountain area.

"Fifth, what the frayg is going on?! You've unmasked us, imbecile!"

Igor stepped back behind the chair and pressed the gun to the back of the pilot's head.

"Answer them!"

The pilot turned on the loudspeaker and shouted in a broken voice, "Spontaneous launch! I told you, there's a problem with the power!"

"Dammit! Turn on the Maverick."

Rokotov looked over the control panels and found the word 'Maverick'. It appeared to be the combat autopilot module.

"Don't touch the sensors," Igor whispered. "If you want to live, figure out a way to switch on manual control mode."

"I'm unable to run the Maverick!" the pilot wheezed.

"Why the frayg not?"

"There are problems in the system! My machine's going out of control! It's targeting the nearest markers! I'm switching to manual mode."

"Fine. Figure it out quickly, I need all the mechanisms ready to go!"

The screen flickered and went dark, then lit up again.

Transition to testing mode.

The targeting monitor settings had been reset.

Two complex servodevices extended from

the base of the control panel, looking like astronavigation controls.

"Have the biometrics been disabled?"

"Yes. How else would the technicians be able to work on the machine?"

"Good, now fold the Legion system into a stowed position."

"I can't. You broke something! We have to go up again."

Igor nodded reluctantly. He hadn't reconnected the cable. "You're going up first. Get a move on, and don't do anything stupid," he warned.

They climbed outside.

"Restore the cable connection. Quickly!"

The pilot made the decision in that moment. He leaped onto Rokotov, trying to push him off, but Igor had been expecting an attack and simply jumped back, making the Terran lose his balance on the armored slope and fall ten meters with a brief shriek.

* * *

AT NOON, THE THREE servomachines: Aquila, Andrew's Hoplite and the autopilot-controlled trophy Phalanger turned towards the mountains.

They didn't talk much. Groves was actively

scanning while Olga tried to get used to the sensations of direct neurosensory contact, but her mind clearly wasn't coping with the cybersystem merge. Everything looked different through the eyes of the machine, as if she was in a different world, and the sense of disorientation caused waves of dizziness to wash over her.

Stip was fixing the mechanics as they walked and Aquila's tread became more confident but the android still wasn't satisfied. He continued to make small repairs, using the internal technical tunnels to move around the machine.

"Olga," She heard Andrew's voice. "You should move to the Phalanger."

"Why?"

"It has an emergency ejection system."

"No. I'm not leaving Aquila!"

"Look at the targeting monitor. I'm sending you data."

Groups of crimson markers appeared and went out on the screen.

"They're Phantoms. Three flights. They're patrolling the area," Groves explained curtly. "If they spot us, there will be a fight."

"What are they doing here?"

"Isn't it obvious? Nadyrov must have found out Cassiopeia's approximate location. Did you really think that we would easily reach the ship, load up and fly away?"

Olga stayed gloomily silent. That had been the plan!

She wanted to call Stip and ask the android if he could take the pilot's seat in an unexpected confrontation but she didn't have enough time. A flash appeared in the distance and the sensors began to alarm. Two heavy missiles launched from the outskirts of Alpine City, flew a short way and then showered the desolate mountain area with a multitude of explosions.

"It's the Pilumi! With multiple warheads!"

Andrew's alarmed voice fell silent. Olga's mind was instantly flooded with a whirlwind of non-human sensations. Her perception of the world suddenly sharpened, stretching forward and upward as Aquila automatically fired a series of probes, erasing the dull monotony of the ruins and illuminating them with bright bursts of detected signatures.

Streams of data poured into her mind, dozens of kilometers suddenly blurred into vague outlines that flashed past her, and a moment later, her vision cleared again: she saw the Phalangers lurking among the ruins in the technology park, Lozin's vehicle, hastily disguised by a pile of rusty pipes, and pairs of aerospace fighters leaving a fading contrail in Cassia's skies.

Her mind was drowning in the images. They were coming from different angles and directions -

the cybersystem would have divided them into streams and projected them onto separate screens but direct contact wasn't designed for it.

There was a moment of complete disorientation and then the load abruptly lessened, giving Olga clarity of thought again, as if she was surfacing from the dark depths of a digital maelstrom, swimming up to the light.

Aquila had adapted, adjusting to the peculiarities of the human mind and guiding her along the edge of the abyss.

Olga took a shuddering breath. The display panels came back into view but the dim glow of the holographic screens looked meager in comparison, not providing even a hundredth of the information available to her beyond the line of safety.

What was she to do? There was a trap up ahead. The new abilities were more likely to crush her mind than help her to control Aquila, but her previous perception was already ruined, seeming slow, clumsy and not very informative.

"Where are the fighters?"

Her nerves were on fire. It was all happening so quickly and inexorably that there was no time to weigh up the options and make a decision. A clear picture appeared in response to her mental query — after the unexplained missile salvo, the Alliance servomachines were abandoning their unmasked positions as three pairs of Phantoms had completed a combat turn and were rushing into attack!

She was overcome with panic and then an icy premonition of death.

Aquila's AI was absorbing the intense human emotions. For a machine with artificial neural networks, they were a shock. The ancient technology affected both of them deeply and the instinctive desire to survive coupled with the cybersystem's capabilities resulted in instant action.

Andrew hadn't even had time to take aim at the leading Phantom when Aquila's cockpit rose and tilted slightly and its lasers sprayed fire.

The head fighter disappeared in a flash, its wingmen suffered damage and veered into different directions, interrupting their attack and dropping closer to the ground. Aquila spun its body around and produced two more scathing volleys.

Humans were not capable of such speed and accuracy. Groves knew this for sure since he'd had plenty of practice. The amount of energy expended in the destruction of the fighters, however, didn't fit into the framework of rational machine logic. Something extraordinary had happened, as if Aquila had responded in a fit of passion!

This thought came and went.

The probes tore off the cloak of invisibility.

The signatures of nine Phalangers, three of whom were preparing to launch the Pilumi, could be scanned straight ahead.

The battle couldn't be avoided. Right now, Groves could count on nobody but himself.

* * *

THE MISSILE SALVO from the heavy Alliance servomachines fell over an area covering tens of square kilometers. The multiple Pilumi warheads showered down in a fiery barrage.

Andrew used the Hoplite's only advantage and accelerated sharply, getting out of the zone of total destruction. Aquila was falling noticeably behind and the explosions burst around it, with shards lashing its ceramic armor like a molten blizzard.

Their only chance of staying alive was to reach Cassiopeia. If the colonial transport's main module had been prepared for launch, not all was lost...

Snapping back with single missiles, he rapidly led the Hoplite to a cluster of industrial buildings at the edge of the technology park. Their walls and ceilings, cast from reinforced concrete, would provide additional protection for a time. He knew that they would try and immobilize the

Aquila and take it with minimal damage but nobody would spare him and his machine.

* * *

AQUILA BROKE through the flames.

Olga couldn't help herself, like any untrained person, she was numb with terror, unable to control the machine in the inferno that had descended around her.

Andrew's Hoplite had disappeared from view. The trophy Phalanger that had been following them sustained several direct hits and she saw flames leap from its cabin before the servomachine was torn apart by the internal explosions.

She shrank back into the chair, shuddering from the nearby strikes, broken, crushed and completely disorientated.

It felt like it would all be over in just a second.

Aquila's AI took a different view. With every second of direct neurosensory contact, rapid and irreversible processes developed in its neural matrix. Having absorbed the shock of human emotions, it reacted in its own way. Powerful and heavily armored, having survived hundreds of fights, it felt for the first time the hot and uneven beating of the human heart.

The firestorm, meanwhile, began to die down.

The ground smoldered. Clouds of dust drifted slowly back down. Large chunks of reinforced concrete fell from the destroyed road junction with a dull clatter.

The enemy servomachines rushed into attack and their signals drew rapidly nearer.

Olga's heart beat hollowly.

No more was required right now. Aquila's artificial neural networks had undergone a qualitative transformation. The daily grind of war that had destroyed Igor Rokotov's soul found its place, forming a layer of experience that neither people nor cybersystems possessed.

Aquila was reborn a second time in less than a day, finally and irreversibly.

The servomotors howled. The frequency variator found Hoplite's signal.

Listening to its intense and updated feelings, Aquila independently changed course and tried to contact Groves but didn't get an answer for an unequal battle had already begun among the ruins of the industrial complex.

Stip, the right activator is damaged. Fix it. I need maximum speed.

* * *

ANDREW GROVES, having avoided any direct hits, took his Hoplite deeper into the industrial zone, where the massive repair workshops formed a dense shield.

The red dots on the map began to move. The enemy split into two groups, and only one Phalanger, the same that had produced an uncoordinated missile launch, stood frozen among the ruins on the southern edge of the technology park.

Alright, no point in counting it right now. There are four others. Andrew had no idea how to defeat them. The Vesuvius Testing Area was used to perfect the tactics of fighting against Aquila-type machines. In the upcoming battles, Hoplites were supposed to carry out reconnaissance, create disturbances, and protect the more powerful but slower Phalangers from air attacks.

There was almost no chance of surviving against them in direct combat. The shells from their heavy electromagnetic guns would penetrate his armor with the first hit.

What did he have? Only speed, maneuverability and the ability to generate false targets. He couldn't really count on his own firepower. The thirty-millimeter EMGs and short-range missiles would be effective only if striking the vulnerable parts of a structure.

Which meant that the only chance of survival came from damaging the Phalangers, knocking out their sensors and forcing them to do what he wanted...

Andrew had made a critical error. Of course, he wasn't planning to abandon Aquila, but he didn't consider the machine from Dabog as a force to be reckoned with. Olga, in his opinion, could not influence the situation. She wasn't a pilot. She didn't have the appropriate training. He could only hope that Aquila would distract the enemy and hold out under fire for a few minutes...

Dropping the last two phantom generators, Andrew took his Hoplite into a huge hangar, where stood several robotic construction systems, which had been brought here for repairs a long time ago.

The four red markers split up. Two pilots fell for the trick and turned their machines around, following the false signatures. Excellent.

Another pair entered the narrow space between buildings. The follower stopped to monitor the intersection while the leader headed for the hangar doors. The thick walls of reinforced concrete didn't allow the Phalanger to start firing at once. Its weapons were currently working against it since the shots would certainly destroy the barrier but would also damage the shooter, and the pilot wanted to work cleanly like he had done on the testing ground.

The steady tread of a sixty-ton servomachine made the ground vibrate. A fierce battle had already erupted in the center of the technology park, but here it was a battle of nerves.

The Phalanger's outline appeared for a second in the open doorway. The guns barked out briefly. The ancient construction complex, a tracked platform with equipment mounted on it, shuddered as it took a hit. The hangar was filled with thunder and smoke, and the metal melted where it had been hit. The holes glowed dully, convincing the enemy pilot that he had struck a false target since the Hoplite didn't do anything in response, didn't even move, and its energy matrix didn't change its characteristics.

"A dummy... This bastard thinks he can get away by dropping some phantom generators! Third, what have you got?"

"Nothing so far."

"Keep looking! He's around here somewhere! He's hiding among this metal crap, probably has switched off the reactor or reduced its power."

The heavy servomachine began to turn as it scanned.

Groves was drenched in sweat. The cockpit side flashed in the reticle and the guidance system immediately highlighted the electromagnetic gun attachments, which were covered by massive armored casings.

Two launches filled the hangar with noise and light.

The Phalanger swayed. Even at such a short distance, only one missile reached the target while the second one was shot down by the laser missile defense system.

There was no time to assess the damage. Peppering the enemy's side with a long volley from the EMGs, Andrew took his Hoplite deeper into the building, hiding behind the ancient mechanisms and heading for the second exit.

Explosions followed at his heels. He'd won himself a few minutes, but would that help? Four Phalangers opened heavy fire. A cloud of bitter concrete dust shot up where the ancient hangar used to stand. The shells knocked down walls but Andrew had already smashed through the ancient gates using his Hoplite and escaped the strike zone, turning and moving along the edge of the technology park. Missiles flew past him with a howl — in addition to the Legions, the heavy servomachines were equipped with medium-range launchers.

Explosions blossomed further ahead and to the left. A growing dust cloud gathered behind him, and directly ahead, the road climbed over a small hill, which led to several overpasses.

Andrew wanted to live. Cold sweat dripped from his brow. Where was Aquila?!

Landing on a rocky platform, Groves scanned the surroundings. There it is...

The robot from Dabog was retreating slowly, snapping at the enemy with laser discharges. Aquila was having a hard time. Large clearings were smoking among the buildings, created by the bursts of heavy Gauss guns. Thick black smoke poured out of a damaged Phalanger. The static signal at the edge of the technology park blinked, changed the marker color for some reason, and began to move hesitantly towards the fight.

Andrew discerned all this in a fraction of a second. The situation seemed hopeless.

"Olga, head to the Cassiopeia! I'll distract them!"

Without waiting for a reply, he discharged a missile volley and, his guns firing, sent his Hoplite charging down the slope. It looked like he wasn't going to get out of this scrape.

Chapter Fourteen

THE SUDDEN FIGHT that broke out so near Alpine City finally snapped something in Olga's mind.

To see the world through the eyes of the machine was shocking enough, but when the first missile salvo hit, and a set of trajectories reached out to Aquila, her mind simply couldn't stand the load.

Olga curled into a ball in the chair, her eyes squeezed shut, shuddering all over, but this didn't make it any easier. The direct neurosensory contact continued, and the realistic sensations received from the sensors bordered on insanity.

Everything human faded away, only the

horror of inevitability remained, together with the logic of numbers.

Aquila's subsystems poured brief strings of reports into her mind, based on the objective analysis of forces:

Available accumulator capacity 63%.

Maximum speed considering existing damage: 30 km/h.

Combat survivability considering current balance of forces: 90 seconds.

She had ninety seconds left to live! That's how long Aquila would last under the barrage from the Phalangers, which were only slightly inferior to the servomachine from Dabog.

They moved across her path in two groups, cutting her off from the gorge leading to Cassiopeia's storage area.

Operational data update: minus one enemy, plus 20 seconds of survivability.

The shock let her go. The missile strike stropped, Andrew's Hoplite suddenly accelerated, drawing the attention of four of the enemies, while one of the Phalangers hadn't engaged in battle, with its marker remaining on the outskirts of the technology park for some reason.

Flames reflected in Olga's dilated pupils. No matter where she looked, the screens showed fire. One of the missiles had landed in an underground storage for crude oil.

Among the thick plumes of black smoke streaming over the ground, flashed the outline of a Phalanger, then came two ear-splitting bursts of fire and a wall of explosions rose. Olga cried out involuntarily. The feedback caused sudden pain and pulled her out of the torturous stupor. Her eyes found a target. Obeying her mental impulse, Aquila's cockpit turned, and a laser volley at maximum power burned through the armor of a heavy Alliance servomachine.

Available accumulator capacity 42%.

Operational data update...

The Phalanger burst into flames, and the other three Alliance machines suddenly swerved aside and shrouded themselves in clouds of anti-laser particles which refracted the light, so that Aquila's subsequent volley was wasted.

Available accumulator capacity 37%. Onboard reactor power 102%. Working fluid temperature critical.

"Stip, take control of the fire!" Olga tried to pry the shunt out of her implant socket with trembling fingers.

No. Please. Stay with me...

The hot whisper stopped her in her tracks.

"I'm not a pilot! I can't! I'm just wasting energy!" she cried.

A system message came as an answer.

Optimizing power. Reducing load on the

reactor.

A technical hatch screeched open overhead and Stip's endoprosthesis, wearing scorched tatters of fabric, slid down. The smell of burning followed him into the cockpit.

Formation of new variable environment.

Analysis of target maneuvering. Failed...

'I don't understand what's happening,' Aquila's whisper weaved into her thoughts and continued to burn. *'They could have struck from behind the screen of anti-laser particles but they didn't. Why? I cannot process the logic of their decisions!'*

"They got scared and are now being cautious," Stip's voice held jarring notes. "There are people piloting the Phalangers. They operate outside the framework of machine logic."

Formation of new variable environment.

The sign flashed insistently.

"Just take the controls!" Olga begged. "I can't do this anymore. I'm not a soldier and I'm not a pilot! We need to reach the Cassiopeia! Just reach it and not destroy everything and everyone in our path!" She disconnected the shunt, buried her face in her hands and froze, almost losing consciousness when the sensation of direct neurosensory contact suddenly faded away.

Formation of new variable environment... Successful. Changing tactical schemes. Taking over control.

"Stip, help me. Connect through the maintenance port. Open the communication channel with Andrew's Hoplite," Aquila's synthesized voice, which was used to announce all the important moments of decision-making, now sounded calm and detached.

*** * ***

THE BATTLE AT THE EDGE of the technology park resumed with new force.

The Phalanger pilots quickly gathered themselves after the first unexpected losses, and now seven heavy Alliance servomachines surrounded Aquila in a semicircle, cutting it off from the Cassiopeia.

The robot from Dabog, despite its genius construction, superior weapons and better protection, was doomed.

"Keep firing at it! Avoid direct hits to the cockpit. We need to wear it down!" the voice of the united group commander sounded more and more confident.

Aquila was retreating. The damaged Phalanger kept burning. Fragments of the Phantoms gave off columns of smoke among the ruins. The Alliance servomachines advanced under the cover of the dust cloud, mixed together with the anti-laser particles.

"Its leg has been hit! It's becoming unstable, it's going to collapse!"

IN THE COCKPIT of the captured Phalanger, Igor Rokotov placed his hands on the manual control levers. The complex servodevices allowed him to set the direction and speed of movement, and to manipulate the independent weapon suspensions to fire, but even that proved to be a daunting task without the proper training. The sixty tons of metal didn't obey him very well. The heavy tread of the servomachine seemed more like an unsteady lurch — the Phalanger swayed, scraping a building wall with its right weapon, smashed through some ancient foam concrete blocks and found itself in a technical parking lot.

Damn... Despite the outwardly similar construction, piloting the Alliance servomachine was proving to be extremely difficult.

Igor gritted his teeth. The stimulants were gradually wearing off.

In that moment, the communication variator tuned into a preset frequency and took over an encrypted channel.

It was coming from the Aquila!

The trophy Phalanger stopped with a fading howl of its servomotors. Igor had to manually exchange data, but he couldn't finish the operation as two enemy servomachines appeared in his line of sight! Rokotov didn't have time to contact Aquila. The enemy was approaching, and he had to take over the controls again.

Five-shot bursts rang out as both guns discharged, but the sight on the manual control wasn't very accurate and the shells smashed into a building on the other side of the parking lot, inflicting only minor damage to the enemy mechanisms.

He heard swearing on the reserve channel and then someone called to the pilot, "Austin, what are you doing?!"

"Commander, it's not him! The implant label isn't scanning. The Phalanger has been captured! I repeat, the Fifth is under enemy control! It's moving under manual control, I'm sending the coordinates."

✳ ✳ ✳

THE DAMAGE SCHEMES were multiplying with every second.

Aquila was still holding on but the situation appeared hopeless. The heavy Alliance servomachines proved to be dangerous opponents. The surprise factor no longer played a deciding role. The pilots of the Phalangers had overcome their confusion and were now using a previously practiced tactic of hiding behind a curtain of anti-laser particles and methodically shooting at the Aquila while avoiding return fire.

There was a little more than a kilometer left to the gorge leading to Cassiopeia's storage area, yet how could they reach it when the enemy was blocking the way? The forces were blatantly unequal.

Aquila kept walking, using the ruins for cover whenever it could. A smoking plume stretched out behind it, and sparks occasionally sprayed from the holes in its armored casing. There was enough energy left for one more volley. The overloaded reactor could not compensate for the loss.

"Olga, I need to know where Lozin is."

"I'm trying to contact him. There's a lot of interference."

"Keep trying. We only have one chance, one attempt."

Olga knew what the AI was planning. Moving among the ruins, it was deliberately drawing the enemy to a specific point in the technology park, despite the inflicted damage.

The communication module finally found Cassiopeia's signal. If only she could contact Lozin and find out where he and Igor were, and transmit the instructions, and then the death trap would have no time to snap shut.

The AI's level-headedness frightened her. It appeared that the Alliance pilots had succeeded in their task and the machine from Dabog would soon be defeated, yet Aquila's internal monitors showed a slightly different picture. The integrity of the structure had a ten percent reserve...

Suddenly, the fire started to weaken. The short respite allowed Aquila to release several reconnaissance probes.

After a few seconds, it became clear that another Phalanger had suddenly entered the fray. It had remained static prior to this, probably due to a fault, but now it started moving and attacking its own team!

"Got it! There's a connection with Vadim!"

"Where are they now?" Aquila used the internal audio system.

"Vadim is on the outskirts of the technology park. He says that Igor left! He thinks that... Oh my God! Rokotov has captured the Phalanger!"

"This may disrupt our plan. But I will try to fix everything." Aquila's synthesized voice sounded cool. "Tell Lozin to get ready to collect Igor. Plan out their route. We are approaching the designated point!"

Events began to spiral out of control.

"Olga, I got it..." Lozin's voice kept dropping

out due to the interference.

"There is contact with the Cassiopeia! Send them the information."

Aquila switched on the reserve drives, suddenly increasing its speed and reaching the edge of the technology park. The closely placed buildings made the five Phalangers draw nearer to each other.

Old, abandoned mines were located underneath. Aquila had just passed a collapsed entrance to one of them.

The dust cloud grew bigger. The Alliance servomachines were creating the shortest path for themselves, moving under the cover of the anti-laser particle suspension.

✳ ✳ ✳

ONE OF THE PROBES released by Cassiopeia had survived. It was now moving ten meters above the ground, circling around columns of fire and breaking through clouds of smoke.

The virtual space generated in the crew compartment was filled with the terrifying details of the battle below.

Maria couldn't breathe, so horrible was the holographic battle unfolding around her.

She simply couldn't process what was

happening, and yet the technological might of the battling servomachines was not the biggest source of shock.

The reconnaissance probe crossed the technology park and was starting to turn at its southern edge when Lozin's SUV suddenly came into view.

The SUV's paint was beginning to smoke and it looked like the car would burst into flames at any moment due to the surrounding inferno.

Where was Vadim?!

She saw him a second later. Lozin was lying behind a pile of concrete rubble. His ears were bleeding, his sallow face was covered in soot, and his limp posture left no hope.

"My God, Vadim, what will I tell Kate?" Maria's lips whispered inaudibly. Hot tears ran down her cheeks.

She shut her eyes, unable to watch, and when she forced herself to open them again, her heart immediately began to pound because Vadim was alive! He came to, staggered to the car, got into the crumpled SUV and disappeared into a growing cloud of dust, leaving Mary Polvin alone in agonizing suspense.

* * *

"GROVES, REPORT when you get into position!"

A couple of minutes ago, when Andrew was preparing to distract the Phalangers to give Olga a chance to reach the Cassiopeia, he wasn't thinking about himself. The events swept him up, racing him towards a certain death, when he was stopped by the data transfer from Aquila.

The plan briefly outlined by the artificial intelligence seemed insane but any options were good with such an obvious imbalance of power.

The Hoplite swerved behind an outcropping of rock and left the fight, giving it a brief break.

Andrew's ears were buzzing from the intense exertion. He needed several seconds to gather himself, to glance at the calculations and tactical schemes.

'Frayg, this might actually work!' came the thought.

Aquila's artificial intelligence had understood Olga Polvin's phrase literally. A fight with the combined forces of the heavy servomachines was doomed to fail, however, they just needed to *stop* them, not destroy them!

Groves turned onto an old road that led him to a small platform located above the branching overpasses. From here, he could see the whole technology park. It was the perfect position except for one thing — he would be spotted and destroyed immediately after the missile launch. The chance of survival was small.

He touched the recharge sensor. The combat escalator howled, changing the type of missile in the launchers.

The catapult calculations had been made by Aquila and there was no time left to check them. He simply entered the data into the system.

"In position. Ready to fire!"

"Wait! We have an unexpected problem!"

"What is it?"

"Rokotov has captured a Phalanger!"

"Then he should head to the Cassiopeia."

"It is not an option," Aquila said dryly. "He can barely move. Either the mechanism is damaged or Igor simply can't manage the controls."

"What are we supposed to do? Can we contact him?"

"I am trying. Yes, got it!" There was a short pause. "He refused."

"What?"

"He refused. He said that he can manage. He'll cover us."

"Igor's going to die!"

"Give me a second! Be ready! Wait!"

Aquila's artificial intelligence knew Igor

Rokotov well enough to realize that he would not change his decision, would grapple with the controls of the captured servomachine and thus doom them all. Time would be lost; the positions would change and all the calculations would become meaningless.

What could it do?

The Phalangers were approaching. Soon, they would be within direct striking distance again. There was enough power in the accumulators for one more volley. Laser systems modified for Operation Dust Moon consumed too much energy, which could not be replenished in a short-lived fight.

It was a moment of despair for Aquila. The thin line that separated the cybersystem's logic from the newborn jumble of feelings was straining under the pressure of current events. A few moments more and it would be too late.

There was too much damage. There was no power. I cannot fight.

"Vadim!" it turned the cockpit and called Lozin at the same time.

"I'm listening!"

"Pick up Rokotov and head to the Cassiopeia."

"I can't! I can't reach Igor! There's no communication."

"Head over here," Aquila sent a navigational

marker.

A new, shocking degree of freedom was revealed to the artificial intelligence. It was no longer playing a game of chess. Logic and emotions fused together, forcing the machine to make an impossible decision.

"Groves, follow the plan! Wait for my command!"

On board the Cassiopeia

Hypersphere jump calculations ready.
Planetary fuel synthesis completed.
Testing of launching autopilots completed.
Begin countdown?

POLVIN STARED DISCONCERTEDLY at the system messages. One touch of the sensor would begin the command sequence and then only one hundred seconds would remain until the engines switched on.

No. It was too early. The others wouldn't make it.

A fine vibration shook the cliffs. A battle was raging among the ruins in the technology park.

"Nicholas, look at the jump calculations!"

Lisetsky sent a simplified graphical image of the course designed by the cybersystem to his terminal. It was based on the data obtained from the navigational crystal on Igor Rokotov's ship, and this turned out to be a problem.

How could they recognize, among the dozens of tension lines in the hypersphere, the only one leading to Dabog's system?

From the cybersystem's point of view, there was only one course of action. They had to turn on the hyperdrive at the point where the Rokotov's ship had materialized, which was below the safe orbit zone around Cassia!

'We have no choice,' Polvin told himself. 'We must accept this risk and hope that the zone of curvature of space will not affect the dense layers of the atmosphere, otherwise, weather conditions over Cassia's inhabited continent may change in catastrophic and unpredictable ways.'

"What are we going to do?"

"Blast off as soon as ready," Nicholas snapped. "But first, we wait for our people."

"Are you sure? We have no idea what the consequences might be."

"So, get the cybersystem to work it out! Let it perform some additional calculations!"

"I have an incoming call! It's an emergency frequency from the time of the Great Exodus. It might be an attempt to uncover us."

"I'll answer. I think we have already been discovered. Get ready to begin the prelaunch countdown."

Polvin touched a sensor on his cyberstack, and his daughter's voice suddenly filled the cockpit.

"Aquila calling Cassiopeia! Hold the countdown and open the cargo portal! Please, nobody argue with me, we have to do this! The consequences have been calculated. We're approaching. Please acknowledge!"

✳ ✳ ✳

VADIM SPENT THE FIRST few minutes after Igor had left in painful ignorance. He couldn't believe that there an ambush up ahead. The fighters made sense but how could have Nadyrov worked out Cassiopeia's exact location and deploy servomachines there ahead of time? No, Rokotov was surely being paranoid and exaggerating the danger.

The sudden missile launches from the closest ruins left him utterly bewildered.

What was he supposed to do now?! Lozin felt lost, watching the growing cloud of dust, and then he heard the sound of servomotors and several Phalangers suddenly appeared in view.

The Alliance mechanisms were barreling straight ahead, crashing through walls and firing their guns.

The burning blast waves almost flipped the SUV right over. Hell rapidly descended over the area. Missile strikes covered a huge part of the technology park and the ancient constructions were torn down like houses of cards, the remaining crude oil in the old underground storage was set alight, and a bitter smoke drifted over the ground, blotting out the sun.

There was nothing that Lozin could do. He got out of the SUV, which offered no protection, and crawled a little way to the side, hiding behind a pile of concrete rubble, pressing his hands to his bleeding ears and knowing that in another couple of close hits, there would be nothing left here but a burnt corpse.

Another explosion struck thirty meters away. The burning shock wave swept over him, sending him unconscious.

He regained consciousness again quite quickly and sat up, coughing violently and looking frantically around him.

Through the curtain of bitter dust, he saw an enemy Phalanger. It swayed as if it had been hit. Lozin's cyberstack reloaded and began to automatically scan through frequencies until it picked up a signal.

"Rokotov to Aquila, I have captured a Phalanger but can barely control it. Mark the targets and I'll try to hit them with my guns!"

It seemed that he wasn't heard and Igor began a fight with two nearby enemy machines before something extraordinary happened. First, Vadim was contacted by Olga, and when he haltingly explained the situation, she replied, "Quickly, grab him and get out of there. Here's the route!"

Vadim had no idea how to contact Rokotov and persuade him to leave the captured Phalanger, and anyway, what for?

Like many others, Vadim didn't yet know that the battle around him did not forgive delays. In a fight between servomachines, humans have almost no chance of surviving and only bare seconds to make a decision.

Stumbling and falling repeatedly, he reached the SUV. The paint had peeled away. He could barely breathe inside the cabin. The engine started up but kept cutting out.

The crumpled SUV skidded onto the old and cracked road. Piles of concrete rubble rose on either side of the street. The frightening silhouettes of three servomachines towered above them.

Aquila's laser volley struck unexpectedly... hitting the turning platform of the trophy

Phalanger!

"What the hell is she doing?!" Lozin almost lost control of the vehicle when the molten metal sprayed over the street.

The cockpit of the heavy servomachine, cut off by the laser volley, separated from its drive and began to slide down, crushing the ruins.

Vadim skidded to a halt. He was surrounded by collapsing buildings and swirling dust. The front end of Phalanger's armor flashed into view. Sparks and flames flickered in the gloom.

"Igor! Igor, are you alive?"

A bluish glow suddenly flickered over several hatches and they opened as the emergency system kicked in. Rokotov climbed out, staggered to his feet and took several steps.

"Igor, over here!"

Rokotov guessed rather than heard Vadim, ran up to the SUV and climbed inside. "Why did it hit my Phalanger?"

"Buckle up!" Lozin said curtly. "I have my orders to collect you and break through to the Cassiopeia!"

AQUILA CONTINUED to maneuver desperately as it watched the movement of the green marker.

Lozin did as he had been asked. His car, moving along the main street, reached the gorge leading to the main module of the colonial transport.

"They're safe! Go for it, Andrew!"

TWO MISSILES with thermobaric warheads[6] erupted from Hoplite's launchers.

The first went into the mouth of an old mine that ran beneath the technology park, and the second one disappeared into a growing cloud of dust and anti-laser particles.

The thermobaric explosions hit within a few seconds of each other. The dust cloud immediately detonated and a roaring ocean of flame flooded the area, with the man-made cataclysm throwing everything together in the next moment.

The ground shook. Huge fissures ran under buildings and streets. The ruins lost their shape and became shrouded in a haze, a fountain of stone shot up into the air, and then everything began to fall apart: the ancient workings collapsed in on themselves and sections of the hill, on which stood the technology park, started to slide into the underground cavity with an almighty crash.

The shock wave swept and burned away

---

[6] The main damage inflicted by a thermobaric weapon comes from the excess pressure formed in the shock wave front, which reaches about 30 kg/cm2 in the center of a fuel-air cloud detonation, with the temperature reaching 2,500-3,000° C in the detonation zone in a fraction of a second.

everything in its path... except the Phalangers, whose heavy armor could withstand the damage from the fuel-air explosion.

The soil was completely burned away within a kilometer radius and now looked like lunar soil. The concrete and stone turned into a big, steaming rubble, buildings were destroyed, and the ancient technology became a useless pile of metal, and all of it, including the Alliance servomachines, were sliding down into the large conical craters formed on the site of the long-abandoned mines...

Aquila was out of range by the time the strike hit, as it had managed to descend the long concrete ramp and was now crossing the warped space of the old loading terminal, skirting around the destroyed technology park and moving in the direction of Cassiopeia.

The camouflage mesh had been torn off the crater but it no longer mattered. The shell of the colonial transport's main module had withstood the explosion. Beside the ship stood Lozin's burning SUV as technical servos scurried around the smoking cables.

"MY GOD, VADIM, you're alive!" Kate rushed to her husband and helped him to hold up Igor Rokotov. For a moment, she stood and embraced them both.

"Where's the medical bay?" Lozin's hand was

bleeding profusely. He was shouting hoarsely instead of speaking, trying to overcome the effects of the concussion. On the last leg of the journey, they were seen and fired upon by one of the Phalangers.

"Here!" Kate touched a sensor and the hatch moved aside with a hiss. "Mary, help me! Quickly!"

Rokotov's legs were buckling under him. He could barely understand where he was and what was happening.

Taking advantage of the general confusion, the Lozins' grandson came out of his cabin and stared around him, surprised and frightened. The holographic display still showed a 3D picture of their surroundings. Beyond the Cassiopeia, smoke swirled into tornadoes and roaring columns of flame kept bursting from the fissures in the cliffs.

He almost started to cry when he noticed the blood. "Grandpa, did someone hit you?"

"It's fine, it'll pass," Vadim held the wound closed. "Maria, tell them that we're onboard! And find out what happened to Aquila. Where are Olga and Andrew?"

The cybersystem responded to his words at once. Lozin saw the servomachine from Dabog. Aquila was walking up the smoking slope. Cinders flew off its armor.

"Grandpa, look at the huge robot!" Little Andrew exclaimed. "Oh, there's another one! Is it broken?"

Groves' Hoplite stood burning among the cliffs.

Polvin's voice came into the crew compartment. "Everyone, get ready! Commencing the one-hundred-second countdown!"

AQUILA WAS HURRYING to get to the Cassiopeia.

It was walking within a direct line of sight of four enemy machines, inspiring horror but not attacking. The clouds of anti-laser particles had burned away but there wasn't enough energy left in the machine's accumulators for even a single shot. The power of the overloaded reactor had to be reduced so that only the drives were receiving energy.

It had won this fight by absorbing human thinking, finding the one defining phrase in the jumble of thoughts and feelings: *they just need to be stopped.*

Looking at the dark outlines of the enemy servomachines, Aquila's artificial intelligence could see the coming horror.

None of the Phalangers had been completely destroyed in the explosions. Their sensors had burned away, and some of the poorly protected subsystems had been damaged, but these faults were being rectified right now. The technical servos released by the pilots were engaged in urgent repairs. In a little while, at least four Phalangers would again unite into a combat group.

Aquila didn't miss the smallest detail.

The battle of the servomachines had lasted seven and a half minutes. The technology park, which was a similar size to a small town, had been wiped off the face of the earth and turned into a wasteland, riddled with fire-breathing fissures.

Olga Polvin, devastated by the battle, had surrendered control and was staring in shock at the screens.

With a screech of damaged engines, Aquila turned into the gorge leading to Cassiopeia.

Hoplite's marker faded. The fate of Andrew Groves remained unknown.

* * *

THE HOT METAL crackled. The bitter smell of smoke seeped into the control room. The damaged consoles spat out sparks and the cybersystem showed no signs of life.

Andrew stirred. Some sections of the external holographic screen were still working, allowing him to assess the situation.

Four Phalangers, damaged but not destroyed, were approaching the gorge that Aquila had disappeared into.

With bloodied fingers, he manually adjusted the frequency until he found Cassiopeia's signal.

"It's Andrew... Launch now..."

"Andrew, where are you?" Polvin responded instantly. "Where can we pick you up?"

"Start the countdown... I couldn't eject from the Hoplite."

"We're not abandoning you!"

"Leave me... I'll survive... Start... If you wait another minute, everyone will die."

"Andrew!"

"Stop... I'm shutting down the comms," he touched a sensor, cutting off the pointless argument.

'As long they listen, as long as they don't do anything stupid.'

After several dull thuds of his heart, a raging wall of flame cut off the entrance to the gorge — it was Cassiopeia's planetary engines.

Andrew wearily closed his eyes. Even through his tightly closed eyelids, he could see the glaring glow, then it began to wane and Andrew's hand yanked the lever that manually triggered the catapult.

Hoplite's cockpit was leaning to the side. The

system couldn't guarantee the pilot's safety in this situation. 'It's still better than captivity.' He thought.

The circuits closed. The armor plates couldn't open so they were dropped using the emergency method. The latches bounced off with a metal ping and the piloting chair, encased in a shock-absorbing frame, was cast into Cassia's sky along a gentle ballistic trajectory.

Groves went dizzy from the G-force and then briefly unconscious, before coming back with a painful sense of weightlessness.

He was falling.

The parachute system had failed.

The forested hillside was rapidly approaching. Due to the angle of the cockpit, Andrew had been catapulted in the direction of the ridge. The emergency segment had flown over the mutilated technology park, reached the peak of its trajectory and was now descending.

At the last moment, the built-in jet engines flashed briefly, reducing the speed and changing the spatial position of the pilot chair, and then the flat armored base crashed into the trees, snapping branches. The crushing blow made Andrew slip out of consciousness again.

$* * *$

On board the Shadow of Earth cruiser

"CASSIOPEIA HAS LAUNCHED! The trajectory has been calculated and the assault carriers are on an intercept course. Three minutes to visual contact, five minutes to forced docking and boarding by the landing teams."

Admiral Nadyrov looked at the updated information.

The Shadow of Earth began to move into low orbit[7] while simultaneously performing a geosynchronous maneuver. If Cassiopeia's main module could not be captured, it would be destroyed by a missile strike from the cruiser.

"Navigation room calling."

"What is it?"

"Latest update on the course and signature analysis!"

"Keep it short, what's the problem?"

"They've activated the high-frequency circuit! They're planning to jump at a height of one hundred and thirty kilometers!"

"Are they nuts?!"

"That's what the calculations are showing

---

[7] Low orbit, given Cassia's atmosphere, is between 180 and 300 kilometers.

us!"

Nadyrov simply couldn't process the meaning of this report. What the frayg? Why did they decide on such a desperate step? The assault carriers maintained their masking, while the cruiser's orbit passed over the southern part of Cassia's inhabited continent until the last possible moment. The handful of colonists had no reason to turn on the hyperdrive at such low altitudes! Why are they engaging in something so risky?

"Overlay our course and current position!"

New data was immediately added to the image.

Nadyrov understood that these people were mad. They wanted to repeat Rokotov's maneuver and drag the Shadow of Earth into another uncontrollable hyperjump!

He had to make an immediate decision. "Forecast for the anomalous region!" he demanded.

"Considering the known hyperdrive power of the colonial transport, the warping and breakdown of space will form a sphere with a radius of fifty kilometers."

"Are we going to get caught up in it?"

"Yes, the cruiser is within the warp zone! The consequences are impossible to calculate!"

"Change course. Cruise thrust. We're leaving!" Nadyrov finally snapped. He was scared.

"Assault carriers to withdraw."

The admiral was not willing to sacrifice everything to catch a handful of lunatics.

* * *

HYPERSPACE WINDOW IS CLOSED.

Cassiopeia's main module was gone.

The veins on Nadyrov's neck bulged and his eyes became bloodshot. He looked like he was about to explode but the admiral kept his emotions on a tight leash and looked at the neighboring screens.

The probe floated over the ruins of the technology park. Five damaged Phalangers walked slowly towards the pick-up point. Another one had completely burnt up and three others had fallen into the underground cavities. There was no contact with their pilots.

The damaged Hoplite stood smoking on a small platform among the cliffs. Its cabin was open and some of the armored plates had been dropped when the pilot had ejected.

Aquila and Igor Rokotov had escaped once again!

In terms of battle-testing the latest technology, the fight between the servomachines had provided valuable information. A recording of the events was already undergoing analysis.

Figures and graphs were flickering at the bottom of the screen. The tactical module was processing the received information. After Cassiopeia disappeared, the cruiser's cybersystem received the freed-up computing power and data feeds were now being processed ten times faster.

Suddenly, the recording wound back to the moment when the servomachine from Dabog struck the first flight of Phantoms.

The aerospace fighters were already on an attacking course and were performing penetrating scans, which allowed them to collect unique technical data.

A separate holographic monitor instantly assembled Aquila's energy matrix, with special programs adding a 3D image of the legendary servomachine. Nadyrov couldn't understand what the analytical modules were so interested in. He had seen this reconstruction dozens of time and noticed nothing new.

Unexpectedly, the data processing programs removed the layer of armor, highlighting and enlarging the pilot chair, which — Nadyrov peered more closely — was not occupied by Igor Rokotov!

A girl sat in the chair!

Who the heck was she? How did she get access to the cockpit?

Now Nadyrov couldn't understand anything at all. There was no doubt that Igor Rokotov had been on Cassia. The former President of Cassia and several officials from the highest echelons of power had been questioned separately, and they had all given the same testimony. But how could some local girl gain access to the Aquila and manage to control such a complex mechanism? It seemed preposterous, causing the admiral to smirk incredulously. It was utter nonsense!

However, the cruiser's cybernetic core, containing AI capabilities, disagreed with him. Several individual blocks were highlighted on the 3D model, associated with a structure reminiscent of the artificial nervous system of colonial series androids, then, in addition, the system highlighted an inconspicuous connection cable curving over the girl's shoulder.

A compatibility search began in a separate window, with images of different devices flickering at breakneck speed.

Signature match found.

Year 2213. A joint project of the Genesis Corporation and Rimp Cybertronics.

The system of direct neurosensory contact. Not used in practice due to potential danger to the human mind.

NADYROV LEANED heavily on the sloping console, carefully considering the meager data.

So that's what it was? Direct contact

between human and machine? A temporary mental symbiosis?

"Has contact been established with the capital?" He asked without turning.

"We have determined the navigational lines of the hypersphere leading to Yuna and Vesuvius. A direct jump to Earth is impossible from here."

"Send it through the hypersphere frequency channel."

He quickly scribbled a few lines.

'To John Winston Hammer from Admiral Tiberius Nadyrov. As a result of a military operation, I have found and captured the planet Cassia, terraformed to Earth Standard and fit for immediate settlement.

Testing of the servomachines can be considered successful. During the fighting, I obtained unique technical information that may affect the future course of the war.'

"Send it at once!"

THE SCAN FILE and full transcript of data from the battle on Cassia changed the fate of many civilizations.

Exactly a year late, in the laboratories on Yuna, Howard Faragney would create a second-generation Maverick, an artificial intelligence for servomachines, equipped with a module for direct neurosensory contact. The designer intended for the cybersystems to learn and gather the combat experience of their pilots, but in practice, everything would turn out to be much more complicated, harsher and inhumane...

A step was made over a line that should never have been crossed.

The war would blossom anew.

Epilogue

ANDREW GROVES REGAINED consciousness under starlight. He could hear voices coming from below him, "...here somewhere. We're within the drop coordinates."

His fingers were caked with dried blood. He undid the harness with difficulty and crawled onto the ground.

The cold autumn night breathed silence. He could see a glow in the distance, it was the fires still burning in the technology park.

Trying not to make any noise, Andrew pulled a survival kit from the base of the emergency segment, checked his weapon, and trudged up the slope, away from the voices, the crackle of twigs and the rustle of crumbling stones.

Step by step, the vague and unfamiliar concept of freedom formed new meanings in Andrew's mind.

He had survived after all.

Dabog Planetary System

THE DEBRIS SWIRLED around in space, occasionally glimmering with the reflected light of the sun.

A few days ago, when Igor Rokotov turned on his hyperdrive and made a suicidal blind leap, the three frigates following the Shadow of Earth cruiser were dragged into the space warp. Two of them had collided and been destroyed, while the third survived but had lost power and was now docked at the repair platform.

Rocket and escort carriers, as well as a group of five corvettes, were all the troops that the Terran Alliance currently possessed in Dabog's system.

"WE WON'T GET another chance. We have to act now!"

The three dozen spacecraft that formed the combined battle group looked rather unimpressive. The largest was the main module of the colonial transport Pursuer from the planet Kjuig. The rest were transport ships converted for military purposes.

"I agree," responded Auguste Dubois, commander of the passenger liner that had shuttled between Dabog and Elio before the war, now rearmed and proudly referred to as a 'small cruiser'.

"The Alliance escort carrier contains at least five Phantom squadrons," Dmitry Dorokhov, pilot of the Needle, reminded everyone.

"We'll come out from behind the dust moon and strike from maximum distance. We'll focus our fire on the escort carrier," suggested the captain of the small rocket cruiser called Lucifer. This ship, reconstructed at the shipyard on the Moon Stellar, was the most formidable fighting unit of the Free Colonies Navy.

"That's right!" added his voice the captain of Parallax. "While the Alliance hasn't brought up fresh forces, we'll be able to break through to Dabog and evacuate its citizens."

"Have we established contact with the planet?" asked Dubois.

"Yes. They're waiting for us."

"In that case, there's no time to waste. Let's

synchronize our cybersystems and start the attack."

* * *

A BATTLE RAGED in space.

"This is the Needle! My main engine's hit! Get the corvette off my tail!"

"This is Artemis! Head to the repair platform! I'm coming to help."

"Lucifer to the group. We're under fire from the rocket carrier!"

The Pursuer was trying to reach the planet. The electromagnetic guns installed in the airlocks mercilessly wasted its ammunition, with missiles firing in all directions. The flagship of the Free Colonies was already gaping with numerous holes from rocket strikes, and turbid plumes of decompression fragments trailed after it.

The Alliance escort carrier had been destroyed. Not a single fighter had been allowed to take off, and now the enormous ship was dying in a fireball of internal explosions.

Dabog's ash-gray atmosphere was boiling. The colonists' transport ships were descending using their planetary engines.

Nevertheless, the situation was critical. The rocket carrier had managed to release a crushing volley and was now reloading its launchers, preparing to strike again.

"The corvettes are in pursuit! They're entering the atmosphere behind us. Help!"

"Flagship to the group. Cover the transports!"

The Pursuer was suddenly illuminated by the fire of its propulsion engines and set a course for the rocket carrier of the Alliance.

The two ships were heading towards each other. There was going to be a collision.

"A hyperjump!"

A space warp suddenly appeared in Dabog's low orbit.

The floating sea of debris stirred and rippled. The anomaly rapidly grew, taking the shape of a funnel pierced with the threadlike charges of hyperspace energy.

The main module of the Cassiopeia colonial transport appeared like a ghostly silhouette, and fully materialized a split second later, triggering another wave of space distortions. The Alliance rocket carrier was thrown off course and sent into uncontrolled drift, while the damaged Pursuer was pushed towards the planet. The situation changed dramatically. It wasn't quite the turning point but the fighting lessened as many ships were knocked off course.

"Flagship to the group!" the voice was

interrupted by disturbances. "We have been contacted by the main module of Cassiopeia. Igor Rokotov is on board. They'll take on the rocket carrier. Everyone, stop attacking secondary targets and follow the corvettes. Cover the transports! We're commencing the evacuation of Dabog!"

As if confirming his words, the Cassiopeia turned on its engines and began to reorientate itself. A cargo door opened. Scans showed that inside stood a combat servomachine of Aquila's class, equipped with heavy lasers.

The commander of the rocket carrier received the same information. He decided not to tempt fate since Aquila's capabilities had been well-studied.

The Cassiopeia had not yet completed its maneuver when the only major Alliance ship performed a hyperjump, deciding to avoid a fight.

DARIA KRETCHETOVA stared at the lead-gray clouds being illuminated from above. The entrance to the bunker was behind her, where two androids were gathering all the children. They had to be evacuated first but the radio conversations spoke of fierce fighting in orbit and left almost no hope of a favorable outcome.

The flame ripped apart the low, swirling clouds.

The transport switched to an antigravity thrust. The planetary engines fell silent and the spaceship was now descending almost soundlessly onto a small, cleared platform.

Scars from laser fire glinted dully on its armor.

The landing gear screeched as it touched the frozen ground. Steam rose into the sky, the hatch hissed open and a short ladder extended with a metallic clang.

"Quickly!" came the voice of an unfamiliar pilot.

Daria couldn't answer him. Her breath caught in her throat as tears streamed down her cheeks.

The blockade of Dabog had been broken.

P.S.

This was the first and most terrible year of the Galactic War.

A year of painful revelations, the consolidation of worlds, the renaissance of technologies, and desperate blind punches through the hypersphere in search of worlds colonized during the Great Exodus.

The Free Colonies Navy, consisting of converted cargo ships and modules of colonial transports, had desperately resisted the Terran Alliance forces, managing to hold onto the systems of Kjuig, Elio and Rory, where the first military base was built on the Moon Stellar.

Breaking the blockade of Dabog did not end the planet's defense. A portion of the defenders and most of the Hugo series androids remained on the planet to continue research into new kinds of technology. They held Dabog for another year, transmitting the design results to the Fort Stellar using hypersphere frequency channels.

In December 2609, the planet was captured by the forces of the Terran Alliance.

As a result, Hammer's Line, consisting of 64 star systems, became a closed circle, and it became impossible to jump directly to Earth's coordinates.

Andrew Groves survived after ejecting himself from the Hoplite and remained on Cassia.

Igor Rokotov went through the whole war and became Admiral of the Free Colonies Fleet.

The First Galactic War would last another thirty years, bringing Humanity to the brink of self-destruction, but this will be told in subsequent books of the History of the Galaxy.

The fate of Daria Kretchetova was very dramatic. The evacuation transport that she was on was destroyed. Centuries later, in the postwar period, she would be found and revived using postwar technology at the Fort Stellar, when Humanity would first encounter an alien space race.

End of Book Two

Version of 2017
Author's web address: https://livadny.ru/

Want to be the first to know about our latest
LitRPG, sci fi and fantasy titles from your favorite
authors?

Subscribe to our NEW RELEASES newsletter:
http://eepurl.com/b7niIL

Thank you for reading *The Shadow of Earth!*
If you like what you've read, check out other LitRPG,
sci fi and fantasy novels published by Magic Dome
Books:

An NPC's Path LitRPG series by Pavel Kornev:
The Dead Rogue

Level Up series by Dan Sugralinov:
Re-Start

**The Way of the Shaman LitRPG series
by Vasily Mahanenko:**
Survival Quest
The Kartoss Gambit
The Secret of the Dark Forest
The Phantom Castle
The Karmadont Chess Set
Shaman's Revenge
Clans War

Dark Paladin LitRPG series by Vasily Mahanenko:
The Beginning
The Quest
Restart

Galactogon LitRPG series by Vasily Mahanenko:
Start the Game!

**The Bard from Barliona LitRPG series
by Eugenia Dmitrieva and Vasily Mahanenko:**
The Renegades

The Neuro LitRPG series by Andrei Livadny:
The Crystal Sphere
The Curse of Rion Castle
The Reapers

The Expansion (The History of the Galaxy) series by A. Livadny:
Blind Punch

Point Apocalypse *(a near-future action thriller)* **by Alex Bobl**

The Sublime Electricity series by Pavel Kornev
The Illustrious
The Heartless
The Fallen
The Dormant

You're in Game!
(LitRPG Stories from Bestselling Authors)

You're in Game-2!
(More LitRPG stories set in your favorite worlds)

The Game Master series by A. Bobl and A. Levitsky:
The Lag

The Naked Demon by Sherrie L.
(a paranormal romance)

More books and series are coming out soon!

In order to have new books of the series translated faster, we need your help and support! Please consider leaving a review or spread the word by recommending *The Shadow of Earth* to your friends and posting the link on social media. The more people buy the book, the sooner we'll be able to make new translations available.

Thank you!

Till next time!

www.ingramcontent.com/pod-product-compliance
Lightning Source LLC
Chambersburg PA
CBHW071640260626
47170CB00001B/181